DOMINION FIRST BLOOD

Book One

RICHARD MANN

**Copyright © 2018 Richard Guy Mann Goldbloom Publishing.
November 2018**

All rights reserved. No part of this book may be reproduced in any form by any electronic or mechanical means including photocopying, recording, or information storage and retrieval without permission in writing from the author. All characters appearing in this work are fictitious. Any resemblance to real persons, living or dead, is purely coincidental. This work is registered with the UK Copyright Service registration number 284713421.

I greatly appreciate you taking the time to read my work. This is the Special Edition with extra chapters, pictures, histories, afterword, and appendices. Please consider leaving a review wherever you bought this book or telling your friends about my books, to help spread the word.

Cover illustration by Denis Turla and Richard Mann. Pictures purchased from Shutterstock. Internal pictures are classified as free to use, share or modify commercially.

Give feedback on the book email: richardgmann@yahoo.co.uk

Follow me and Like my Facebook Page:
facebook.com/richardgmann.author
Join my Richard Mann Author Sci-Fi Group on Facebook
Sign up for news and book releases at www.richardmannblog.com
Follow me on Twitter: @richardgmann

First edition
Printed in the USA by the wonderful people at CreateSpace

"Fabulous book! Science thriller with a feel of history. It pulled me from the first page. Plenty of action, adventure and unusual twists. The characters are masterly written and author's attention to details deserves a lot of praise. At times I felt like I was traveling in time and space and it reminds me Star Wars and Lord of the Rings. Highly recommend this book to all Sci-fi lovers. Looking forward to your next book Richard Mann!"

By Iryna Dudinaon 25 November 2017 | Verified Purchase

"An outstanding piece of work. Destined to be a classic. It's the best action adventure book I've read in years, gripping, edge of seat excitement, a real page turner. It's a mix of sci-fi action thriller horror and historical fiction…Frederick Forsyth and Bernard Cromwell on steroids..

This is quite a long book..but it needs to be. There is real depth on the characters..they feel alive and real. I really love Cockney Vinnie the sexy femme fatale vampire lucia and the flawed complex hero Bullet Proof Pete. I felt I could relate to the characters. There are many funny moments (esp. When 2 tough SAS heroes dress up as women).

There's also an interesting love triangle but I won't go into it here as it will spoil the story. There is plenty of fascinating backstory….WWII and Roman times.i felt like I was there..i like the old fashioned chapter titles pictures appendices and history. Can't wait for book two."

By Dan 8 November 2017 Format: Paperback | Verified Purchase

"A tried and tested formula, aliens invade earth destroying and enslaving humanity. But this has an unusual twist. Humanity fights back with vampires as allies. A well-written book that will have you hooked from the first to the last page. It's reminiscent of Lord of the Rings in scope and adventure. Can't wait for the sequel."

By Celine 16 September 2017 Format: Kindle Edition | Verified Purchase

"Excellent effort by a new author! Full of ambition and wide-ranging scope. Something for lovers of Sci-Fi, action heroes and with vampires thrown in for good measure!"

By DejiDeal 15 September 2017 Format: Kindle Edition | Verified Purchase

"Although I'm not a big reader this book was very easy to read which kept pulling me closer and closer. The characters were very interesting and the plot twists and surprises kept the reader engrossed in the story, it's clear to see the author has put a lot of effort into the research that's gone into this book.

The quality of the book itself is also very good, however you wouldn't expect less for the price. This book has definitely peaked my interest in reading more books and I can't wait for the sequel."

By David on 5 September 2017 Format: Paperback | Verified Purchase

"What a vivid imagination the author must have. The story is so well laid out one has virtually to be arrested to put the book down. I will not go into the story here except to say that it covers the globe and ventures into space. I'm looking forward to book 2. Don't be long Richard mann."

By Chris 22 August 2017 Format: Kindle Edition|Verified Purchase

This book is dedicated to my family
who are the rock of my life. To
my mother Patricia you have always been there for us.

"Sometimes doing your best is not good enough.
Sometimes you must do what is required."
Sir Winston Churchill

"A time to love, and a time to hate, a
time of war, and a time of peace."
Ecclesiastes 3:8

Contents

Cast of Characters 11
Prologue 15

Chapter 1:   Natural Selection 23
Chapter 2:   Freak of Nature 27
Chapter 3:   Dreams of Mountains 31
Chapter 4:   Mental Torture 36
Chapter 5:   Getting Badged 39
Chapter 6:   Home Sweet Home 43
Chapter 7:   East End Welcome 48
Chapter 8:   007 51
Chapter 9:   Yemen 56
Chapter 10: Halo Drop 60
Chapter 11: The Empty Quarter 65
Chapter 12: Ice Cold in Alex 70
Chapter 13: The Holy Desert 74
Chapter 14: The Bedouin 79
Chapter 15: The Mission 85
Chapter 16: Justice is Done 90
Chapter 17: On Her Majesty's Secret Service 94
Chapter 18: Black Op 97
Chapter 19: Goldilocks 100

Chapter 20:	Peter's Promotion	104
Chapter 21:	Ancient Discovery	109
Chapter 22:	Count Cassian's Castle	112
Chapter 23:	Search for the Book of Berossus	116
Chapter 24:	Of Questionable Character	121
Chapter 25:	Primordial Instinct	126
Chapter 26:	Vampire and Human Summit	129
Chapter 27:	Physic Vampires	134
Chapter 28:	Invasion	138
Chapter 29:	Panic in the Oval Office	140
Chapter 30:	Where the Fuck is Grimbald?	143
Chapter 31:	Alien Contact	145
Chapter 32:	Sirius Protocol	150
Chapter 33:	Sirius HQ	155
Chapter 34:	A Rat in the Pack	158
Chapter 35:	The President's Speech	161
Chapter 36:	Vinnie's Business	164
Chapter 37:	Leaving Home	166
Chapter 38:	This Cannot Be Happening	170
Chapter 39:	Buck House	175
Chapter 40:	Alien Agenda	180
Chapter 41:	Queen's Speech	183
Chapter 42:	It's a War, But With No Rules	188
Chapter 43:	Surprise Visitor	193
Chapter 44:	Alien History	198
Chapter 45:	The Emperor Speaks	202
Chapter 46:	Atlantic Storm	204
Chapter 47:	Incoming	208

Chapter 48:	New York	212
Chapter 49:	Nazi Speech	216
Chapter 50:	Domination	221
Chapter 51:	Fighting a Losing Battle	225
Chapter 52:	New Horizons	227
Chapter 53:	Kidnap	230
Chapter 54:	Roman Mistress	234
Chapter 55:	Terror in the Forest	237
Chapter 56:	Terror in the Whorehouse	240
Chapter 57:	Terror in Virginia	244
Chapter 58:	Traitor Uncovered	246
Chapter 59:	Launch Depth	250
Chapter 60:	Nazi Blood	253
Chapter 61:	Shapeshifter	258
Chapter 62:	Vampire Lair	260
Chapter 63:	Vampire Moon	266

Amazon Review	271
Acknowledgements	272
Appendices	273
About the Author	275
Feedback to the Author	276
Book Movie Trailer	277

Cast of Characters

Captain Peter 'Bulletproof' Morgan—SAS soldier / MI6 agent

Corporal Vinnie 'The Terminator' Carson—SAS soldier

Lucia—Vampire Elder and member of the Vampiri Grand Council

Count Cassian—Vampire Elder and Head of the Vampiri Grand Council

Jennifer Morgan—Peter's wife

Frank Wilson—US President

General Bill Scott—US Chief of Defense Staff

General Julian Grimbald—Head of US Space command

Professor Picard—Eccentric French Polymath

Father Sebastian Harris—Priest. Ex SAS

Sir Nigel Goldbroom—MI6 Chief

Ergtuk the 82nd—Sumeri Alien Clone

Herr Herg-Zuk—Sumeri Alien Emperor

Marshall Zurg-Uk—Sumeri Alien Defense Chief

Lord Grim-Uk—Sumeri Alien Narzuk SS Chief

Himm-Uk—Sumeri Alien Narzuk SS Deputy Chief

Gill Carson—Vinnie's wife

'Handsome' Mike—US Navy Seal

General Mike Schmitt—Sirius Defense Chief

Captain Duke Miller—CIA agent

Colonel Bradley—21 regiment SAS Colonel

Colonel Stan Wight—Sirius base Colonel

Please note: The Appendices: Cockney Slang table and Vampiri and Sumeri Alien command structure are at the back of the book. Additional material is available in the Special Edition only.

"I imagine they might exist in massive ships, having used up all the resources from their home planet. Such advanced aliens would perhaps become nomads, looking to conquer and colonize whatever planets they can reach."

"To my mathematical brain, the numbers alone make thinking about aliens perfectly rational."

"The real challenge is working out what aliens might actually be like." "We only have to look at ourselves to see how intelligent life might develop into something we wouldn't want to meet."

"If aliens ever visit us, I think the outcome would be much as when Christopher Columbus first landed in America, which didn't turn out very well for the American Indians."

Professor Stephen Hawking

Prologue

SUMERIA (ANCIENT IRAQ) 4000 BC

A huge object lands silently in the desert, next to a primitive settlement of mud huts. A temple and pyramid of polished white limestone stand nearby. The moonlight reflects off the massive alien craft.

Alien shapes move out of the craft, closely followed by snarling hounds with yellow eyes glowing in the dark. Spines project from their backs, saliva drooling from their large fangs.

'Inim en-lil-la-ta sa šu gal bi-šu,' barks a tall alien. 'Take the human women—kill the men if they resist.'

The aliens enter the mud huts and drag out wide-eyed women dressed in simple, cloth tunics, screaming for their lives. The tallest of the marauders shouts orders to his troops, showing sharp, jagged teeth. A cynical smile appears on his long angular face as he looks at the scene before him—so many worlds conquered, such a weak enemy.

His thin, wiry arm points to a group of men and his hounds leap into action. His angular head looks up to the moonlight, and his large black eyes squint, as he scratches at the diseased pale green flesh on his hand.

'Attack—attack!'

The hounds leap forward and tear the men to pieces, the dog's saliva arcing in unison with the victims' blood. The green-skinned commander grins in satisfaction as the women are herded like sheep into the spaceship, still screaming, calling for their husbands and children.

Nearby, on the top of the pyramid, an ancient vampire with long blond hair looks on in disgust, his ice-blue eyes squinting at the macabre scene before him. As he stands, his strong and wiry body is framed against the moonlight. He opens his mouth to reveal sharp fangs that could tear an animal or human to pieces in just seconds. His name is Cassian, and he is the oldest vampire on Earth, and now his deep guttural voice fills the night.

'Disgusting filth! Why don't they leave the humans alone?' Cassian's eyes slowly turn red. Large and black leathery wings sprout from his body. One of the alien troops looks up and freezes, standing open-mouthed and speechless, for Cassian is transforming into an ancient demon, his eyes blazing red, his hands now giant claws, his teeth huge fangs, drooling saliva. Cassian leaps into the air and swoops down the side of the pyramid, his leathery wings gliding silently towards the group of alien invaders. The alien soldier looks up as he sees the red-eyed vampire swooping towards them.

'Nergal tuk! Nergal tuk!'

'Night-crawler, Night-crawler!' screams the terrified alien as Cassian swoops down.

'I am Nergal, ancient demon, God of The Dead—come to me!' he speaks in deep guttural tones, the alien soldiers slow their advance, their black eyes wide with fear.

Other vampires appear out of the darkness, slipping through hidden crevices in the pyramid, their red eyes glinting in the moonlight. As Cassian lands on the sandy soil he tears apart two frozen aliens with his talons. His red eyes glint in joy and, with a swoop of his sword, he slices two alien dogs in half, then with lightning speed, bites the head off a green-skinned soldier, the head tumbling across the sand to a group of shocked soldiers who back away slowly, looking to their leader.

'Run for your lives—run!' orders Cassian to the women.

The freed women huddle in a group, clutching each other for support. Wailing children clutch at the skirts of the women. A woman looks at her husband, who is fatally wounded, the sand stained red with his blood. She screams as she picks up a rock and throws it at the retreating aliens.

The tall alien commander points at Cassian and tells his troops to attack, but they run back to the spaceship instead, closely followed by the commander, shouting over his shoulder as he scrambles up the ramp, knowing the battle is lost, his soldiers no match for the night crawlers.

Cassian watches as the remaining aliens flee to their ship, dropping their laser weapons as they run up the ramp, the door closing behind them. The engines whine and the craft takes off, slowly at first, then shooting off at lightning speed until it is out of sight.

'Good riddance to the alien filth,' mutters Cassian, as he looks at the scene of carnage around him, then back at the disappearing ship.

'We are hungry,' a vampire says as he goes to take the blood of an injured man. Cassian puts his hand on the vampire and throws him off.

'We only feed on dead humans—let the others go.'

A bruised and bloodied woman, tears flowing from her eyes, approaches Cassian, his demon red eyes glowing red.

'Thank you—thank you,' says the frightened woman. Cassian nods as the woman runs off to find her children and to mourn her dead husband.

They will be back, Cassian thinks, as he watches his vampires feed hungrily on the dead. His eyes return to their natural blue color and his black leathery wings shrink.

Cassian walks back to the pyramid, over the sand, his black cloak flowing behind him. He places his hand on the cool stone, utters ancient words of magic and where before, there were large blocks of stone, now a stone door appears. It opens to reveal a dark passage lit by torches. He walks into a room with a sarcophagus, and inside the tomb is an alien, with large black eyes and a tall, thin body, preserved for study. He examines the body and takes a sample from the green diseased skin.

Why is the alien filth coming here, pillaging and kidnapping human women, are they declining, as a race? Their green skin is flaking they are not in good shape. We are not prepared for another attack, not nearly enough. The humans do not deserve to suffer at the hands of these despicable aliens. We need the humans, and they need us.

If he helps the humans can he be redeemed? Can a demon redeem himself in God's eyes, through good acts? He now regretted his decision to follow the one called Lucifer, The Shining One, The Morning Star, who charmed one-third of all the Holy Angels to fall away from God and follow him. He was so jealous of God's plan to create the human race – *and to use his own DNA in their making*, and so he rebelled, along with his followers. If only the human's knew they had the Creator's DNA. And they were cast out by Prince Michael, thrust down from Heaven, into the Abyss. Regret now fills his heart—a tear falls down his pale cheek, as he relives the shameful memory. He will help the humans and hope that, one day, he will be forgiven. The die has been cast. *One thing however, is for certain. The alien filth will be back.*

DESERT TOWN IN IRAQ 2006

Peter, Vinnie and two other soldiers in desert smocks and Shemaghs, walk stealthily down the side of a building in a dusty desert town. They are a four-man patrol from A squadron of the 21 SAS Regiment. Each patrol has a soldier skilled in signals, demolition, and is either a medic or is a linguist. Peter himself is a skilled linguist and medic. Vinnie's skills are signals and demolition, as well as being an expert sniper. As Sergeant, Peter leads the patrol.

They move into a street, looking backwards and forwards, on rooftops, down alleyways, looking for insurgents. The Iraqi townspeople eye them suspiciously and move inside doorways, ushering their children inside. Eyes peek out behind shuttered windows – there is silence now. Dust swirls down the street from a desert breeze. They squint their eyes against the dust and harsh sun. A lonely figure, an old woman bent with age, face-baked and wizened from the sun, points at them as she hobbles across the street.

'Crusader! Crusader!'

On a rooftop, Peter's quick wits spots a flash of light.

'Vinnie, 1 o'clock roof top!'

A Kalashnikov fires from the roof. Peter flinches as bullets spray three inches from his face, but the two other soldiers behind them are hit. Peter and Vinnie level their M16's, butt in the shoulder, sights on target, all within a split second, and return fire. Peter's heart is racing with adrenaline as he grabs another M16 from one of the downed soldiers and they dive behind a car. They studiously ignore their fallen colleagues as they view the rooftop.

'Time for mourning later,' whispered Peter.

They return fire in three second bursts to conserve ammunition. The car is peppered with bullet holes from return fire and the fuel tank is leaking onto the dry sandy street. The air is filled with the smell of cordite, petrol and choking dust.

Peter retaliates with two M16's, one in each hand, as he shouts a battle cry. One insurgent falls from the roof and hits the ground. 'Fire in the hole!' shouts Peter as he fires a grenade at the rooftop. As it explodes against a wooden barrier, two Iraqi insurgents are blown clean from the roof, and seem to fall in slow motion through the air.

'Oi Terminator, let's move before it blows!' Peter shouts as they run down the street. They had only gone ten yards when the car explodes behind them, Peter taking the full force of the explosion in his back, and they are thrown to the ground. A bullet explodes one inch from Peter's face, Vinnie takes one in the leg and screams.

'Vinnie, house on the end, first floor!' shouted Peter. Then Peter sees Vinnie's ankle and takes the sniper rifle from Vinnie, a Barrett M107.50, but Vinnie is having none of it, and takes it back. Vinnie calmly adjusts the sight and elevation. 'Ten knots east', Vinnie took account of the wind. A bullet grazed Peter's ankle. As Vinnie fired, the shooting stopped and there was silence.

'That's why they call him "The Terminator"', said Peter.

'You're the luckiest bastard alive – "Bulletproof Pete." Vinnie grunted in pain. 'There's no way you can be shot!' winced Vinnie as he grabbed the radio.

'Two men down. Evac required. RV delta four 1330, over.'

'Let's get out of here!' shouted Peter, as the townspeople started poking their heads out of their houses on the street. Then Peter's sixth sense kicks in - he turns round as a wild-eyed machete wielding Iraqi insurgent brings down his arm to slice Peter in two, but fast as lightning he pushes out his hands hitting the shocked insurgent in the chest who flies back twenty foot through the air, landing in the smoking blackened remains of the burning car. Vinnie looked at Peter quizzically through his pain - no normal human had that strength.

They raced for the rendezvous, Vinnie hobbling from his wound, Peter carrying both dead soldiers, one on each shoulder, quick as an Olympic one-hundred meter champion. He can hear a helicopter approaching. Shots from another Kalashnikov sprayed against the wall behind them as they reached the clear ground of the RV pickup – he can see the helicopter landing fifty feet away. Within two seconds Peter had hurled himself and their dead colleagues into the Royal Navy Lynx, then grabbed Vinnie into the helicopter, which touched the ground just for a second before lifting off again.

They slumped in the back of the helicopter taking off their gear. Vinnie looked at his friend Peter, 'Lucky bastard', he thought. Not so much as a scratch, and he wasn't even out of breath – no wonder his nickname was "Bullet Proof" Pete. Vinnie on the other hand was covered in scratches and bruises, had a bullet grazed his thigh, and blood oozing from his lower leg. He breathed heavily, out of breath, as he tended his wounds, Peter putting a bandage on his leg.

Peter looked at Vinnie fixing his wounds and thought about his friend. Vinnie – he could always count on Vinnie. Dead reliable, saved his back more than once. And in life that's what's important - finding people you can rely on. Vinnie's a scruffy bastard and he's got no manners. I mean, you wouldn't take him to have tea with the Queen or anything, but Peter loved him like a brother, and that's what counts, someone you can trust one hundred per cent.

Peter thought about his reputation of never being shot in a firefight, and not even getting a scratch, his amazing speed and agility, and the best soldier in the regiment, which made him curious. In the squadron they called him "Bullet Proof" Pete. Vinnie is a fearsome fighter and a great shot, so they call him "The Terminator". They both passed SAS selection first time, and it was hard training, but they loved it, it was natural for them. They took to it like ducks to water. He recalled the look of the directing staff as he completed the sixty-five k endurance march in three hours, they could not believe it. Many thought it was unnatural.

Supernatural some called it.

His mind then wandered back to his home in the valley, his sanctuary away from the madness, by the stream that ran through the woods, those ancient enchanted woods. His vision of the old man, the priest, and what was he saying as he was pointing at him? And an ancient name that resounded in his mind - Destiny was shouting at him.

"You are the one."
"You are Caius."
What the fuck does that mean?

Chapter 1

Natural Selection

BRECON BEACONS 2005

Two fit young soldiers are running up a mountain in military fatigues and full Bergen, sweat drips into their eyes, and down their backs in the searing heat. Other soldiers are lagging behind—one collapses exhausted. The fitter soldier reaches the top of Pen y Fan in the Brecon Beacons and pauses for breath.

The sun bounces off Peter Morgan's bald head as he shields his sharp blue eyes, surveying the majestic scene. His super-vision picks out a struggling soldier miles away, then spots his friend Vinnie further down the mountain, trying to keep up. As he looks around him, he feels on top of the world, the king of the mountain. Peter looks at the raw beauty of the green valleys and rugged hills and mountains, and at that moment he feels alive.

Then he has a moment of reflection.

Why did he become a soldier? It seemed like the best career move. Besides, he left school at sixteen with only one GCSE, in geography, and followed his father into the army. His father had died overseas on some clandestine mission, so he had to support the family. His teachers said he had huge potential and urged him to stay on at school and study, but his family came first. He loved looking at maps and reading about exotic places in the world. Besides, growing up in Merthyr Tydfil—the back end of nowhere, it was either wade through cow shit as a farmer or join the army.

So he chose the army.

Besides, he could travel the world and experience those exotic places for himself and send money home to the family. He had been to Gibraltar with the Royal Regiment of Wales, but he knew that if he passed SAS selection, he would have real adventures in far-away places, just like his father, who had also been in the service. It was in his early twenties that he and Vinnie both decided to join the army, and now in their mid-twenties, they were taking the ultimate test, SAS selection.

He loved the mountains and the green valleys, more than anything else. The fresh spring water that sprang from the rocks, the smell of the air that filled his lungs—the dirty air of the city wasn't for him. He remembered the fairy stories that his grandmother used to tell him about the hidden and ancient places in the Welsh valleys, places that time forgot, where old memories lingered. Places of magic and wonderment, witches and wizards and cave-dwelling hermits, and an ancient legend about an old wood in a hidden valley where a priest had lived since time began.

Peter's super-sensitive hearing picks up a conversation between two struggling soldiers six hundred yards down the mountain, 'You know what they say about that Pete Morgan, he isn't human!'

Peter's friend, Vinnie, eventually catches up. 'We'd better get a move on, they're catching up,' pants Vinnie in his East End accent, his face sporting a cheeky grin, his short brown hair sticking up.

'They won't catch us,' replies Peter, his deep, resounding voice has a slight Welsh accent, but also an older quality about it. They speed off again, Vinnie struggling to keep up.

Two tough, weather-beaten, directing staff, Des, and Artie, both veteran SAS sergeants in their mid-thirties, watch through binoculars at the bottom of Pen y Fan.

'Artie, did you see him run, full kit and all, up Pen y Fan? Never seen anything like it, left the rest in the dust.'

'It ain't natural Des. Never seen anything like it,' said Artie, brewing tea in his mess tin, 'and I've been in the service for ten years.'

'And me. Been a DS for five years, Artie.'

'I know Des. And?' said Artie patiently.

'He is the fittest bugger ever to be entered for selection, and that's saying something. Tougher than any Para or Royal Marine—and they're hard bastards,' replies Des lighting a cigarette.

'Nothing seems to faze him,' says Artie.

'Remember the thirty-kilometre march in the pouring rain with a forty-pound Bergen?' says Des eating a sandwich and drinking tea from his mess tin.

'Yep, gruelling by any standard,' replies Artie. 'But he left them all standing. Did it in record time too.'

Des recalls the extra endurance test, which many candidates fail. They have to run up a steep hill carrying a dead weight, like a heavy log. At the top of the hill, they have to perform a burpee jump up and then go straight to a press-up. Ten burpees must be done within twenty-five seconds, or else it's a fail. Then they must run back down the hill and do it all again, ten times.

'Remember extra endurance, Artie? Pete Morgan did it twenty times, beating all the rest. I almost failed his mate Vinnie, think he has a bit of asthma,' said Des.

'Get to the point, Des.'

'Anyway, Morgan comes up to me, without breaking a sweat, and says, 'Staff, can I do ten more, please? I need a proper workout.''

'Ten fucking more Morgan!' I screamed.

"Yes Staff,' he replied, cool as you like.'

'Go on then son,' I said. 'Meanwhile, all the other guys were laid out on the grass, chin-strapped. One of them had to be taken to the hospital. Suspected heart attack,' says Des slurping his tea.

'Built like fucking Bruce Lee as well. Ain't natural,' replies Artie.

'Heard a rumour the Yanks are after him,' says Des.

'Yep, I heard the same. CIA,' replies Artie, raising his eyebrows, taking a swig of water in the heat.

'You know what his nickname is, don't you?' says Des.

'Yeah. Bulletproof Pete.'

'Bulletproof my arse. Nobody can stop a bullet,' says Des drinking his tea.

'His mate Vinnie. Reckon he's an East End gangster,' says Artie.

'That's what I heard. Don't cross him, Artie.'

Chapter 2

FREAK OF NATURE

Peter knew that people were talking about him. Was he a freak of nature? His hardened physique, built by years of training, gave him muscles and sinews like Bruce Lee. He had the same lightning agility and the strength of ten men. He felt superhuman.

Nobody could outrun him on the marches.

No one.

Peter knew the SAS selection process would either make him or break him. He needed to know. It was a stepping stone to greater things—his dreams had told him this. But he knew he would never be the same person again. It would be something akin to a spiritual awakening, that was how he saw it—the supreme test of mind and spirit.

He knew that some soldiers die of heat exhaustion in the summer selection, or hypothermia in the winter selection, others simply collapse from fatigue.

Peter, however, felt elated. His blue eyes blazed with light.

He felt alive, the adrenalin coursing through his veins.

He felt as strong as steel, as if another force was within him, something stronger than himself. This is what he was meant to be, a warrior, he and Vinnie together, conquering the world. He had a vision of fighting dragons with a sword, and winning against all the odds. Maybe he was fighting himself, and the dragon was his own inner demons whom he was trying to defeat, in this supreme test of endurance.

Peter thought about the other soldiers on selection. He knew some of them, and Vinnie of course. He had prepared Vinnie by doing extra training with him otherwise Vinnie would certainly have failed.

Peter reflected on the selection process. Any member of Her Majesty's Armed Forces can be considered for Special Forces selection, but most candidates are from the Parachute Regiment. All instructors (*directing staff*) or DS's like Des and Artie are full members of the Special Air Service. Selections are held twice a year, in summer and winter, in Sennybridge in the Brecon Beacons. Selection lasts for a total of six months.

Less than ten percent pass.

There is the hill phase, jungle phase, weapons and combat survival phase, the week-long escape and evasion phase and finally the resistance to interrogation. Peter knew it was the ultimate test of mind and body, and it was the humble, quiet guys who passed—those who are reliable, dependable and level-headed. In a firefight, you had to depend on your comrades, your mates, your brothers in arms. It wasn't normally the loudmouths or show-offs who passed, they didn't have the right temperament.

On arrival, Peter had completed a personal fitness test (PFT) and an annual fitness test (AFT). He remembered the doctor's comments. 'There must be something wrong with my equipment,' he said, shaking his head. 'Mr. Morgan, you are the healthiest candidate ever to enter for selection. Your high-density lipoprotein, the good stuff, is off the scale and your resting heart rate is thirty-nine beats per minute.' He then amazed the doctors when he dead-lifted two thousand pounds, without breaking a sweat.

Then he marched cross country against the clock, always leading the pack, the DS struggling to keep up with him. The distances increased each day, culminating in what is known as Endurance: a sixty-five-kilometre march with full equipment, including a sixty pound Bergen on his back, scaling and descending Pen y Fan.

Even before the endurance, more than eighty of the hundred or so who started had dropped out, either collapsing or simply quitting. There was no shame in quitting. Des and Artie treated each man with respect, even giving them a lift to the train station.

Peter now relived the endurance march, designed to bring out personality defects, which must be completed within twenty hours. They were woken at 4 a.m., Des, and Artie shouting at them to 'move their arses.' Their Bergens were topped up with bricks to weigh sixty pounds, but for Peter, it felt like 6 pounds. One candidate tried to cheat, by removing bricks from his Bergen when he thought no one was looking, but Des regularly checked all Bergens, and he was "RTU'd", *returned to unit*, in short order.

Peter recalled the journey by truck to the start, all the soldiers are silent, knowing what lay ahead. It was dark and raining as they clambered out, retrieving their rifles and Bergens. Good job it was summer, or else he would be freezing his bollocks off. He felt the cold like everyone else, and the weather in the mountains could change dramatically within a few minutes—sunny one minute, torrential rain the next.

They were given compass bearings and the route of the march. Peter got off the lorry, put his Bergen on, slung his rifle over his shoulder, and got off to a fast start leaving everyone behind, including the DS. By 6 a.m. he was alone with no one else in sight, and he started to think about his dreams.

Strange dreams.

Chapter 3

Dreams of Mountains

Last night Peter dreamt he was on a mountain, Vinnie was with him but was unwell. The sky was blue above him, it was warm; he walked on ashes and sharp rocks, a lava flow, now crusted over was on his right. He could see steam vents. It was a volcano. There was a woman with him, with long black hair, pale skin, red lips and blue eyes. She was beautiful. But it wasn't his wife. She seemed familiar, an ancient memory perhaps, from a different life.

Who was she?

Up ahead he could see a cave, dark and forboding. Something was inside. He felt a pang of fear in his stomach as he approached. But he did not want to go inside, it felt ominous. There was something in there, something ancient and primal. The mountain shook as he stood there, deciding whether or not to go in.

Peter's thoughts were broken when he stumbled on a rock and fell flat on his face, the Bergen full of bricks falling on top of him. He cursed as he lay on the grass, drank some water and took a short rest. What did the dream mean?

Then he looked around him at the raw, rugged landscape, his deep blue eyes shining with a light. Peter loved the Welsh mountains, the beauty and wildness of it all, hinting at ancient mysteries and magic. He felt part of it.

No office job for him.

He felt a sense of peace as he set off again, running down the hills and then half trotting, half running up the next. He was filled with a wild joy as he ran, like a deer running through the forest, at one with the Earth energy all around him. It was the same energy as Cernunnos, the green man-god, with antlers, walking the forest, the oak tree, the deer and forest animals—the energy of nature all around him. The green energy of the dragon ran through his veins, ancient and powerful, like an ancient warrior god. Nature sang to him as he ran, as did the trees, the grass, and the wild animals.

He felt alive.

The endurance march was completed by Peter in just three hours, a record. Vinnie just scraped through in just under twenty hours. Peter did have some aches and pains, the Bergen had chaffed the skin on his back, and it was red raw, but that was nothing compared to Vinnie. He was a physical wreck.

Pen y Fan, at 2,907 feet above sea-level, is the highest peak in South Wales, situated in the Brecon Beacons National Park. Peter recalled the run at the top of Pen y Fan.

It was 3 a.m.

It was pitch black.

There was freezing rain and a 60 mph wind. The conditions were atrocious. Everyone was struggling. Of the 20 that set out that night, 12 had given up and were wrapped up in their survival bags, shivering. Peter didn't have much sympathy—they knew what they signed up for.

Vinnie was bent double against the wind trying to catch Peter, who egged him on. 'Don't give up now Vinnie!' Peter screamed. Vinnie collapsed, blown over by the wind, Peter went back and picked him up. 'In one hour we will be off the mountain, having a brew!' he screamed into his ear. Vinnie had lost all his toenails and was limping, but he carried on. 'That's the spirit,' cried Peter to the mountain gods, who were throwing their worst at the pair.

Then Vinnie tripped in the darkness and fell 20 feet down the mountain, into the blackness of space. Peter felt his way through the darkness, through the driving rain, and found him in a depression in the ground, just two feet away from a 1000 foot drop.

A precipice.

Death was only one footstep away. Vinnie was wild-eyed as he recovered back up the slope, and Peter's excellent vision found a safe route down the mountain. Peter was silent as he walked, he had nearly lost Vinnie.

His brother Vinnie.

As he approached a lorry, he could make out Des and Artie, handing out cups of tea. Vinnie hobbled up beside him, looking like a ghost as Peter warmed his freezing wet hands on the steaming mug of tea that Des gave him.

'You're the first two back,' said Des, handing him a cigarette.

'It's hell up there, DS,' replied Peter, feeling the wonderful-tasting liquid warm his insides.

'That's the idea,' said Artie handing Vinnie his tea.

Peter took his boot off. He had lost two toenails on the previous march but amazingly grew them back within one day.

'How come you got all your toenails, Morgan, nobody else has?' said Des sipping a mug of tea.

'Ain't natural,' added Artie, eyeing Peter with suspicion.

Following the Hill phase in the Brecon Beacons Peter's wish came true and he traveled to Belize for the jungle phase. Exotic places. He was taught jungle survival skills: patrol formation, movement and navigation. If anything, the jungle phase was the toughest of all the phases, with its hot, sticky, energy-drawing heat, dehydration, mosquitoes, fatigue, as well as the constant dampness—everything was damp.

He marvelled at the wildlife: monkeys, snakes and spiders. He didn't like the spiders. Another batch of candidates dropped out in the jungle phase. They were gradually being whittled down, but he would stay the course, for he was Bulletproof Pete, toughest of the tough. He returned to Stirling Lines *(Hereford)* to finish training in foreign weapons, battle plans and to take part in combat survival exercises.

The final phase of selection is the weeklong escape and evasion. Peter and Vinnie were formed into a patrol, an SAS four-man unit, with two other candidates, dressed in old Second World War uniforms and carrying only a tin can filled with survival equipment. They were told to head for a point by first light. Peter was worried about Vinnie, he wasn't keeping up, and for the last few miles Peter had supported him as Vinnie had sprained his ankle, but nobody talked about it.

He would do anything for Vinnie.

They were being hunted by half a battalion of infantry and off-duty policemen with dogs and helicopters. They clambered over the rough and uneven ground, the damp and cold starting to chill their bones. They climbed over a wooden fence and found themselves in a field, but it was misty. They had gone 50 yards when out of the mist they could hear hooves approaching. Out of the darkness came a charging bull! Vinnie turned to run and fell over. He looked frightened as the charging mass of muscle came towards him.

Peter stood his ground between Vinnie and the oncoming bull. As it came close, he dodged to the side like a bullfighter and grabbed the horns of the ferocious bull, which bellowed like a caged beast. The bull could not move as Peter held its horns. He twisted the head of the angry beast, its eyes blazing with anger, then flipped it onto its back, without harming it.

'Run Vinnie!' shouted Peter as they got out of the field. They both laughed as they climbed over the fence.

Most soldiers would be captured within a couple of hours, but Peter and Vinnie managed to evade capture by hiding in a ditch and covering themselves in branches and grass. They could hear the voices of the hunters and the barks of dogs as they lay shivering and motionless daring not to breathe—then Vinnie gave a loud burp, and it was all over.

'Come on sunshine,' said the off-duty policeman, as he pulled back the branches, holding his dog on a leash. Then Des walked up, a half-smile on his face. 'These are the last two.' As they were put in the back of a truck with the other captured soldiers, filthy and exhausted, Peter had to laugh, Vinnie had the uncanny, and anti-social habit, of being able to burp and fart at the same time.

Only Vinnie. Peter watched the dawn rise as he looked out of the truck and exchanged smiles with brother Vinnie.

Nearly there.

Back at the base, two Americans in military fatigues, wearing dark glasses were talking to Des and Artie. 'Did endurance in three hours,' said Des, addressing the Americans, who nodded.

One of the Americans got on his satellite phone. 'Yes sir, I will talk to his Colonel.'

Chapter 4

MENTAL TORTURE

Up until this point, the phases tested physical fitness, which Peter excelled in. The imminent final selection test was possibly the most difficult: resistance to interrogation, RTI, which lasts for 36 hours, and tests a candidate's mental toughness. Only if the candidate passes this test, do they pass for selection.

Peter was pushed into a cold, featureless concrete room and put into a 'stress position', his hands on the wall, legs apart.

Disorientating white noise was blasted at him as Peter focused his mind, going into a meditative state, losing sense of time and space. He didn't know how much time had passed, it could have been hours or a whole day as he was bundled out of the cold, soulless room.

He was in the interrogation room proper, sitting opposite the two interrogators, Des and Artie. Up until this point, Peter had played along with the interrogators, knowing he could walk away. He only gave four pieces of information: name, rank, army number, and date of birth.

But now, they sat there in silence for a while looking at him, impassive, looking for an angle, a lever, to make him crack. Then the real interrogation began.

'Artie told me your penis is so small it's a wonder you can pee,' smiled Des. Artie laughed. It was expected—the personal insults. Peter was silent, *they were trying to bait him.*

'I bet you used to sleep with your mummy, didn't you?' Asked Artie, an evil smile on his face. Peter's blood started to rise, the ancient warrior blood—an insult could only be repaid in blood. Should he kill them both?

As Peter stared at Des and Artie, his countenance changed. Shadows flickered in the corner of the room, the atmosphere changed, becoming darker, denser, malevolent.

Des and Artie hesitated as they looked at Peter, he seemed to grow larger, maybe it was the light playing tricks, but his appearance had changed. His eyes shone a fierce blue like ice fire. Artie looked at Des, then leaned forward.

'Were you a mummy's boy. Were you Morgan?'

'I bet you wanted to fuck your mother didn't you?' The room seemed to grow even darker. The atmosphere seemed heavy, like a thunderstorm approaching. The room shook a little, as Peter gripped the solid steel table legs, his biceps flexed, and he bent the sturdy steel table in half, before their very eyes. Des and Artie stood up and backed away, genuinely frightened, but Peter was silent.

'Interrogation over!' said Des as they hurriedly left the room. Peter sighed, they had tested him, but he had not killed them, as he had wanted to. He had kept his mouth shut, and he had passed the test. He sat there for a while, then walked out into the open air.

He had passed the test, but he had come very close to killing them.

Vinnie was there, looking like a sack of potatoes. Peter was glad it was all over as he joined Vinnie outside. Vinnie, coming from an East End crime family, had struggled with the insults.

'I nearly nutted Artie,' said Vinnie, 'especially what he said about my mother.'

'Good job you didn't, I was tempted myself. Des and Artie didn't know how close they came,' replied Peter, then added, 'it's all over now, don't get emotional, it's just training. Relax mate. Why come all this way to fail at the last minute?'

Then they saw Des approaching them, 'No hard feelings eh?' as he gave them a cigarette each. Peter nodded as Des lit his cigarette for him and he felt the nicotine kick as he sucked in the smoke—his first cigarette for two months.

Peter looked around him, but they were the only two waiting in the cold drizzle, looking like tramps.

Des let them finish their cigarettes, then instructed them to go to the Colonel's office. Des managed a smile and had a look of admiration on his face. At that point Peter knew that he and Vinnie had done it.

Chapter 5

GETTING BADGED

Vinnie and Peter wait outside the Colonel's office in the SAS headquarters. Vinnie tucks his shirt in and tidies his hair. They are filthy and exhausted, both mentally and physically from the RTI, Peter much less so than Vinnie, who looks haggard. Peter feels calm and at peace as they are invited in and stand before Colonel Bradley, who is busy reading a document.

They stand before the gray-haired, stony-faced Colonel, then he looks up. His hard eyes soften a little, and he manages a smile. He stands up and hands Peter and Vinnie the SAS badged cap—he has an inquisitive look in his eye as if not quite sure what to make of Peter. That morning he had taken a call from an old CIA contact, asking about this young man. What was he—*a freak of nature?*

'Congratulations Gentlemen. Of the 102 who started, you and three others are the only ones to pass final selection. Welcome to the SAS. You will both join A Squadron, Mobility Troop. Dismissed.'

Peter is happy, he knows how desperately difficult it is to get in. But he is in. The SAS has four squadrons: A, B, D and G. Each squadron has four troops: Air, Mountain, Boat and Mobility. Each troop has sixteen men when fully manned, *(four 4-man teams)*, but as the SAS is so difficult to get into, it is generally fewer than this.

Peter and Vinnie grin at each other as they salute and walk out, a feeling of exhilaration and accomplishment filling their souls as they look at their new caps, which sport a badge with a dagger, the sword of Excalibur—with wings on either side. Peter studies the sword on the badge—it seems to resonate with him for some obscure reason. The SAS motto is "Who Dares Wins," and the emblem is a dagger with wings. Their philosophy is to train hard, fight easy. 'I can live with that', thought Peter.

'We did it Vinnie—we did it!' Peter claps Vinnie on the back.

'My old man will be so proud,' a tear wells in Vinnie's eye.

'So would my father, if he was alive', thinks Peter. Now he is in, he can find out what happened to his father, even if he had to kick some butt to do so.

He watches as he recognizes one of the soldiers on selection who has collapsed, being stretchered into an ambulance—he does not look good. He is shaking and moaning incoherently—as though he has had a breakdown. He is a fellow candidate from the Royal Regiment of Wales, Lefty—he does everything with his left hand. Lefty is a bit awkward and clumsy, and Peter used to stick up for him when the lads took the piss out of him. As he watches Lefty being put on the ambulance he reflects—Lefty knew what the risks were when he signed up for selection. That was the discipline, but he hopes he will be ok.

As he stands there, reflecting on his achievement, he can see the SAS instructor team, Des and Artie, walking towards them. 'That guy has supernatural powers, it ain't natural,' whispers Artie, thinking Peter cannot hear, but of course, he can.

This time, instead of shouting at him, they are smiling and shake his hand, congratulating him and Vinnie, a look of pure admiration on their faces.

Des and Artie—hard, experienced SAS soldiers, battle hardened, with the scars to prove it, look at Peter as if they have a question that needs answering. No one has finished the selection process more easily than this man. No one has completed the soul-destroying marches quicker or survived the mind-numbing torture in the interrogation sessions more easily, than this man. Their experience in the interrogation room with Peter had shaken them.

Des looks at Peter. A look of disbelief, was this man human? Maybe they would find their answers later. It's impossible to cheat selection, so how did he do it? He would certainly be fast-tracked for promotion. Des feels a bit jealous—it took him ten years to become a staff sergeant in the SAS.

Peter looks at each of them in turn, knowing they have been through the same experience and come out the other side. They are made of the right stuff. He feels humbled.

'I see the truth of it,' he smiles.

'How did you do it?' asks Des. Peter just smiles again, his blue eyes shining.

He shakes their hands again, then they walk off none the wiser. Vinnie claps him on the back. 'I'm taking some leave to see my old man and Gill. You?'

'I'm going home to see Jennifer and the kids, before the action starts again. She's probably forgotten what I look like'. Peter hugs Vinnie and claps him on the back.

'See you soon brother, don't get into any trouble!' shouts Vinnie as he walks off.

Peter collects his gear and gets a lift to the train station from two Americans who have studied him. Silently. As he gets out of the car, they give him a card with a telephone number on it.

'If you ever need a change of scenery let us know, we could use a man of your talents,' the taller American drawls in a Southern accent.

As he stands on the platform, he reflects. He has passed selection, but who are the two Americans who gave him a lift? He has seen them hanging around the Colonel's office. They looked, and felt like spooks.

As he sits on the train he looks at the card. It has a Virginia code, he knows because Jennifer's parents live there. As he watches the countryside go by he looks back on his life and how he met his wife, Jennifer. In his late teens he had a hollow feeling in his soul that he needed to finish his education, so decided to study, part-time, and did an Open University degree course in Geography and Languages, which is where he met Jennifer on one of the study days at the campus. It was love at first sight over tea and sandwiches in the canteen. It had taken all his warrior courage to ask her for a first date—a picnic and walk in the Brecon Beacons. He had strolled over to her, his heart beating fast. 'You're American, aren't you?' he said.

She smiled. 'Yes, I am,' her brown eyes sparkling at this handsome, rugged, Welshman with ice blue eyes, and bulging muscles.

'You're new here.' smiled Peter. 'Let me take you on a picnic, the countryside is beautiful in Wales.' She nodded, admiring the charismatic bald man with blue eyes. They ate their food in a wood, in a hidden valley surrounded by bluebells and lush green grass, the sun shining through the trees. It had been Peter's favourite place since childhood. They were married soon after. Life seemed to be working out for him at last.

Chapter 6

HOME SWEET HOME

Peter thought about how long it had been since he last saw his family, as he walked up the country lane past his local pub, up onto the moor. It had been nearly a year—too long. Would his children recognize him? He stood there a while breathing in the air and admiring the view of the surrounding hills; wild, rugged and ancient. He walked down into the small wooded, hidden valley in the Brecon Beacons where his home was. Home, where he would find peace from his memories of the selection course.

The air was fresh and full of the smells of spring as he trod through the dewy morning grass. All he could hear were the birds singing as he made his way along an old worn path through the woods. As well as the flowers he could smell horses; up ahead was a wild pony chewing the grass. As he passed it on the woodland path, he stroked its back, it turned his head and looked at him, then continued chewing the grass

He would be home soon. The sun shone through the oak and pine trees, then he could see bluebells, and he stopped for a moment to admire the beauty. A squirrel stopped and looked at him, then scurried up an oak tree carrying an acorn. He loved this place, it was so peaceful.

Magical.

As he stood there in the silence, he could hear a stream trickling through the woods. He walked near some rocks and looked at the clear stream as it made its way down through the trees near to his house. He was sure there were fish, maybe trout in there. He would fish with his son, and they would have fried fish for dinner. His son used to drink from the stream. Jennifer used to tell him off for it, but he seemed none the worse for wear. It was good, clean water, trickling down from rocks at the top of the valley.

As he looked at the water in a dreamy, half-trance he seemed to enter a different reality. Time seemed to stop, and there was silence, as he experienced a vision of a large, ancient black book with gold embossed letters that he didn't understand. He could see the book in front of him. He looked at a bird frozen in mid-air. He could see a man, a bearded priest.

When Peter awoke, it was late afternoon; at least several hours had passed, and his family was expecting him. Had selection driven him mad? He shrugged off the visions and put it down to fatigue as he quickened his pace through the woods to his house, in the centre of the valley. There were stories that these woods were haunted by a wise old man, a Celtic warrior priest from early Christian times when the Celtic and Christian religions were one. He lived in a cave in the woods at the edge of the valley. Some say he had traveled all the way from the Eastern Mediterranean. Was it the man in his dreams?

But he dismissed this as he came out of the woods to a small clearing. His heart felt glad as he saw his timber house, strong and sturdy with flowers growing up its walls. He stood and smiled as he looked at his wooden house, which seemed to grow out of the woods. His absence was telling—the grass was overgrown and the gutters needed clearing out.

But he was home.

He could see Jennifer, his darling wife in the kitchen window, her long brown hair and bright brown eyes; he suddenly remembered how beautiful she was. Everything about her was perfect. Her skin, her hair, her smile—which could light up a room.

His children were playing in the garden as they looked up at the stranger coming out of the woods.

'Daddy, daddy!' they came running down the garden path and threw their arms around him.

Jennifer looked up from the kitchen sink and ran out of the house, her eyes tearful as they all hugged each other, laughing and crying.

Jennifer stood there, pensive.

'Well, how did you do?'

Peter showed her his new cap, and Jennifer threw her arms around him. 'Does this mean you'll be spending more time at home?' asked Jennifer, her bright face looking hopeful, her brown eyes lighting up.

'We'll see,' replied Peter, trying to sound optimistic. He smiled at her but inside he knew he would be away a lot, perhaps putting his life in danger, but he needed to find out who this warrior was inside of him; find some explanations for his dreams and visions.

Why did he have the strength of ten men?

How could he run so fast?

Why did he have super vision and super hearing, and why did he feel like there was someone watching over him?

His gut told him he had a destiny to fulfil. He knew that meant leaving his family.

Again.

They all sat on garden chairs in their small garden, surrounded by pine and oak trees, the late afternoon sun beaming down on them. Brilliantly coloured butterflies were fluttering around. Peter had never felt happier than he was right now. He was finally home with his family. The sun was shining, and Peter and Jennifer could not stop looking into each other's eyes. Then Peter kissed Jennifer and held her in his arms.

Peter took his young son into his arms and stroked his blonde hair.

'Let's go fishing tomorrow, in the stream, in the woods, son.'

'Yes, Dad,' Robert replied, his face beaming.

Peter then lifted his daughter Sally onto his lap, and she gave him a big kiss on the cheek.

'Did you miss Daddy?' he asked.

'Yes, can I come fishing too, Daddy?' as she kissed and hugged him.

'Of course, you can, sweetheart.' He thought back to his vision of the priest in the wood by the stream.

Peter looked at his family, and he was filled with the warm joy of contentment as he thought back to the time when he and Vinnie had built this house from scratch. Peter had asked permission for extended army leave so he could start building his house. He and Vinnie would scour the woods for wood in the deep hidden valley in the Brecon he called home. They looked for fallen oaks and pines that were not rotten, and selected oaks that he could legally cut down with a felling license from the forestry commission, without orders signed in triplicate—Peter hated paperwork and bureaucracy. He used to tie a rope around the trees and drag them back singlehanded, with Vinnie secretly admiring his strength, and they used a mini sawmill to cut and shape the wood for the beams and tresses for the house. Jennifer and Gill would make lemonade as Peter and Vinnie collapsed in chairs in the garden, sweating like pigs and gulping down the cold drink, seeing who could make the loudest burp, laughing childishly.

In the evening, they would make stew from local lamb on a roaring log fire, the Dutch oven sizzling the roast lamb, potatoes, and vegetables. They would look up at the stars in the clear night sky, getting drunk on wine, often falling asleep in their chairs. Jennifer and Gill would keep on talking into the early hours, listening to their husband's snoring, then help them to their beds, 'magical days,' he thought. This was as much Vinnie's house as his, he helped to build it after all.

It was beautiful in the spring and summer, the bluebells sprouting forth, the clear stream meandering its way through the woods, the sunshine breaking its way through the treetops. At Christmas they would collect chestnuts, then go home and cook them around the wood burner, warming their hands.

Jennifer had a longing look in her eyes as she gazed at Peter, imagining his rock hard muscles, and iron grip, on her soft body.

Peter smiled at her, the warrior lust in his blue eyes.

'You two go and play. Me and Mummy are going for a rest.'

They went upstairs to the bedroom, tore their clothes off and made frantic love, making up for lost time. Afterwards, Peter fell into a deep sleep, dreaming of battle and a shining sword—and a name, it was on the tip of his tongue. Then he woke up shouting, 'Caius! Caius!'

Jennifer put her arms around him, shaking him - 'What is it? Who is Caius?' Peter looked at her, his piercing blue eyes like jewels, the eyes of a warrior. Jennifer thought he looked like a god as she ran her fingers over his bullet hard, sinewy muscles, resting her head on his chest, then reaching downwards with her hand.

Chapter 7

East End Welcome

Vinnie, strong, muscular, fit and wearing an expression of permanent aggression on his face walks down Whitechapel Road in the East End of London. He reflects on his life, how he met his friend Pete, how he joined the army, and how he had the choice of working for his father, as an East End gangster, or joining the army. He remembers the conversation with his father, Reg.

'Son, you're a good boy, and I'm very proud of you. Me and your mother love you very much, but this is not the life for you. I don't want you to be like me, it's too late for me, but you have a chance. Join the army son, see the world. Make me proud.'

Vinnie has never forgotten his father's words. He smiles as he looks around. It is familiar territory, the place, where he grew up, his manor. His father Reg is a local businessman, as Vinnie calls him, but everyone is afraid of Reg, even the local law enforcement.

He smooths down his leather jacket and jeans as he walks into the Blind Beggar, a notorious pub in the East End. Everyone turns to look as he walks in, and stops talking. In one corner of the bar stand four very large, serious-looking heavies. They are wearing smart Italian suits, and they sport combed back hair. In the silent pub, in the middle of the bar, are his wife, Gill and his father Reg, who is wearing a white shirt, black tie and has combed back hair. Reg's granite features crack as he sees his son. Vinnie walks towards his father, trying to contain his emotion. As Reg hugs him, there are loud shouts and cheers from around the bar. "Hurrah for Vinnie!"

'We're so proud son, so proud!' Reg wipes away a tear as he stands back and admires his son.

'My son, a member of Her Majesty's Special Air Service.'

Vinnie looks at Gill, at her long blonde hair, and cuddles her, as he beckons for a pint of beer. Reg claps him on the back. They clink glasses as they down the real ale. Everyone cheers again.

'It's supposed to be a secret, Dad—getting badged,' whispered Vinnie. 'Don't worry son, your secret is safe with us. Where is Ron? He's supposed to be here'. At that moment, as if by magic, Ron walks in and walks up to Vinnie, an expectant look on his face.

'Hello, Uncle Ron.'

'Well, son?'

'I did it—me and Pete passed!'

'I'm so proud, me and Reg, were so proud, so very proud,' says Ron as he puts his hands on Vinnie's shoulders.

'Drinks are on the house,' shouts Reg as the piano player begins a rendition of Knees up Mother Brown.

'Have some jellied eels son,' offers Reg as Vinnie tucks in. Vinnie puts his arm around Gill and kisses her again, as he looks at his family, his gangster family, and feels proud. His father Reg had insisted that he join the army, rather than become a gangster; looking back on it, it was a good decision. But then again, does the gangster blood flow in his veins?

Can he ever escape it?

Does he want to escape it?

After all, they are his family. Bonded by blood and an oath of loyalty; *they have their own code of honor,* which they observe religiously. You never rat on anyone, and you always follow orders, to the letter. Family and loyalty.

Vinnie thinks about his best friend Peter, and how they met in Wales as teenagers, spending weekends camping and hunting rabbits. Vinnie wanted to sharpen his air rifle skills, so he went to Wales camping, and shooting rabbits. He met Peter, practising his hunting and trapping skills. They hit it off straight away, hunting and trapping rabbits, and roasting them over a wood fire, under a starlit sky, Peter telling tales about old Welsh legends and Vinnie bragging about his pranks in the shadier parts of the East End of London.

Happy days.

In the Blind Beggar, they carry on drinking and partying until the early hours, but nobody complains about the noise. Later that night, a policeman patrolling alone hears the noise from the pub, thinks about having a chat with the landlord, then thinks again, besides he has a family to think about.

Chapter 8

007

MI6 HEADQUARTERS, VAUXHALL CROSS, LONDON

Peter arrives with Colonel Bradley at the MI6 building, River House, in Vauxhall Cross, London in a blacked-out Range Rover. The official name for MI6 is the Secret Intelligence Service (SIS), but everyone at Hereford refers to it as 6. Peter hasn't been told what the meeting is about, and when he asks his Colonel, he just smiles at him. 'You will see.'

On the way down from Hereford, he has asked about his father. 'It's classified,' was the curt reply. Peter felt miffed; *he would have to use some leverage.*

They go through airport-style scanners and a body search. Their SAS IDs are checked against a database, the smart-looking security guard checking their faces. 'Sorry about the extra checks gentlemen. You are clear to proceed.' Peter has heard a rumour that they had nearly let in a terrorist the previous week, who had explosives on him. It never got into the papers, of course, it would be too embarrassing. They are escorted into a lift which goes down to the lower levels of the building. Peter glances at their black-suited and silent escort—definitely ex-military, probably Special Forces.

Silent man.

He remembers the James Bond movies, with a suave debonair 007 driving an Aston Martin. If only the public knew the truth, it is people like him—battle-hardened SAS soldiers who have been recruited by MI6 to do their dirty work. Civvies are simply not up to the job of being a secret agent—not the 007 kind anyway. No going to casinos in tuxedos, but spending hours, days, holed up in a dingy room, eating unhealthy food, monitoring suspects, gathering intelligence. When in the field taking enough Imodium to constipate an elephant—an SAS operative must leave no trace of their presence there. No DNA evidence, smelling like a tramp. Boredom. Then moments of extreme danger and adrenaline.

And extreme violence.

Kill or be killed.

The lift opens, and they are escorted into a huge white room, which is empty except for a large rectangular glass room in the centre. It seems out of place. From a hundred yards away Peter can see someone sitting at a table in the glass room. Mid-forties. Posh looking. Pinstriped suit, combed back hair, old school. Their footsteps echo as they walk in silence towards the sterile looking glass room.

Silent Man punches a code into a panel, and the door slides open. The man sitting opposite them beckons them to sit down. Peter can see a perfectly ironed shirt with a motif, hand-made. Expensive. Gold cufflinks, old school tie—bet he went to Eton, but there is a hardness about him—as if he has seen military service. He has a scar on his left cheek.

His face cracks open as he smiles, 'Ah welcome Colonel Bradley and Sergeant Morgan. I am Nigel Goldbroom. Peter—can I call you Peter?' as he looks at Peter, questions in his eyes. Peter takes an instant liking to him, he seems genuine, not a bureaucrat.

Not a politician.

'Yes, Sir Nigel, I just wondered why I was brought here?' Peter asked.

Colonel Bradley and Sir Nigel smile, as the SIS Chief leans forward.

'Myself and the Colonel were thinking of entering you into the Olympics young man!' Colonel Bradley sniggered, and his blue eyes sparkled.

'But then you wouldn't be secret anymore would you?'

Sir Nigel looks at some papers on his desk.

'You did the 65k endurance in three hours, a record unlikely to be beaten. The strength of ten men, super hearing, and vision. Everyone's talking about you, Peter. And clever, a degree in languages, including Arabic. You can be a great asset to us. I have agreed with the Colonel here that you can work for us occasionally. Is that ok with you?'

'Sir Nigel, I like you—you seem genuine, so I will say yes.' Then Peter adds, 'As long as Vinnie works with me. That's my only condition.'

'Ah yes but he doesn't have your abilities.'

'He's my wingman, I don't do missions without him.' Sir Nigel looks through his papers again.

'Corporal Vinnie Carson, of questionable character, rebellious, father a suspected gangster. Ok but you must vouch for his behaviour.'

'Could provide useful intel—his father I mean,' suggests Colonel Bradley brushing back his silver hair,' raising his eyebrows.

'On London terror suspects. Mmm,' Sir Nigel rubs his chin.

'Me and Vinnie are a team,' prompts Peter.

'OK agreed,' smiles Sir Nigel who now leans forward, a worried look on his face.

Peter's demeanour becomes intense as he stares at Bradley, then at Sir Nigel, 'One more thing. I want to find out what happened to my father. And no bullshit.'

'That's classified,' replies Colonel Bradley. Sir Nigel looks sympathetically at Peter. 'Peter, I wish I could help you, but as the good colonel said, it's classified.'

'Maybe I will go and work for the Yanks then,' says Peter, arms folded, the muscles bulging in his smart sergeants uniform, knowing that will set the cat among the pigeons. Leverage. They thought they could keep it secret – but he knows the CIA are looking to hire him.

Sir Nigel gives the colonel a panicked look.

'Peter, please be reasonable. Look, as soon as you get back from the mission, we will have a chat. Promise.'

'What mission?' asks Peter, his blue intelligent eyes blazing.

'This is a secure room, a sealed room, sound and bug-proof, for what we are about to discuss is above top secret. There will be no record of our conversation.' Sir Nigel drinks some water, clears his throat, then continues.

'Thing is Peter, we have a problem here at the Intelligence Service. A serious problem. We think we have a mole in our organization. A rat. We have a few suspects but nothing concrete. We suspect they are working for the other side. With the terrorists. In Yemen. We are not sure if its Al Qaeda or some or other terrorist group. They have kidnapped the ambassador to Saudi Arabia. It's a black operation, no-one will hear about it. You will receive a full briefing when you get there. The thing is—and this is the important bit—I have arranged for all the suspects to go with you as MI6 liaisons with your SAS team, which you will be leading. Keep an eye on them. There's Saunders, Ponsonby, and Ahmed. Here's a file on each of them. Read it then give back to me. It cannot go outside of this room.'

Peter reads through the two-page report on each suspect. They all appear to be clean—good service records, no suspicious activities. Ahmed is a Muslim, but Peter will not hold that against him. He knows many good Muslims himself—hardworking and good family men. Saunders is from South Africa. Ex-military, a Christian, church-going. Immaculate record. Another good family man. Ponsonby. Single. Went to Eton.

'Did you go to Eton with Ponsonby Sir?' asks Peter. Sir Nigel, surprised at Peter's perception leans forward, 'Yes he's a good man. He was my roommate.' Peter looks Sir Nigel in the eye. There is a look of sadness in it, then it is gone.

'Sir Nigel, let me be frank, these missions are dangerous enough, without rats in the pack. I need to trust people. I trust my men implicitly. It's a dangerous variable.'

'I understand Peter, but we want you to find out who the rat is.'

They sit silent for a while.

'Thing is Peter, I don't trust anyone,' Sir Nigel said unhappily.

'Here is my personal number, it's a secure line.' Sir Nigel looks desperate, as he hands Peter a card.

'I have one more condition,' asks a poker-faced Peter.

'Yes…what is it?' asks a desperate-looking Sir Nigel.

'I want brown leather trim on my DB9 please.'

Colonel Bradley and Sir Nigel nearly fall off their chairs as they laugh. 'Excellent, excellent, priceless Peter. I will enjoy working with you,' laughs Sir Nigel, 'brown leather trim,' he chortles—then his face became serious again.

As they come out of the MI6 building into the fresh air, Peter thinks he will enjoy working with Sir Nigel.

The Range Rover with blacked out windows pulls up outside.

'You are going directly to RAF Lyneham and flying out tonight. Good luck Peter. I don't have to tell you how important this mission is,' says Colonel Bradley as he shakes Peter's hand.

Chapter 9

YEMEN

Peter and Vinnie are sitting in a bone-shaking C130 Hercules military transport with five other men from A Squadron of the SAS. It is a rushed operation—only twenty-four hours' notice—and it shows. It was supposed to be two four-man teams, but one operative was pulled at the last minute. No explanation. The planning?

What planning? Peter and Vinnie have had no time to do their normal triple checks on their kit, as they normally do, apart from anything else. They have prepped their mission at the hangar back at the British base in Qatar - RAF Al Udeid, which is used to support military operations in the Middle East.

Peter's mind races at a million miles per hour: not enough time to check their weapons *(an M16 M203 with grenade launcher)*, ammunition, radios, maps, survival kit, food. Not enough time to beg, borrow and raid the stores for all the kit they need. Not enough time to get some food down their necks before the early evening flight. Something is bound to have been missed in the rush. He likes attention to detail, but he supposes time is of the essence. And last but not least, flaky MI6 liaisons.

A rat in the pack.

'I cannot fight on an empty stomach,' Vinnie keeps complaining.

Peter feels uncomfortable, in the noisy, cold C130—a flying box basically. No first-class loungers, no champagne and steak dinner, and certainly no pretty stewardesses. Peter wishes he was back home, but he is here, and he has to make the best of it, for his men. But he has that uneasy feeling in his gut again.

The noisy C130 hits some turbulence; Vinnie winces and whispers to Peter about his sore arse. Vinnie is not a good flyer. Peter is busy looking at the map again…remembering the rushed briefing by the CO. A young, fresh looking MI6 man, a short, thin officer type with a posh accent called Ponsonby.

One of the suspects.

Peter and Vinnie took an instant dislike to him and nicknamed him Pencilneck. He has no military experience—seen no action, has no idea what it's like out in the field. Ahmed and Saunders are there, but they keep themselves busy, avoiding the SAS men, avoiding their gaze, then looking at Ponsonby. Peter thinks there is an agenda here, and he doesn't like it.

Not one bit.

Pencilneck begins the briefing. 'Chaps, some terrorists, probably Al Qaeda, are holding the Saudi ambassador to Yemen, possibly in a group of villages on the edge of the Rub' al-Khali desert. The villages are near Thamud in north-eastern Yemen. We don't know the ambassador's exact location, but we think it's here.' Pencilneck points to a map on a board. 'We suspect there are least four terrorists, but there may be as many as twenty.'

Peter quickly calculates that it's a thousand square miles of territory. Not enough intel he thinks, how can they plan their mission? Pencilneck continued.

'He was kidnapped some twenty-four hours ago. Their demands are that we release ten Al Qaeda terrorists being held in Riyadh, Saudi Arabia. We, of course, do not negotiate with terrorists. The Saudi government wants to keep this quiet, and there is a news blackout, so this has been classified as a black ops mission, no one will ever hear of it. So if you get in trouble, you know the score.'

The assembled men winced; if things go pear shaped they will leave us with our dicks hanging out, thinks Peter.

'Mission code name is Desert Fox One which will be commanded by Sergeant Morgan. Wheels up in minus 30.'

Pencilneck gives a false smile at this point, trying to look confident, and receives dagger looks from the seven-man SAS team, particularly Vinnie. 'If we don't make it back I'm going to kill him,' Vinnie whispers.

'Vinnie, if we don't make it back…never mind,' Peter reassures Vinnie, 'I will make sure we get back.' Peter stands up to address Pencilneck.

'Target appreciation. We need more intel. Number of terrorists, photographs, weapons. We need a precise location of our target; our men are at risk without more information. This is not how we work. We also need to formulate an immediate action plan, in case we get into trouble, besides this is a black op, we don't want to be left with our dicks hanging out.'

His fellow SAS men admire Peter for his directness with the Rupert . They like him because he doesn't stand for any nonsense from officers, and this has made him some enemies. Pencilneck looks with disdain at Peter as if to say, 'Impudent fool.'

'We will provide further intelligence as we get it, Sergeant Morgan. Dismissed.'

Out on the tarmac, Peter is chatting to the C130 pilot. He is nicknamed "Kojak" because he has a bald head and wears dark glasses, just like Telly Savalas. He looks worried.

'Pete laddy, I've had no weather reports for Christ's sake. I canna fly without up-to-date weather!' says Kojak with a deep Scottish accent. Peter looks ready to kill as he speaks to his Scottish pilot, 'We got fuck all on target appreciation. I don't like this mission Kojak I don't mind telling you, too many variables.' Kojak nods.

At that moment Pencilneck strolls up, eyes squinting in the bright sunshine. 'We need wheels up in twenty minutes.'

Kojak looks Pencilneck straight in the eye. 'I canna fly without weather reports laddy, I'm responsible for these men, I need the METAR report before I fly!'

'You will fly in twenty, and that's official,' is his reply, then adds, 'Besides, there's little chance of bad weather this time of year, particularly over the desert.'

Kojak shakes his head, muttering, as he strolls off to his C130 to make final checks. Peter looks at Pencilneck and swears that if this mission goes to rat-shit, he will do him himself. In military missions, especially the high-risk missions the Special Air Service carry out, any small error can soon escalate out of control. Men die. That's why preparation is the key. Men's lives depend on it.

Peter is responsible for these men. They are his brothers. Brothers in arms. Pencilneck looks at the fearsome presence of Peter,: bald-headed, blue-eyed, six-foot frame, built like Bruce Lee, the SAS man who is called "Bulletproof." He has read his personnel record, and it is impressive, if insubordinate, but then again the SAS does not recruit "yes" men but operates a system of democracy, where each man can have his say, even if it contradicts a superior officer. Each SAS man is an elite soldier, qualified to have his say, at any planning meeting.

He gives that false smile again and goes to shake Peter's hand, but Peter just looks at him, eyes burning.

Chapter 10

HALO DROP

Peter looked at Pencilneck in silence, with his thousand-yard stare, keeping his counsel. He didn't wear his heart on his sleeve like Vinnie, but he would ensure justice was done if required. It would be a HALO drop—high altitude, low opening—for secrecy and stealth so they could land quietly and surprise the terrorists. They would be flying at 30,000 feet.

On the C130, Peter looked across at Sebastian. He was rough looking, had a lived-in face, looked foul, but felt fair. He was a Geordie and had an earthy Geordie accent. He had turned religious, was reading a Bible, and had a nervous twitch. Peter was a bit worried about him, Sebastian had been showing signs of stress recently. Understandable, but that was the job they did, that was the discipline.

They were in the life and death business. Peter and Vinnie both liked him and looked to him for spiritual guidance and advice like a father figure. He would often read quotes from the Bible, and Peter would listen, trying to squeeze out an ounce of wisdom to explain what they did.

Peter looked at the other members of his team, all oddballs, all super fit, all with a touch of that resourceful fighting spirit: Baz, Mad Mike, Des, and Artie. He had forgiven Des and Artie their insults about his mother at RTI. Their maturity and experience would be useful on this mission.

On top of their flying suits, they had oxygen lines, and strapped to each of their backs was the BT80 Special Forces parachute. By necessity the straps were very tight, the last thing you need is a loose strap at 10,000 feet.

Peter recalled with humour, back at the RAF base on the ground, how Vinnie, with help from a parachute dispatcher, had put his parapack on in a hurry and had trapped one of his nuts inside the strap. Peter, Sebastian and the dispatcher all rushed to adjust the strap and free his trapped nut. They all had a good laugh about it afterwards, but at the time, it was serious. Peter had never seen Vinnie look so relieved.

On their fronts were strapped their Bergen's with the kit and an M16 strapped to their sides. They wore their helmets and breathing apparatus getting ready for the jump.

As they sat in the C130 checking their oxygen masks and lines, and making sure the parachute straps were okay, they felt a shudder as they hit another bit of turbulence. Vinnie swore again.

Then another shudder.

The noise inside the C130 was deafening and it was difficult to talk, so he could just about hear Kojak's announcement that they were hitting turbulence.

'No shit Sherlock' thought Peter. The turbulence was even making Peter uncomfortable, and Vinnie, who didn't fly well, was cursing every other second. Peter suddenly realised—they had just started the pre-breathing period before the jump, they needed to breathe 100% oxygen in order to flush nitrogen from their bloodstream, to prevent the risk of hypoxia and falling unconscious during the jump. But only for five minutes.

What if they had to jump now?

This mission was fucked up already.

Peter could hear thunder. Then he caught a flash of lightning. He couldn't see it but he could feel and hear it. The hairs on his body stood on end under his suit with static electricity. His sixth sense told him they were in danger, he had that feeling in the pit of his stomach. His warrior instinct, his Caius nature kicked in.

He would have to act soon.

He looked at Vinnie. Then he felt the C130 get hit by a lightning strike. The plane lurched. As Kojak struggled with the C130 controls, he heroically righted the plane, but both port engines were now on fire. The C130 is as tough as old boots, and he had flown many times in bad weather, but this was different.

They were flying into hell.

Kojak shut down both port engines and was now flying on just two starboard engines. He adjusted his flaps in a desperate attempt to keep the plane flying through the storm and driving rain.

Peter could smell smoke.

'Fuck!' he said through gritted teeth.

The C130 lurched to the left this time, and Vinnie took off his oxygen mask just in time, as he threw up onto the floor. The plane shuddered again. Then it lurched to the right.

Then suddenly it dropped a hundred feet in a few seconds, in a freefall, then it came upward sharply. Harnesses broke as some of the men landed in various positions on the floor, bruised and battered. The Jumpmaster lay on the floor, injured. It couldn't get any worse thought Peter.

But it did.

'Starboard engine out!' screamed Kojak. They were now flying on one engine. The SAS men, hard as nails, now looked nervous and looked to Peter as their natural leader. He read their minds.

He was responsible for these men, he trained with them, ate with them, drank with them, fought battles with them—they were like his brothers.

Then the C130 was hit by a lightning strike again, near the cockpit, and a fire started. Most of the instruments went dark, as Kojak grabbed the controls, hanging on for dear life, while the co-pilot struggled with a fire extinguisher, smoke filling the cockpit. They put oxygen masks on as Kojak glanced back, mindful of the men he was carrying.

'We might need to jump!' shouted Peter to the men and pointed to the tailgate of the C130. But it was closed. He had to talk to

Kojak. He got up and grabbed the headset from the unconscious jumpmaster.

'Kojak, release the tailgate, we need to jump now – before it's too late!'

'Releasing!' shouted Kojak. Then Peter had an afterthought.

'Where are we?' shouted Peter above the noise around him.

'In the desert, Empty Quarter, near the border with Yemen, about two hundred miles from target!'

Peter hesitated, 'Empty Quarter. Shit—middle of nowhere!'

Then he saw flames and smoke coming from the cockpit. The tailgate was not moving.

'Kojak, the tailgate!' Peter shouted at the top of his voice.

Kojak tried the tailgate switch again. He burnt his hand as the fire spread in the cockpit.

But the tailgate would not move.

Peter stood up and walked awkwardly to the tailgate. If he couldn't move it they were all dead. He knew his own strength, the strength of ten men, but was it enough?

He grabbed the tailgate as high as possible to get maximum leverage and pushed down with all his might. He could hear the tail-gate creaking under the strain – but it didn't move. He pushed down again, like a bull – this time it moved an inch, creaking, and complaining.

He had some leverage now. Two inches, then a foot. Then it gave way and came down revealing the blackness of the night. Lightning streaks illuminating storm clouds.

He nodded to the team, and they checked their helmets, breathing apparatus and suits, then followed Peter to the edge of the tailgate ramp.

He stood there looking out into oblivion.

Out into darkness, into the maelstrom of the storm. He looked at Vinnie.

'Follow me!' he shouted.

And then he walked out from the tailgate and launched himself into the air, closely followed by Vinnie and the rest of the team. Visibility was non-existent, as he went through cloud, through rain, through the inky darkness. Flashes of light lit the clouds from the lightning. He would wait until he was through the storm before opening his parachute. It grew less windy, and the clouds started to clear, the thunder became less loud as he plummeted through the air. He thought he spotted Vinnie, but it was too dark to tell. He looked at his Day-Glo altimeter: 20,000 feet. Then the oxygen system packed in, nothing was coming through. His heart raced as he gulped for air.

Nothing.

He tore off the mask and gulped in the air as it rushed by him. But the air was thin. He needed to get to 10,000 feet, where there was oxygen. His heart was racing as he looked at his altimeter again.

Eighteen thousand feet. He needed to calm his breathing and slow his heart rate.

Seventeen thousand feet. His heart slowed as he speeded through the inky darkness, which was now strangely quiet.

The storm had passed. He felt faint and blacked out for a second.

Chapter 11

The Empty Quarter

Peter came to. He had to open his parachute now. He pulled the cord, and the silk parachute opened out above him.

Then he blacked out again.

He felt the warmth on his face as he was sleeping. It felt kind of dreamy like he was on a beach somewhere, somewhere nice like Spain. But it was quiet.

Deadly quiet.

And he was alone.

How long had he been out? Several hours at least.

Then he opened his eyes and was blinded by the sun - he still wasn't sure where he was, as he dug around his pockets for his sunglasses.

Then reality hit him like a lightning bolt.

He sat up. He still had his jumpsuit on, and the parachute was still attached to him. He stood up and detached the parachute, and buried it in the hot sand. The sun blazed around him as he dug around his Bergen and changed into his desert smock and Shemagh (Arab) headscarf. He took a swig of water from one of his water bottles and surveyed the scene.

Sand dunes, great rolling sand dunes, golden brown against a light blue sky, for as far as he can see. He could feel the heat radiating from the sand. Then he remembered Kojak's last words: "Empty Quarter, the desert.'

And it was quiet. Dead quiet. Just the soft sound of a light breeze sifting the sand around him.

On the transport to the Gulf from the UK, he had read up on the region, focusing on geography *(his favourite subject)*. Rub' al-Khali, also known as the Empty Quarter, is a huge desert in the southern Arabian Peninsula, covering about 250,000 square miles, that includes portions of Saudi Arabia, United Arab Emirates, Oman, and Yemen, and is about the size of France. It holds roughly half as much sand as the Sahara, which is fifteen times the Empty Quarter's size, but the Sahara is mostly comprised of rocky outcrops and gravel plains.

He remembered one fascinating fact. It is the largest area of continuous sand in the world. But it has rainfall of less than 1.2 inches and daily maximum temperatures average at 47 °C (117 °F), reaching as high as 51 °C (124 °F). Then he jolted awake as reality hit home.

Vinnie! Where is brother Vinnie?

He looked around himself. He was with Vinnie until he blacked out on the way down. He left his Bergen and walked up a dune. The soft sand shifted underneath his feet as he walked up. He adjusted his Shemagh as he battled his way up the dune. The sun beat down on his head as he climbed about two hundred feet, then stood on the top. He shielded his eyes against the sun and used his eagle eyes to survey the silent landscape.

More sand dunes. Sand dunes as far as the eye could see.

What was that? In the hollow of a dune.

He walked towards the shape in the sand and shouted 'Vinnie!' Then he saw a hand come up and started running. He jumped over the top and into the hollow. It was Vinnie.

'How are you mate?'

'Sprained my ankle I think. Where the fuck are we?' answered Vinnie blinking in the sun.

'Empty Quarter, near the border with Yemen.' Peter looked around him. 'Any sign of the others?'

Vinnie shook his head.

'Let's get our kit sorted and come up with a plan,' decided Peter.

Peter retrieved his Bergen and dumped it in the hollow with Vinnie, which offered a small amount of shade. They stuck the butts of their M16s into the sand and put a canvas sheet over them to make a make-shift shelter. Vinnie dug out his tommy cooker and put some water into a mess tin, and got a brew going. Peter nodded in approval.

They lay with their backs against the sand with the shelter above their heads and sipped their tea. It is amazing how a simple cup of tea can improve morale—critical on any mission, thought Peter as he dug into his army rations and they shared some biscuits. Then Vinnie dug out the radio, switched it on, selected a channel, and tried to make a transmission. It crackled with static.

'Alpha One Zero this is Desert Fox One. Over.'

He was met by the crackle of static.

'Channel 14 Vinnie.'

'Yes, its' set to Channel 14!' Vinnie shouted in frustration.

'Repeat - Alpha One Zero this is Desert Fox One. Over.'

Static again.

'It was definitely Channel 14 Vinnie. It's encrypted so…'

Then Peter stopped and stared at Vinnie, a look of horror creeping over his face. 'You don't think...?'

'They put the wrong encryption codes in?' Answered Vinnie. Vinnie tried again, but it was no use. They tried other channels, but he was met with more static.

'Who was responsible for setting the encryption codes?' asked an angry Vinnie, trying to control himself.

'It was Pencilneck,' replied Peter. They sat there for a while and finished drinking their tea in silence, their minds moving at a million miles per hour, attempting to assimilate their situation, which was very serious.

Peter retrieved his map of Yemen and his GPS, which was working. He calculated the route they should take to the nearest point of civilization, which happened to be Thamud, a town in north-eastern Yemen. The village where their target was being held was near Thamud. Could be any of four or five settlements. A thousand square miles of territory. But for the moment their mission was aborted, well, it had already gone to rat shit. The mission was now a low priority, they just needed to get out of the desert.

Alive.

This was their immediate action plan. Thamud was directly south, about a hundred miles, as the crow flies, through the vast desert. A simple enough plan, but it was harsh terrain. It would be tough going, even for the infamous Bulletproof Pete. Worse, Vinnie had sprained his ankle on the parachute landing.

Peter looked at Vinnie, he was hobbling on his leg.

'Vinnie, fuck the mission, let's just get out of this desert.'

Vinnie nodded and winced again in pain.

They went through their Bergens and decided which kit to keep and which to throw. Food, water, clothing, survival kit, medical kit, M16 rifles and ammunition they would keep. Everything else, including claymore mines, they would bury, along with the parachutes. This was a Black Op operation, where normally they would even keep their poo inside a plastic bag, in their Bergen, to avoid DNA identification. But their survival was now the most important factor—how to get out of the desert alive, that was their driving need.

It would require all their training, just to stay alive.

Peter made the decision to put most of the kit inside his Bergen, while Vinnie would just carry the radio *(that didn't work)* in his. If there was a chance they could get it working, they would take it. They slung their M16s over their shoulders and put the Bergens on their backs.

Peter, having the strength of ten men, could easily manage this. But like any human, he still needed water, and was subject to exposure to the sun like anyone else. Even though his ancient warrior ego seemed to be taking over more and more of his persona these days, he was still human. Peter had the sense to pack some factor 50 sun cream, and they shared this, smearing it onto exposed areas.

Peter plotted a course, using his GPS and map, then double checked the course to his compass, just in case. Then he pointed south. 'That way.'

And they set off.

Chapter 12

Ice Cold in Alex

'Ice cold in Alex,' smiled Peter to his friend, recalling the famous World War Two drama, in which John Mills, after walking across the Sahara Desert, walks into the officer's bar at the British base in Alexandria and orders an ice cold beer. He remembers the look on John Mills' face just as the glass touches his lips.

'Ice cold in Alex,' replied Vinnie imagining sipping an ice cold lager in the Blind Beggar, the cool refreshing liquid going down his throat.

Peter looked at his watch, it was only 8.00 a.m. local time, but it was hot already. Vinnie panted as they climbed a steep dune—three hundred feet high, hobbling on his sprained ankle through the shifting sand. They reached the top and took a breather. It was a fantastic spectacle, beautiful golden sand dunes as far as they can see. It was quiet and peaceful, just the sounds of the soft breeze blowing the sand on the shifting dunes, little lizards scurrying across the sand.

Peter felt a deep connection with the desert, it was a very spiritual place, never-ending, like infinity, and he had a sense of timelessness and oneness with it. A little lizard dashed past him, stopped, looked up at him, then buried itself in the sand.

Peter smiled. He felt a sense of himself and his place in God's universe—in this harsh, hostile environment, which seemed to cut to the spiritual truth of everything.

Life and death.

He felt the presence of God all around him, silent and omnipotent, the potential of all things. Maybe this was a test. Maybe God was testing him.

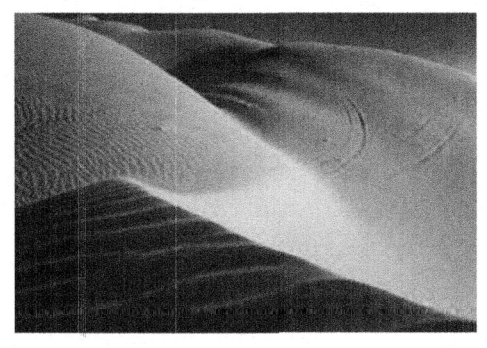

'It feels lonely out here mate,' muttered Vinnie, wiping sweat from his eyes.

'In the final analysis, we are all alone Vinnie,' replied Peter. 'Each of us must face our destiny. It is inevitable.' Peter stopped walking. This was Caius, his alter-ego talking, not Peter. Was he going nuts? Maybe it was the heat.

Peter was thoughtful as they continued down the far side of the dune, its top blocking the sun, so it was cooler there, like a darkened valley. They sat back on their Bergen's and let themselves slide down the hill to the bottom. Peter laughed, it was fun, this sand dune surfing as he looked at Vinnie, who was wincing a bit in pain.

It was noon, and they stood on top of another massive dune, the sun now floating above their heads like a halo. The sun was very hot, and they adjusted their Arab headscarves and rubbed on more factor 50 to prevent burning. Peter reckoned they had travelled all of six miles.

Six miles in four hours. Not good going.

He had tabbed sixty-five kilometres in three hours on endurance, *(an SAS record)*, so this was poor going by comparison, but then again this was very difficult terrain.

The heat was unbearable, so they stayed in the shade of the valley of the dune for an hour. Peter had a look at Vinnie's ankle; it was swollen and bruised, this was more than a sprained ankle. Peter touched Vinnie's ankle joint, and he winced again. He took Vinnie's boot off and examined his foot.

'Bone might be fractured.' Peter put some cream and some bandages around the ankle and foot, and gave Vinnie some painkillers. They waited until four in the afternoon when it would be cooler, and they got moving again, but Vinnie was getting slower. Peter put the radio into his Bergen to ease Vinnie's burden, and they carried on.

'Come on Vinnie – we need to cover some ground mate.' Peter checked his GPS and compass again - they were slightly off. He adjusted his course, with Vinnie lagging behind again.

'Do you want me to carry you?' Peter joked. Vinnie grunted as they soldiered on. It would be getting dark in a few hours, and they needed to cover some miles.

They stopped at sunset, and watched the sun go down – a golden haze on the golden sand dunes, Peter liked the peace and quiet of the empty desert as he watched the sunset, trying to make sense of their situation, and how they had got into this mess, in the first place. On the positive side, there were no wild animals or enemy to worry about out here. They ate in silence as it slowly became cooler, and then crept into their sleeping bags. Not even Vinnie's loud snoring could keep Peter awake.

He dreamed of an ancient warrior in chain armor, and carrying a huge silver sword of power. A holy sword, which vibrated and emitted a blue light, and which his enemies were terrified of. Then he dreamt of being on a plane in a storm, flying through the air and walking through a golden desert. When he eventually awoke, he half opened his eyes but wasn't quite sure where he was. Was he in Wales in his nice comfy bed? But then he realized with a shock that he was not in Wales, but in a desert in the middle of nowhere, trying to stay alive, with his best friend, Vinnie.

He checked their water supply; he had two full NATO Osprey water bottles, and he was halfway through a third. Vinnie had one and a half bottles—four litres, not enough. He reflected on his survival training, which was extensive. In the hot, dry desert with temperatures approaching 50 degrees Celsius at peak, they would need three litres per day, each, as it was the hot season.

They didn't have enough water.

He looked at his watch: 6.00 a.m. They would need to get going soon before it got too hot. Vinnie winced as he stood up and limped behind Peter, who put on his Bergen, then put his arm around Vinnie to help him. Vinnie was his oldest childhood friend, and he would go to the ends of the earth to help him. They were brothers, blood brothers, brothers in arms, and they needed a miracle.

With Vinnie hobbling they were making very slow progress. Vinnie could feel Peter's impatience as they made their way up and down sand dunes. In the end, they found the easiest way was to walk along the top of the dunes, as long as they were headed south, towards Thamud.

Around noon when it was baking hot, they stopped for a drink in the shade of a dune. Vinnie took a gulp, Peter just took a sip, in an attempt to conserve water. He looked at Vinnie's ankle again. It was swollen and looked infected. He put a new dressing on, then helped Vinnie to his feet, then Vinnie looked at him, his lips cracked and sore, his face burnt by the sun, his eyes misty and confused.

'Leave me, Pete, I can't walk. Leave me here to die. I'm not worth it. I'm a burden…tell Gill - I love her. Tell her I'm sorry.'

'Vinnie shut up. I'm not leaving you here to die, mate. We carry on.' With that, Peter switched his Bergen round to his front, and Vinnie climbed on his back piggy-back style. Peter did not complain as he carried Vinnie's weight under the baking sun.

As he trudged in the burning heat, the dead weight of Vinnie on his back, he thought he could see something. In the distance, Peter could see an object in the desert—an aircraft, definitely an aircraft. As he got closer, he could see it was a C130—their C130. It was broken in two, but the wings were intact. They looked inside, then looked in the cockpit, the co-pilot was dead, but no sign of Kojak. Where was he? He searched the fuselage for water, but there was none. Did anyone know it had crashed? Was the transponder working? Why were they forced to fly in bad weather?

Was there another agenda here?

Do they stay or go?

Chapter 13

THE HOLY DESERT

Peter is tempted to stay in the shade of the C130 fuselage, but they continued to their destination of Thamud for two more days, making progressively slower progress. Vinnie's condition becomes worse.

They don't have enough water. One bottle left between the two of them. Peter tries to push this thought from his mind as they watch another sunset go down.

He has never been much of a churchgoer but living in a beautiful and isolated Welsh valley, he has a sense of the nature of God, the stillness and the beauty, the perfection of his creation in all its forms. He doesn't like cities—too much concrete and glass. He respects mother nature and feels closer to God in this lonely desert, but they need a miracle. He bows his head and says a silent prayer in the sunset. Then they sleep.

When they awake, they drink the last of the water and get going again. But Peter's throat still feels parched. He hasn't peed for two days now. As he carries Vinnie, he can feel the heat of the sun, beating down on his head. He feels dizzy and disorientated as he staggers forward, the desert seems hazy; the desert and sky appear to become one.

Peter's mind wanders, and he thinks about when he and Vinnie first met. As a teenager, Peter used to spend weekends shooting rabbits in the Welsh hills. Vinnie used to come up from the East

End of London to get away from "The Smoke" as he calls it. Vinnie could shoot a rabbit at three hundred yard, he was a natural. They hit it off immediately and became best mates, camping out in the hills, eating baked beans and sausages from a tin can, as well as roast rabbit of course. They talked about joining the army together. It all made sense at the time. For Vinnie, it was either be a gangster, like his father or join up. For Peter, it was either the army or work on a farm, after all, there weren't many jobs in Wales.

Peter could always count on Vinnie. Dead reliable, saved his back more than once. And in life, that's what's important—finding people you can rely on. Vinnie's a scruffy bastard, and he's got no manners - I mean, you wouldn't take him to have tea with the Queen or anything, but Peter loves him like a brother, and that's what counts, someone you can trust one hundred percent.

Peter thinks about his reputation of never being shot in a firefight, and not even getting a scratch, his incredible speed and agility, and being the best soldier in the regiment, which makes him curious. Many of his SAS colleagues and friends thought it was unnatural, supernatural some called it. There is something greater than himself at work here.

His mind then wanders back to his home in the valley, his sanctuary away from the madness, fishing with his son in the stream that runs through the woods, those ancient enchanted woods. His vision of the old man, the priest—what was he saying as he was pointing at Peter?

"You are the one." What the fuck does that mean?

Peter staggers as the desert shimmers in front of him. Then in front of him, he has a vision of a massive black ship in the sky, monstrous and foreboding. It fills the horizon, making a thunderous grinding noise, as it turns slowly above him. It seems alien—as if it is not from Earth. Then it shimmers and is gone, but it doesn't seem like an illusion.

It feels real to him.

He reaches for his water bottle, to get some water on his dry, cracked lips, but it is empty, and he falls to his knees, weak and confused, Vinnie's arms around his neck. 'Leave me…leave me

Pete, I'm a burden…' Vinnie whispers incoherently, then becomes unconscious.

Then in front of Peter, the desert shimmers again, and he can see something in front of him.

His heart races, as through a mist, a man in a dark habit is pointing at him. He has a brown tanned face, wise, kind eyes and a small beard. He has the look of a priest and wears a hooded cloak, and has an aura of patience and understanding that some priests possess. The wise man opens a large black book, with ornate gold lettering on the cover. The man beckons to Peter as he turns the old, heavy script-like pages—it looks like Greek text, and then the man looks at him.

Peter hesitates, confused. Who is this man? What is this book? Peter looks at the priest, he has a kind and gentle face. Is this the man he saw in the wood when he fell asleep? His heart slows as he begins to trust him. He lays Vinnie in the desert and joins the man, looking at the ancient black leather-bound book.

There is a picture in the book of an ancient warrior, a knight with a sword. Peter is transfixed as the wise man shows him the sword in the book . It has a gold handle and pommel, and the silver blade gives off a bluish light. The priest calls: "Caius, Caius you are Caius." Peter feels confused, 'My middle name is Cai, he thinks, an old Welsh name meaning Kay, not Caius.' His father had told him it was after one of King Arthur's knights, the one closest to him.

The indestructible one.

The priest continues: 'That is your name, your name of power, Caius, remember it. The sword is ancient. It is your birth right. It is one of the seven holy swords of Prince Michael, the Lord of all Angels, the one who is like God. You may call your sword only in time of great need. It will give you power, just call it three times and you will see it in your hand. It is Caledfwlch, an ancient Welsh name. Later it was called Excalibur, in Latin, the sword is called Caliburnus. It has other names. Listen to your heart, you will choose the right one.'

'One more thing: You have the ability to grow as tall as the tallest tree in the forest if so pleased, and the ability to radiate supernatural heat from your hands. Now sleep," says the priest. Peter lies on the sand and sleeps. He has confused visions of battles, strange flying craft, and beings which are not human, but all around him is an aura of blue light.

When he awakens, he has another vision—A golden-haired being surrounded by blue light, with white angel wings, dressed in white robes, with a gold belt, and a gold necklace with a blue jewel. He stands nine feet tall. Not human.

In his left hand, he holds a golden cup, and in his right hand, he holds a silver jewelled sword. It is the same sword the priest showed him. It has a gold handle and pommel, and the silver blade gives off a bluish light. The being walks towards him and smiles benevolently, and Peter is filled with hope.

The being speaks no words, but Peter feels comforted and reassured that in the end, all will be well.

As Peter looks on the angels beautiful face he witnesses an emotion: infinite love, then infinite joy, then infinite intelligence—a gateway to God.

Infinite power.

He is surrounded by a bright light, but not blinding—soft and gentle. The entity puts the golden cup to Peter's mouth, and drinks a cool liquid, like crystal water, and he feels invigorated; the being does the same for Vinnie. It must be an angel thinks Peter, like in the bible stories? Is he dreaming? But Vinnie is with him. It must be real.

Then the being speaks.

'I am the Archangel Michael. You are Caius, and I am your patron. You may only call me in times of great need. I have existed before time itself. I have existed before the creation of the Earth, before men, before the dinosaurs roamed the Earth. The sword will give you power, strength, and the will to succeed and conquer your enemies. It was created at the beginning of time by the Creator and given to me.'

Peter stood open-mouthed.

'It can only be wielded by one such as yourself, a demi-god, else you would be obliterated. With my sword you will conquer your enemies and destroy evil, for that is its sacred purpose. You have been chosen for this task, and you must complete it. You agreed to this task before you incarnated onto this earthly plane.'

Michael solemnly gives him the sword. As Peter stands in the desert he admires the blade, and it vibrates in his hand, like it has a life of its own - the power running through his body. He takes a sharp intake of breath and feels invigorated and indestructible. The silver sword shines with a blue light and rivulets of lightning spring from it – he can see four words written on the sword, but written in an ancient tongue.

He has a vision of an ancient battle, knights in armour, shouts of joy and terror, and horses and mayhem. He tastes grass and dirt in his mouth. Then a desert and a large river nearby and an advancing army – the sun burns his face. Then another vision of a black ship towering above him, and his heart pumps with adrenaline as unhuman beings approach him from all sides. The tall being places his mind on Peter's shoulder.

'The water from the cup will sustain your mind and body in the battles ahead. I have spoken.'

Peter drinks from the cup again, and gives some to Vinnie, then asks, 'What task?' but the entity smiles and then is gone, the sword also is gone, and then they fall unconscious lying in the sand.

They awake, and Peter continues walking, energy renewed, but he is carrying Vinnie again, who is moaning incoherently. 'Vinnie is not going to last much longer,' thinks Peter.

They need a miracle.

The heat becomes unbearable, like an oven, the air hot and still with no breeze. 'Just over the lip of that dune, I must make it to the top of the dune.' Peter summons all his remaining strength and manages to crawl over the top, and Vinnie falls on top of him. They lie there in the shade of the dune, but it is midday, and the heat is stifling.

'You look like shit,' laughs Vinnie. 'This is the end,' thinks Peter, just before they both fall unconscious.

Chapter 14

THE BEDOUIN

Peter is being prodded by something. His eyes are half open and his parched mouth and cracked lips try to speak. His eyesight is blurred as he tries to focus. He can see a dark brown, leathery face looking at him with keen eyes—kind, gentle eyes.

He is wearing a traditional red check headdress with a black band around it and white robes. He puts a goat water skin to Peter's lips. The water is cool and pure as Peter gulps the water down his parched throat.

In perfect English, he speaks, 'My name is Abd Al-Wali,' and the Arab man bows. Peter feels refreshed as his quick mind analyses the name in Arabic. Peter bows to the man and shakes his hand.

'Servant of the Guardian.'

'That is correct,' says Abd Al-Wali, 'You are most knowledgeable for a Westerner.'

'I studied Arabic,' replied Peter. The kind Arab helps Vinnie to his feet and gives him more water from the skin.

Peter looks at the Bedouin nomad, for that is what he is, for no other Arab is as welcome to strangers. He is small and thin, for food is scarce in the desert, and being thin helps to dissipate body heat. His face is fierce, with a pointed, hawkish nose, olive skin, and sharp little beard. His eyes are kind, but wrinkled by years of squinting in the sun. He looks a bit rough but Peter's gut instinct told him to trust him.

'Come, you will be guests in my home.'

'We are saved!' thinks Peter as he reflects on the chance meeting in the desert. He and Vinnie climb onto a camel each, strap on their gear and follow their new friend. The camel looks back at Peter and sneers at him, showing its crooked teeth, and drooling saliva.

Late in the afternoon, they descend into a valley in the dunes, and it feels a bit cooler. Some Bedouin tents are arranged around a herd of goats and camels. Peter sees a small cluster of date palms and a few hardy plants—a small oasis in the middle of nowhere.

This peaceful, place of quiet and solitude. Is this the peace he has been seeking, thinks Peter?

They walk into the tent, and there is a flurry of activity, as their Arab host issues orders to his wife, daughters, and relatives. They scurry around preparing food and offering tea to their honoured guests. Peter watches as their new Bedouin friend's son holds a goat by its neck.

Abd Al-Wali calls out to God, then makes a swift, deep incision with a sharp knife on the throat, cutting the jugular vein, windpipe and carotid arteries of both sides, but leaving the spinal cord intact. He carefully collects the blood from the goat in a jug.

'Dhabīḥah,' says Abd Al-Wali. Peter understands that the slaughter of an animal must be done in a certain way, it is Islamic law.

Outside the tent, they heat stones over charcoal and grill the freshly slaughtered goat meat. Peter has read up on Bedouin culture. Bedouins are expected to boil their last rice and kill their last sheep in order to feed a stranger. Hospitality is regarded as an honour and a sacred duty.

Peter and Vinnie are invited to sit and share a cup of thick, gritty coffee. Vinnie grimaces, but Peter nudges him, and he thanks his host graciously. Then they are introduced to his wife, two daughters, and son. The women wear long decorated robes, which cover their heads, but they are not masked. The two friends sit on soft cushions while Abd Al-Wali's family smile and stare at them.

'Be on your best behaviour, Vinnie,' Peter warns, but Vinnie is very grateful and thanks his host again.

Their Bedouin host approaches Peter and Vinnie in turn and smears blood from the goat onto the mouths of his guests, in a show of hospitality. Peter knows this is a great honour and thanks him again.

Soon they are sitting down to a feast of goat, rice, honey and beans, and mint tea. It is delicious; Peter nods and thanks each family member in turn for the food. Then Vinnie gives a loud burp. Peter looks sharply at him and then at his host, as the Bedouin's grin widens and the family clap.

'Allah be praised,' says his host in thanks for their food.

'Why is your English so good?' asks Peter.

'I listen to the BBC World Service with my family.'

One of the sons plays an oval-shaped guitar while the other beats a small drum. They watch as their host's two daughters perform a traditional Bedouin dance, in time with the music, their deep dark eyes over their veils, telling a story. Their dance is hypnotic, the long black-haired daughters smile shyly at Peter and Vinnie as their hips gyrate. The dance lasts for half an hour then they all applaud.

Peter thinks this Bedouin Arab man, whose race has lived in the desert since before recorded time, has more honour in his little finger than Pencilneck had in his whole body. Peter stands up, bows to his guests, then addresses Abd Al-Wali in fluent Arabic.

'You are a man of honour, and you will always be my friend.' With that, his host kisses Peter on the lips in a show of great affection. Vinnie also bows and shakes his hand, but refrains from kissing him.

Then they are shown to their beds: blankets and soft cushions. 'We will talk in the morning, Peter.' With that, they both fall into a deep sleep. Peter wakes at dawn and strolls out of the tent to stretch his legs and is greeted by his Bedouin host.

'Your friend Vinnie is injured. You are welcome to rest a while.'

'Thank you. We will stay for two days then we need to get going again,' says Peter, liking this man more by the minute. But can he trust him?

'You are a military man. You are on a mission.' Peter smiles at his intuitive friend. Can he still complete his mission?

'I'm looking for a village near Thamud where an important man is being held.' Abd Al-Wali nods and understands.

'My Bedouin brothers told me about this. I will take you there in three days.' As if reading his mind he looks at Peter, 'There are other soldiers like you nearby.'

Peter is elated—some of his team must have survived! He tries the radio again, changing frequencies to try to contact his team, but no luck. He will not attempt to contact Pencilneck yet he needs more information—there were too many unanswered questions. Peter watches while Vinnie is nursed and his ankle bandaged by the Bedouins family, and wonders how they could have survived.

Was the angel real? It felt real. Peter begins to believe in miracles as he rests in the Bedouin tent regaining his remarkable strength. On the third day, they load their gear onto camels and set off with Abd Al-Wali, leading the convoy of three camels, and their riders.

As they set off through the desert again, the scenery changes and they see ancient temples built out of the rock, with stone pillars, made from pink and brown rock. Peter looks at the holy sites, and ponders upon what may transpire, but decides that nature will take its course and everything will work out okay. It was a miracle being saved by the Bedouin man, he knows that, after his mirage of the angelic entity dressed in white robes.

Is he dreaming?

Soon they are on the outskirts of a village. Abd Al-Wali points to a mud hut near the edge of the village, gets off his camel and greets another Bedouin man, who stands guard outside, carrying an old Enfield rifle. Peter and Vinnie follow him into the mud hut, and in a dark corner, he can see Sebastian sitting, his head nodding back and forth. He is holding a bible and chanting something, repeating himself. He looks up at Peter, but his sunburnt features show no recognition of him.

'Sebastian, it's Peter from A Squadron.' Sebastian looks up again, this time he recognises him.

'You are Peter, they call you Bulletproof Pete.' Then Sebastian starts reading his bible again. In another room, Peter finds Des and Artie.

'All right lads, where's Baz and Mad Mike?' he asks. They shake their heads, they look sunburned, with cracked lips, but otherwise okay.

'Lost in the desert,' replies Des shaking his head. Sebastian joins them, mumbling to himself—as if he is talking to someone who's not there.

Has the desert driven him mad? ponders Peter, as he looks at Sebastian.

They all gather round, while Vinnie gets a brew going.

'I'm very grateful and everything, but don't you think it's odd that this Arab just found us in the desert?' said Vinnie.

'He saved our lives, Vinnie. If he were one of the terrorists, he would have killed us where we lay—if we hadn't died of thirst first.'

'Yes you're right mate,' said Vinnie.

'Besides I know these people. I studied Arab languages and culture at university. The Bedouins—this Bedouin I think—is genuine. What do you think lads, shall we trust him?' Peter looks around the room at his sunburnt colleagues.

'He saved us,' said Des. Artie nods.

They are joined by Abd Al-Wali.

'Ok lads time for a Chinese parliament. First off, a big thank you to our friend, Abd Al-Wali. Without him, we wouldn't be here now,' says Peter looking warmly at his new Bedouin friend.

They all nod and shake his hand warmly. Peter decides they need more than Vinnie's tea to boost their morale.

'I think we should make our friend here an honourable member of our squadron, for services rendered. Hands up who agrees.'

They all put their hands up.

'Abd Al-Wali, you are now an honourable member of the Special Air Service.' They all cheer. The Bedouin's eyes water as he looks at his comrades.

'It is an honour for me, thank you'; he bows his head.

'Now down to business. Did any of your radios work?' They all shake their heads.

'Wrong fucking codes,' swore Des as he sips his tea.

'It's Bravo Two Zero all over again.' Vinnie has found some biscuits in his pack and handed them round, which go down very well.

'Who was responsible for setting the codes?' ask Des.

'Pencilneck,' replied Peter. They all nod and look at Peter.

'I will do it,' replies Peter, acknowledging their need for justice. They are silent for a moment, then Peter continues.

'Anyone seen Kojak? We saw the crashed C130 in the desert. Co-pilot's dead, but no sign of Kojak.' They all shake their heads. 'I spoke to him before we left – he never received any weather reports from Pencilneck.'

They all look in disbelief at Peter and shake their heads again. The weather report was a big detail that was missed in the rush.

Or was it deliberate? Peter wonders.

Chapter 15

THE MISSION

'Cheers Vinnie, best cuppa tea ever,' said Des. The lads nodded at Vinnie as he handed round more biscuits. Peter admired Vinnie, he had the incredible knack of brewing the best tea you ever tasted, and the lads loved him for it.

'Yorkshire Tea,' said Vinnie.

'Now back to the mission. Our Bedouin friend here has some information about the Saudi Ambassador.' In perfect English, the Bedouin addressed the rough looking, super fit, sunburnt soldiers around him.

'My Bedouin friends tell me the Ambassador is being held in a house just one mile from here.' He drew a map of the target house and its environs in the sandy floor.

'More tea please Mr. Vinnie,' the Bedouin asked politely. Vinnie obliged, and Abd Al-Wali smiled, taking two more biscuits.

They all warmed to the Bedouin man who had saved them from the desert, and brought them to this place of safety; they appreciated his great compassion and kindness towards them. The man who, through his Bedouin network in the region, had gathered all the required intelligence for their mission. Peter had always tried to befriend the locals in any mission; they could always give intelligence that wasn't available elsewhere.

Hearts and minds.

'How many terrorists?' asks Peter.

'Maybe ten. Four outside keeping guard, four in the backroom with the ambassador and two in the other room. They are armed with Kalashnikovs and RPGs. But they are not good shots—praise be to Allah.'

'How do you know?' asked Peter.

'We saw them practising,' replied the Bedouin.

'I want you to get a message to the Ambassador to stay in his bed, lie flat at all costs, ok?'

'One of my kinsmen delivers food to the house. It will be done. When will you attack?'

'Five a.m. tomorrow morning.'

'My kinsman will have to go tonight,' answered the Bedouin.

'Thank you, my friend. We cannot wait, we need the element of surprise,' said Peter and shook his hand, pleased as punch with the intel. The rest of the team shook the Bedouin's hand again, hardly believing their luck in finding this man.

They decided to rest up and strike before first light. They cleaned their M16s of sand and oiled the parts before reassembly. They packed enough magazines in their belt kit and webbing for the following day's mission. Then they scrounged in their Bergen's for what was left of their rations before Abd Al-Wali saved the day by inviting them to another house where they ate a delicious meal of goat, rice, and beans. Vinnie tried his best to keep good table manners and when he burped he was a bit embarrassed, but his hosts smiled and clapped.

Then they gave their heartfelt thanks and went back to the mud hut to get an early night. Peter had grave reservations about Pencilneck and decided not to call him in case he alerted the terrorists, there had been enough fuck-ups for one mission.

Zero hour was set to 5.00 a.m. precisely.

The target house was not much more than a mud hut. They would not risk any surveillance in order to avoid detection and retain the element of surprise—there were no suitable lying up points available.

Peter ordered Des and Artie to take up positions in front of the target house in order to take out the four guards at zero hour, and then take out the terrorists in the front room. Vinnie would set a charge and blow the back of the target house at zero hour. This was where the Ambassador was being held, his codename was Hotdog. Then Peter and Vinnie would clear the backroom and acquire Hotdog.

They were up before 4.00 a.m. rechecking their kit and blackening their faces to stop reflective light, before changing into traditional Arab clothing. At 4.00 a.m. they moved stealthily into the cool desert night, a large moon lit the sky. A Bedouin friend of Abd Al-Wali smiled showing rotten teeth, then beckoned for them to follow him. As they made their way in silence, the only people they met were two Arabs, but they were ignored. They were careful to keep their magazines in their belt kit underneath the robe and their M16s covered.

At 4.30 a.m. they were at the target and started taking up positions. Outside the mud hut were four guards, but two of them were sleeping, slumped against the mud hut wall. No sign of any other activity. Des and Artie took up positions at the front of the house, hiding in an alleyway, while Peter and Vinnie, along with Sebastian, moved quietly up the street, down a narrow gap between two houses, and went to the rear of the building, hiding behind a low wall.

All was quiet. The moon was still out and lit the night; there was no cloud cover. A mouse scurried in front of them. Then two rats started sniffing Vinnie's boots before they became bored and went on their way. There were just fifty yards between them and the target house. They absorbed all activity around them, every shadow where someone might be hiding, every noise.

Peter beckoned Vinnie to fit the charge. It was 4.40 a.m.—twenty minutes to zero hour. Sebastian shifted nervously behind Peter as they watched Vinnie place the charge, then stoop low and get back to safety. Peter had decided to use Sebastian as backup in case they needed it, but he was nervous about using him for the main assault, he just wasn't up to it.

'All set,' whispered Vinnie as he got back behind the wall. Sebastian crossed himself and said a prayer for them while they waited.

It was 4.50 a.m., ten minutes to zero hour.

They had no other comms so Peter assumed Des and Artie were good to go. At the front of the mud hut the two terrorists who were asleep were now awake sharing a cigarette. Peter could see smoke drifting over the mud hut, and the faint smell of cigarette smoke touched his nostrils.

It was now 4.55 a.m. Five minutes to zero hour.

At that moment, Peter could hear the sound of bells and looked round to see a young shepherd boy, walking towards them, the bells around the goats jingling away in the silent night. They crouched lower down behind the wall further to get out of sight. The shepherd boy stopped behind the mud hut with his goats and looked around him, unaware of the explosives just ten feet from him. Peter looked at his watch nervously.

Now it was 4.59 a.m., one minute to zero hour.

'Sebastian, I want you to grab that boy, and keep him quiet till it's over. GO NOW!' Peter whispered. Sebastian crept forward behind the boy and put his hand over his mouth. The boy struggled, eyes wide with terror, as Sebastian dragged him back behind the wall the others were crouching behind.

'Ten seconds,' said Peter.

They readied their M16s on semi-automatic, as Peter looked at his watch.

Five.
Four.
Three.
Two.
One.

Nothing.

Peter looked at Vinnie, horror-struck.

The charge had not gone off. Peter could not afford this mission to fail they had come this far, walked across a desert, nearly died, only to fail again.

'Follow me!' shouted Peter as he rushed to the rear wall of the mud hut, clutching his M16, closely followed by Vinnie. Peter could hear rapid bursts of fire from Des and Artie from the front of the mud hut as he rushed at the rear wall and using his bare fists, punched two holes in the rear wall. A second later he had made a hole large enough to get through. They rushed in, threw two stun grenades making a loud bang, and saw four pairs of shocked white eyes looking at them, eyes watering from the smoke—with the Ambassador on a low bed.

Everything seemed to move in slow motion as Peter and Vinnie dropped the four terrorists in two seconds flat, each downed with a double tap. Then they dragged the frightened Ambassador out of through the hole and back to the safety of the low wall.

They could hear firing from the front of the house and panicked shouting in Arabic, but then it went quiet. Then shots were heard from inside the house, and the sound of running boots as Des and Artie came rushing through the door to the backroom and out the hole in the wall.

'All clear!' shouted Des.

Peter retrieved a mobile he had borrowed from one of the friendly Bedouin and called the commander at RAF Al Udeid Airbase.

'We have Hotdog. Repeat we have Hotdog. Require immediate Evac. Over.' He then gave his coordinates breathing a sigh of relief.

Chapter 16

JUSTICE IS DONE

The base commander had put a crate of beers, packed in ice, on the C130 Hercules bringing them home, which they demolished in good order.

'Ice cold in Alex,' said Peter as he raised a one-litre bottle of Becks to Vinnie. Vinnie burped and did a good impression of his arch-enemy, Lieutenant Ratti. They all laughed, even Sebastian.

Then Peter raised his beer again. 'Here's to Mad Mike and Baz—fallen heroes, may they rest in peace.'

'Amen to that,' said Sebastian. They all clinked their beers and became silent, remembering their fallen comrades—the missions, the piss-ups and the football matches.

Then they slept for a while, but Peter was wide awake, he didn't sleep much, or rather he didn't need much sleep. Had Pencilneck deliberately sabotaged the mission, was he in league with the terrorists, or was he just incompetent? Was he responsible for the death of Mad Mike and Baz?

They were now back at the British base in Qatar, RAF Al Udeid, sitting alone in the mess—which was more like a restaurant—laughing, eating and joking. Vinnie then did a very good impression of Pencilneck, which Peter thought was very funny. Then Peter did his impression of Pencilneck which made Vinnie fell off his chair, and Des, Artie, and Sebastian all fell about laughing again.

As they recovered from their fits of laughter, Peter thought about how they had not seen the object of their merriment since they got back—*which was unusual.*

He was obviously avoiding them.

He had chatted with Ahmed and Saunders when he arrived back at the base, and they had apologized profusely for the shocking planning cock-ups. Peter had given a full report to SAS Colonel Bradley, which filtered down to Sir Nigel at M16, being a joint mission. But Peter felt uneasy. Something wasn't right.

He smelled a rat.

Then the coin dropped.

He walked away from the table to a quiet corner, retrieved the private number of Sir Nigel and dialled.

'Goldbroom,' came a curt reply.

'It's Morgan Sir.'

'Ah Peter, I read your report. Tough mission.'

'Yes, sir. I think we have a problem. It's Ponsonby.'

Silence at the other end.

'Go on.'

'Things don't stack up. Radios didn't work, C130 crash, explosives didn't work, scant intel on the targets. He has avoided me like the plague since I got back as if he wasn't expecting to see me. I want you to run another financial check on him.'

'He was clean. But I will do it again, and dig a bit deeper this time. I trust your instincts. I have had my eye on him for a while. I will meet you when you get back,' Sir Nigel seemed reluctant as if he was hoping it wasn't Ponsonby, his old Eton buddy.

Then the room went deadly quiet as they all looked in the direction of the door. Pencilneck, (Ponsonby) strolled in trying to look casual. As he came up to where they were sitting, there was a deathly silence, five pairs of eyes looking daggers at him. He was accompanied by two tough looking military police sergeants, who looked like they worked out every day.

Ponsonby shifted nervously.

'Hi, chaps! Glad you made it back ok, and great job on rescuing the Ambassador. The Saudi Arabian Government wishes to convey their thanks for your efforts.' He coughed slightly.

'Listen I know there were some shortcomings in the mission, but we have taken these on board for the future. We have learned lessons, and I have conveyed these to our Chief Sir Nigel and your Colonel Bradley, Sergeant Morgan. Why don't you take a few days R and R *(rest and relaxation)* and we can talk again, about another mission.' He coughed nervously again.

Peter's demeanour began to change, and he seemed to grow in size. The menace oozed from every pore of his body as he stared at Pencilneck, who tried to avert his eyes, as Peter strode over to his target.

The atmosphere became heavy as thunder. Peter's blue eyes blazed like fire as he now stood just two inches from Pencilneck, staring him out.

The thousand-yard stare.

Pencilneck's eyes began to water, and he began to shake. The two military police sergeants took one step forward. Peter's six-foot frame muscles flexed underneath his T-shirt, his blue eyes burned with fire. The military police took a step back, genuinely frightened.

'Baz, Mad Mike, lost in the desert. Presumed dead. Why? Radios didn't work—because you put the wrong fucking codes in. The C130 went down because Kojak never got any weather. We nearly died out there. This is the worst planned mission I have ever been on!'

Peter stepped back and punched Pencilneck in the face with lightning speed. He flew back through the air ten feet, landing on his back semi-conscious. He slowly got up on his elbows, his jaw broken, his nose bleeding; two teeth fell out.

'I will have you court-martialled Morgan!' as blood and saliva dribbled from his mouth. He nodded to the two policeman who moved towards Peter who, in the blink of an eye, pushed his hands out impacting them both in the chest, and the two men flew backwards twenty feet, landing hard on the floor, lying moaning, unable to move.

Then, to their shock and amazement, Kojak, the C130 pilot strolled in, looking sunburnt, thin and above all, angry. He nodded at Peter and his team then walked up to Pencilneck and gave him a good kick in the nuts. Pencilneck rolled up in agony, moaning incoherently.

'Standard operating procedure: we never fly without weather reports!' Kojak's face turned red as he unleashed a verbal torrent at the hapless Ponsonby.

'We could have avoided that weather. My co-pilot Chris died because of you, he was my friend. He has family, these men nearly all died out in the desert,' pointing at Peter and his team. Ponsonby clutched his balls in agony, moaning.

Peter's blood started to cool as he reflected on his actions. He had probably just ended his military career. He thought about Jennifer—she would not be pleased if he got a court-martial, he had a family to provide for. Still, it was done now, and he felt better for it.

Justice was done.

Chapter 17

ON HER MAJESTY'S SECRET SERVICE

Peter, in civvies, is sitting in the SIS chief's office in River House, London. Colonel Bradley has given him strict instructions to go to MI6 and see the Secret Intelligence Service chief himself. He has not seen Sir Nigel since the last meeting in the glass room.

The chief walks in, wearing a blue, three-piece pinstripe, ignores Peter, and sits himself down at his luxuriant desk, going through some papers. Then he looks up, and leans across his teak desk to speak to Peter. Sir Nigel Goldbroom is an old Etonian, his family has old money, and he is rich. He is much respected, having had a distinguished military career—a successful soldier rising to the rank of General before taking on the role of SIS Chief. He has seen real action and has the scars to prove it. He has that disciplined air about him that senior military officers have.

'Sergeant Peter Morgan. How are you?'

'I'm good sir thank you for asking.'

'I didn't update you on Ponsonby. He was the rat. You were right. Found out he had a girlfriend in Egypt, with links to known terrorists, and a secret bank account. We also found some emails on his home computer that link him to a Yemeni based terror cell. But we turned him. We turned him all right. We extracted a lot of information on the terrorist network in the Middle East. Thanks to you Peter.'

Sir Nigel walks over to the drinks cabinet inside an old wooden globe.

'He is now a double agent, he feeds false information to the terrorists, and we get valuable intel in return. You have distinguished yourself, your Colonel Bradley thinks very highly of you. And so do I.'

'So I won't get a court-martial for hitting Ponsonby?'

'No, no, don't worry about all that. You did well,' Sir Nigel laughed adding, 'I gave him a good kick in the bollocks myself, but don't tell anyone.' Peter laughed, he was beginning to like Sir Nigel, he was the genuine article. He becomes more serious as he looks at his single malt whiskey selection.

'Ice?'

'Yes please,' replied Peter.

'With the agreement of your good Colonel, you are being seconded to MI6 permanently. The thing is Peter, we need you. I need your guile, strength, intelligence and your military skills. I've just had a meeting with the Prime Minister; we need to stop the terrorist funding network in Saudi Arabia. It will take tenacity, patience and possibly extreme violence. What do you think?'

'Yes sir, I'm up for it.'

'Good man, good man!' Peter paused then added, 'But Vinnie comes with me—he's my wingman.'

Sir Nigel pours them both a drink. He would not normally do that for an operative, but there is something special about this man. Are all the stories true?

'That's fine, I will arrange it. I know you two work together.' Peter tastes the whiskey. Single malt, it slides smoothly down his throat. Sir Nigel then becomes more serious.

'All we have is a picture, we don't know his name, we don't know his whereabouts, but it's probably Saudi, Riyadh perhaps. Your mission is to find him, get intel on this terrorist funding network, and then extract him for questioning. His code name is Goldilocks.' Sir Nigel tops up his glass, adds some ice, then continues.

'It will be a joint mission with the CIA. Your CIA contact is Captain Miller.' Peter looks at the Goldilocks picture, trying to find something, anything. He looks at the one page of data about him. Real name: unknown. Associates: Ali Ab-Dala, Address: possibly Jeddah. Goldilocks last known address: unknown, maybe Riyadh. Then he looks back at the picture of Goldilocks. His super-vision spots something. There is a tiny label on his Arab robe, his thawb – it is almost undetectable.

'Do you have a magnifying glass?' asked Peter. Sir Nigel digs around in his drawer and finds a large old-fashioned magnifying glass. He hands it to Peter who focuses on a tiny label on the Arab garment.

'There we go…' Peter writes down a name.

'Let me use your computer and Google this name, it's the name of an Arab tailor, I think.' Peter types in a name.

'Abdul Gents Tailoring, King Fahd Dist., Riyadh.'

'It's come back with an address of a tailor, in downtown Riyadh sir. That will be my starting point.'

'Excellent, well done.' In five minutes flat, he has accomplished what his MI6 operatives had failed to do in one month. Sir Nigel shakes Peter's hand warmly.

'Good luck Peter.'

'Thank you, sir. The other matter we discussed?'

'Oh yes, your father, Frank Morgan. Now, what I am about to tell you stays in this office, ok?'

'Agreed, sir.'

Chapter 18

Black Op

Sir Nigel poured Peter another drink, added some ice, sat looking at Peter for a while, then began.

'It was during the Bosnian conflict in the 1990s. Back then I was a major in the SAS. Not many people know that.' Peter's respect for Sir Nigel grew enormously. He knew what it was like on these missions. He had been bloodied in battle. A fellow soldier.

'Your father, Frank. He served under me.'

Peter sat there open-mouthed in shock. 'Go on,' he said, hardly believing what he was hearing.

'It was a black op mission. There was a Bosnian Serbian warlord who was committing atrocities in Bosnia and Herzegovina. His name was Jusak Mosovich and was heavily involved in the Srebrenica massacre, ending with the deaths of 8,000 innocent civilians. Our job was to take him out. Unofficially of course.'

Peter nodded, absorbed.

'It was a four-man team, including Frank and me. I would provide reconnaissance and intelligence, and Frank would be the one to take the shot. Mosovich had stationed himself on Mount Igman on the outskirts of Sarajevo, so he and his cronies could take potshots at the innocent civilians. We knew his position was heavily defended with mortars and heavy ordnance, so we hid among some trees on a nearby mountain, watching their movements, waiting for an opportunity.'

Peter leaned forward, taking a gulp of whiskey.

'We ate and slept in that cold trench on that mountaintop for three days watching, taking shifts. Frank had a Barratt 0.50 sniper rifle. I gave Frank wind and weather data so he could make his calculations for the shot. Fog was a problem, especially in the mountains.' Sir Nigel paused, recollecting his memories.

'On the third day, the fog had cleared, and we spotted him, directing mortar fire at Sarajevo. Frank, cool as a cucumber, took his shot, and I confirmed the kill—1.5 kilometres. He was a brilliant sniper. He had to shoot a bit higher because of the distance and the heavy damp air. We executed our exfil plan and headed to our RV, in the valley on the other side of the mountain, for pickup. But what we didn't know was that they had spotted us. They were tracking us. And we didn't fucking spot it Peter. We didn't spot it!' Sir Nigel banged his fist on the table, scattering some papers.

'Just as the heli came in for the pickup, Frank was hit by a sniper shot and was killed instantly. We carried his body to the heli and that was that.'

Peter nodded and was silent for a while. 'Thank you. I needed to know. I know him as a father, but what was he like to work with?'

'He was brave, fearless and plain speaking. Called a spade a spade. A bit like you Peter,' said Sir Nigel as he poured his operative a large glass.

Peter sat in silence for a while, drinking more whiskey, as he looked at Sir Nigel, who was busy leafing through some papers, scratching his head, and occasionally glancing at Peter. After a few minutes, Sir Nigel looked up, a fatherly look on his face.

'Peter, I have decided to give you top secret security clearance. There's something I want you to look at. Something very odd. Can I pick your brains?' he asked, as he picked up a document from his desk marked 'Top Secret, in red, and handed it to Peter. 'We've had reports of women going missing from the UK, it's not the usual missing persons either, tramps and dropouts etc.'

'What age are the women?' asked Peter, curious as he read the top-secret papers.

'That's the thing. All aged between 18 and 35,' replied Sir Nigel.

'Are there other common denominators? asked Peter, piqued by it all.

'Yes, they are all in perfect health. It's not just the UK, it's the US as well. Langley and ourselves are trying to keep it out of the press. It's a real mystery. We don't like unknowns Peter.'

Peter suddenly had a vision of a darkened sky, like an eclipse—all was in darkness. People were running and screaming in terror. There were explosions—and then silence. He was standing alone, holding a fiery blue sword, surrounded by flames. He recovered himself and looked at a shocked Sir Nigel.

'The world is about to change,' he said, then he got up and walked out of Sir Nigel's office, tears in his eyes.

Chapter 19

GOLDILOCKS

SAUDI ARABIA

After spending the whole summer in Saudi Arabia, Peter looked like an Arab. His skin was dark and leathery due to the harsh, dry climate. He was wearing a thawb, traditional Arab dress. The white cloth reflected the harsh summer heat, and he was glad of that. He had also grown a beard. In addition, he could speak fluent Arabic, and it was impossible to tell him apart from any other Arab walking down the street in Riyadh, his thawb covering his large, muscular body. But of course, he was not an Arab, he was on secondment from the SAS working for MI6 tracking down terrorists, and their funding network.

Using his natural charm and wit, and five hundred dollars in hard currency, the Riyadh tailor had given him an address. There was no need for violence. He had been following Goldilocks discreetly for about a month now and had gained valuable intelligence about his contacts. But now he suspected that Goldilocks knew he was being followed. He had to be careful, or he would lose him completely.

Peter looked at a thermometer sign on a building, the temperature had hit 50 degrees centigrade as the unrelenting heat reflected off the pavement. 'Too fucking hot,' thought Peter, as he followed Goldilocks at a discrete distance. Peter was glad when his target turned into a shopping precinct. It would be cooler there. The tall, thin Arab was not a terrorist as such, but a financier, a middleman, who oiled the wheels of terror. He was wiry and dark, with shifty eyes which darted about, here and there. Vinnie, in western civilian clothing, followed a discrete distance behind Peter and the target.

Using his hidden radio and earpiece Peter radioed Miller. 'Have eyes on Goldilocks, following him into Riyadh Avenue Shopping Centre. Standby. Out.' Miller waited in a blacked out Mercedes down a side-street.

Peter remembers their night out in a secret Riyadh drinking bar, discretely hidden down an alleyway. He immediately hit it off with Miller. Ex-Navy Seal, black hair, moustache, fit as a fiddle—from New Orleans with a southern drawl. He was blunt-talking but a gentlemen to boot. He provided great kit, which was a blessing, and the radios worked, unlike the unreliable British ones.

In the dimly lit bar, in a basement two floors below the street, they sipped their beer taking in their surroundings, their backs to the wall—*you never know*. It reminded Peter of the bar in Casablanca, full of shady characters in dark corners, whispering secret conspiracies. Miller was eyeing a pretty Indian girl in a red dress. She touched her hair and kept smiling at them.

'I think she fancies you,' Peter said. Miller smiled. They downed at least ten bottles each, and the last thing Peter remembered that night was sirens and running feet as the bar was raided by the local plod.

Peter followed his target up an escalator, and into an internet café. Air conditioning, thank God. He ordered a coffee and one hour's surfing time from the man behind the desk. Goldilocks sat down at a terminal, Peter sat in the cubicle next to him, sipping his coffee, blending in, looking normal.

Goldilocks glanced over at his cubicle neighbour and curiosity piqued him, as he raised his eyebrows and studied Peter with his blue eyes and tanned face. Peter's fluent Arabic at the counter, and the local accent, had allayed his suspicions, and he continued typing with his thin fingers.

Peter studiously ignored him, knowing the slightest slip would give him away. He put a USB into his computer which ran some special software, which could pick up keystrokes from nearby PCs. The USB flashed letters onto his screen as he picked up Goldilocks' keystrokes. Peter could see what Goldilocks was typing: a bank in Yemen, an account, Golden Brotherhood Society, an account number, even a mobile number—BINGO! Peter took a screenshot, logged into a secure MI6 site and emailed the screenshot to his contact at MI6. His job was nearly done, he could get back to Jennifer and the kids now, get out of this bake oven climate, and relax at home.

Goldilocks looked again at Peter, as another Arab man, a huge, swarthy man with a military demeanour, built like 'The Rock,' walked behind Peter and saw his screen, the MI6 secure website page. Peter had left it there a second too late.

Fuck it!

The Arab man shouted and put a knife to Peter's throat. Quick as lightning, Peter's instincts kicked in as he held the man's sinewy arm, the blade a millimetre from his Adam's apple. A bead of sweat ran down Peter's nose as the men struggled, his attacker had monstrous strength. Even though Peter had the strength of ten men, he struggled, as the man's grip tightened around the blade.

Peter slowly stood up, pulled back his arm, the knife just grazing his cheek, as he launched his body and flew backward, hitting a wall, breaking several of his attacker's ribs and winding the monster Arab, as he hit the wall. At that moment, Vinnie rushed in, and in a split second, had fired off two shots. The swarthy Arab man dropped to the floor lifeless.

Goldilocks swung around in panic, eyes wide with terror and surprise. Peter and Vinnie manhandled him out of the café door before onlookers knew what was happening. Peter took off his bloody headdress as they rushed along and radioed Miller: 'Require immediate evac. Have Goldilocks. Repeat, have Goldilocks. Out.'

'If you make a scene, my friend here will kill you,' whispered Peter in fluent Arabic.

Goldilocks nodded and walked between his two captors, looking for an escape route, but of course, there was none. He relived the last thirty seconds in his mind as he saw his minder being shot—once in the head, and once in the neck, and his feeling of desperation.

Peter looked at his thawb, it was covered in blood, and passers-by were looking at him, including two security guards, who started following them. The officers shouted a warning and started running after them.

Peter carried Goldilocks out of the shopping precinct as a black Mercedes with blacked out windows pulled up outside, skidding to a halt. The two friends bundled Goldilocks into the back, he started screaming, but one punch from Peter knocked him out. The two security guards started running towards the car shouting, but the Mercedes took off at high speed, wheels screeching. In the back seat of the car was a silent Goldilocks sat between Peter and the CIA man, Vinnie in front, as they sped off to the secret CIA station in Riyadh.

Peter relaxed. He would be home soon.

Chapter 20

Peter's Promotion

Peter sat in the SIS Chief's office in Vauxhall Cross, London, the MI6 building. The chief was looking at one of his paintings, dressed in an Italian wool bespoke suit. Peter looked around him, 'Different world', he thought. Deep pile carpets, wood panelling, gold-framed paintings, teak furniture, and leather-backed chairs. Peter thought he recognized a painting by John Constable, he had seen one like it in the National Gallery. He liked landscape paintings, they reminded him of his native Wales. But this painting did not have a signature. As they sat opposite each other, the Chief offered Peter a glass of Glenmorangie, in a proper whisky glass. 'Excellent whisky, I shall buy a bottle with my bonus', contemplated Peter.

'Single malt, my favourite,' Peter smiled as he looked at his new boss and relaxed in the comfy leather-backed chair again.

'Glad you like it. Take the bottle with you. With the agreement of Colonel Bradley you're being promoted to Captain', Sir Nigel smiled. Peter smiled back, he had heard through the grapevine, and he felt very happy about it.

'Thank you, sir,' said Peter taking another very satisfied sip.

'And please, no more late night phone calls from Riyadh, Peter. If you want to go drinking, be more discrete.' Sir Nigel tried to look serious, then smiled. He handed Peter a card. 'It's a get out of jail free card Peter. Use this number next time, I need my sleep.'

They both laughed.

'Thank you, sir,' smiled Peter, liking Sir Nigel even more.

Sir Nigel leant on his polished teak hardwood desk and looked at this Peter Morgan, this amazing operative who had done so much to fight terrorism and the funding network. Intelligent too, thinks on his feet, and the strength of ten men. Likes a drink, but who doesn't? He would forgive his minor misdemeanour in the Riyadh drinking den. Peter is his best operative, he was seriously thinking of taking him on full time, that's if the CIA didn't get him first, of course. He was hoping to appeal to Peter's British patriotism. He was trying to fend them off, as he knew this young SAS man had already been offered a role across the pond—they were going to overlook the rule that he had to be a US citizen.

There was something different about him; not so much as a scratch in all his operations, no wonder his nickname was "Bulletproof" in the squadron. There was an aura, a charisma, about him, but he couldn't quite put his finger on it.

'Captain Morgan, congratulations on a job well done.'

Sir Nigel refilled Peter's glass and topped up his own, adding some ice as he smiled at Peter. 'With your help, we have shut down a major terrorist funding network. It will set them back years.'

'Sir Nigel, I haven't seen my family in nearly a year,' Peter said as he sipped his whisky.'

'You have six months paid leave from today. Enjoy it, and again well done.' Sir Nigel stood up and brushed his bespoke suit. Then added. 'There's a bonus coming your way too.' Peter smiled.

'By the way, Langley is interested in you, they like your work. But we would like to keep you if that's ok?'

Sir Nigel looked for a response from his young secret agent but did not get one. Peter was busy looking at a painting. Sir Nigel could see Peter was distracted.

'I see you like the painting.'

'Yes, it reminds me of my home in Wales.'

They both stood up and walked over to the painting, admiring its beauty in silence, Peter felt a warm rush from the whisky as it made its way down his throat. This was a good moment, one to savour, a moment of success, 'Enjoy it' he thought. Sir Nigel's mind went back to the mission in Bosnia where his father was killed; he felt partly responsible.

'It's an unknown, but I suspect it's an early Constable,' ventured Sir Nigel. 'I like this painting,' he added.

'So do I, very much,' Peter nodded.

'You can have it,' said Sir Nigel looking directly at Peter.

'Thank you,' replied Peter, genuinely thankful for the gesture. Never turn down a good thing, he had learned that much in life.

'So you will stay with us?' a desperate tone in his voice.

Peter didn't respond, the CIA probably paid better than the Secret Intelligence Service, and Jennifer could see her parents, who were also in Virginia. But he was loyal, and besides, he liked Sir Nigel. After all, he was British, a warrior of the Isle of Albion, the ancient name for Britain. Peter had a vision of himself as a warrior wielding a sword, centuries ago, in an ancient war, in the mountains of Wales. He was a warrior, it was in his blood. But then the vision passed, and he was in Sir Nigel's office again, drinking whisky.

'I thought I had lost you there for a minute,' said a concerned Sir Nigel. 'I sometimes get visions…' Peter replied, coming out of his dream state.

Then his thoughts turned to his brother Vinnie.

'Don't forget Vinnie – he saved my life,' responded Peter.

'Of course, of course, Corporal Carson we will, er, give him a pat on the back,' the Controller smiled patronizingly.

'Pat on the back, I bet Vinnie will be pleased!' Peter said as he walked out of Sir Nigel's office.

Sir Nigel shouted, 'Peter, come back!' aware that he had offended him. He had not realized how close he was to Vinnie. He did not want to upset this fellow - he looked fearsome when angry.

'Peter—Peter I am sorry!'

He came back into the office and sat down on the leather-backed chair again, his demeanour angry. 'Vinnie deserves a bonus too. And leave.'

'Okay I will arrange it,' replied Sir Nigel, eager to please.

There was a knock on the door.

It was a quiet knock, tentative. Ponsonby poked his head around the door - Pencilneck from the ill-fated Yemeni mission.

Peter stood up, even angrier now, as Ponsonby crept past him. The rat who got two of his men and Kojak's co-pilot killed. He gave Peter a sideways frightened look. 'Ah I understand you have already met Ponsonby,' said Sir Nigel with a wicked smile.

'Yes, I have Sir Nigel,' as Peter gave Ponsonby an icy stare.

'You are a fucking rat Ponsonby, and you got two of my men killed. Good family men. By all rights, I should kill you where you stand. But I'm not allowed, Sir Nigel needs you.' Peter now stood an inch from the terrified Ponsonby's face, cold sweat pouring down his face.

'But if Sir Nigel tells me you're giving him false information, or if you lie to him, I will find whatever rat-hole you're in and tear your limbs off, one by one. That's a promise.'

'Yes, yes, of course, Captain Morgan, anything you say,' stuttered Ponsonby, his frightened eyes shifting furtively from Peter to Sir Nigel, looking for a way out. Sir Nigel turned his attention to Ponsonby. The thin weasel stood to attention.

'Ponsonby, you heard Captain Morgan. Make sure your contacts in Yemen give us the location of the terror cell in London. You're dismissed.' Sir Nigel winked at Peter as Ponsonby scurried out the door behind him.

Sir Nigel then smiled at Peter. 'Don't worry Captain I will look after Corporal Carson.

'Have a safe trip back to Wales.' Sir Nigel now stood, then paused as he looked at Peter, that fatherly look on his face.

'Your father, you know he died fighting for what he believed in. Ridding the world of scumbags. Peter, myself and your Colonel are recommending your father for the Military Medal. It's what he deserves.'

'Thank you, sir, it is the right thing to do. You are an honourable man.'

Then Peter stood up straight and saluted the SIS Chief. Sir Nigel saluted back. They stood there for a moment in silence remembering Frank Morgan, soldier and father. Peter remembered his father coming home from missions, down the garden path, carrying presents—smiling and hugging him—he had happy memories, and he smiled. He didn't see his father often, but the times he did were special times.

Sir Nigel then closed the door, opened a file marked 'Top Secret' in red and looked sharply at him. 'Last time we met you said the world is about to change – what did you mean?'

'Sir, I get visions, sometimes of my life centuries ago, sometimes in the future it is difficult to tell.' Peter shrugged his shoulders then added, 'We face a threat, but unlike any we have encountered before Sir: *expect the unexpected.*'

As Peter walked through the corridors of MI6, the staff looked at him. They had heard the rumours, *everyone had*. As he walked out of the building he breathed a sigh of relief, he would be glad to get home. He could trust Sir Nigel, but he didn't trust Ponsonby as far as he could throw him. The question was, what other enemies did he have?

Chapter 21

Ancient Discovery

IRAQI DESERT

In Iraq, which was once known as Sumer, an aging, bearded archaeologist, Professor Picard, excavates under a rock statue of an ancient Sumerian goddess. The perfectly preserved goddess wears a headdress, she is naked, her breasts prominent. In her hands, she holds what looks like an ankh, she has wings like an angel, and her feet are claws. On either side of her are two owls. Next to the goddess is another statue that has a sword, and jagged teeth with the face of a skeleton, and it has wings. He smiles and nods to himself.

'This is the one,' then looks at his skinny, bespectacled, male undergraduate assistant.

'Sumer was the first civilization you know. But there is a mystery: how did they go from mud hut dwelling fisher folk to pyramid building mathematicians, and so quickly? That is what I hope to find out, mon ami.'

'If anyone can find out you can, professor,' replies the sweating assistant. His reputation is legendary. PhDs in archaeology, anthropology, philology, biochemistry, physics, mathematics, and electronics. President of Mensa, consulted by world leaders. Eccentric, but his intellect is unparalleled.

Under the blistering hot sun, the professor uses a brush to wipe away the dust, revealing a stone slab. Then he uses a handkerchief to wipe away the sweat and dust from his face. As the hot desert sun beats down on his back, the professor takes a swig from his water bottle. Along with his young male assistant, they manage to move the slab to reveal a dark chamber.

They struggle through the small entrance and fall heavily onto a stone floor. There is Sumerian cuneiform writing on the ancient stone walls, and in the middle of the chamber is a sarcophagus. The professor studies the writing, running his finger along the cuneiform characters. "Ah oui…oui, 'The Shining One from the stars—here he rests.'" The assistant listens intently as inside the chamber, it is cold, and there is an eerie silence. He shivers and looks at the professor.

'This place gives me the creeps,' he whispers.

'Let's move the top slab,' gestures the professor.

'What do you think is inside, Professor?' asks the assistant almost too afraid to ask.

'Only one way to find to find out!'

'Christ, it's heavy! Here it comes,' replies his assistant.

They manage to move the slab just enough to reveal what is inside. Professor Picard is shocked at the sight that confronts him. In the sarcophagus lie the mummified remains of an alien creature. It has a large oval head and large eye sockets, where the eyes were. It has long thin arms and legs.

'Sacre bleu! Sainte Mère de Dieu—it's not human!' exclaims the professor.

'Look at the size of the eyes!' whispers his assistant. They cross themselves, the professor whispers a prayer, and they edge closer to look at the alien mummy. Professor Picard takes photographs of the ancient writing and mummified alien, while his assistant takes flesh samples from it, being careful not to damage the alien.

'We can analyse these later, back at the university,' orders the professor as they make their way out with their equipment. While the assistant loads the gear into their jeep, the professor stands silently looking at the sky.

'Penny for your thoughts Professor,' as his young student stands by him.

'Mon ami, there is a change in the air.'

'What do you mean, Professor?'

The professor looks at the young man but doesn't want to frighten him unnecessarily. He needs to talk to his adopted father, his secret protector, from early childhood. He turns and smiles at the curious young man.

'Take the equipment and samples back to Berkeley. I must travel to Europe, to see an old friend.'

Chapter 22

COUNT CASSIAN'S CASTLE

MOUNTAIN CASTLE – ROMANIA

Professor Picard and Count Cassian, who is wearing a black hooded cloak, stand on a stone balcony, overlooking the mountains under a blue sky. Cassian is deep in thought, his piercing deep blue eyes hide ancient wisdom, the cloak hiding his long blond hair. They are in Cassian's home in Romania, his ancient castle, forgotten by time, nestling in a remote valley in Transylvania. Due to its remoteness, and inaccessibility by road, it has very few visitors, which is just how Cassian likes it.

'I know you like to keep a low profile Cassian, mon ami, but you could have found a home…well, a bit more accessible,' complains Professor Picard.

'It suits my purposes, Professor,' replies Cassian as he turns to look at his old friend, giving one of his rare smiles.

'Your finding that ancient tomb was no mistake, Professor.'

Cassian looks again at the mountains, searching the skies, looking for something. 'I have become aware of an ancient threat. Our old enemies, that ancient filth, da aliens, are coming back to haunt us. I suspect they are coming in numbers this time, and we are not prepared. Not prepared at all,' he says in his East European accent.

Cassian slaps the stone balcony in frustration.

'Not prepared at all.' He turns to the professor.

'Cassian, if you are right the humans will need our help. You must meet with them.' The professor has an urgency in his voice. Cassian is thoughtful.

'The humans?' Cassian raises his eyebrows.

'Professor, you are right, of course. In the past, I have been reluctant to meet with them, they could not be trusted, but now, things are different. It is time.'

Cassian puts his head in his hands.

"We have been complacent Professor, we must start to make preparations, make plans. We cannot meet this threat alone. We cannot.'

'Cassian, we must consult the old book,' Picard touches his protector's arm hoping to lighten his burden.

'I have always trusted your counsel Professor, but the book, it is full of riddles.'

'And perhaps wisdom, my old friend.'

They are joined by Lucia, a vampire elder, wearing a cloak. She puts her arm in the professor's and looks at him with her deep blue eyes, brushing back her long black hair. 'Lucia my dear, exciting times are ahead,' announces the professor, looking serious.

'Yes, Uncle Louis,' as she rests her head on his shoulder. 'I missed you,' as she kisses his cheek.

'It's good to see you smile my child.'

As they stand there, a large crow lands on the balcony, still as stone, its black beady eyes looking at Cassian, hiding great intelligence. It blinks then waddles toward him on the balcony, then jumps onto his shoulder.

'Morfran, Morfran…wise old bird, give me news.'

The cunning old crow caws into his ear as Cassian strokes its head. The ancient vampire listens intently and nods as the wise old bird caws away. He feels inside his pocket and digs out some walnuts and acorns which Morfran eats hungrily, nuzzling his head against Cassian, who strokes his pet's neck then looks up concerned.

'We have less time than I thought.'

In the distance, a huge black swarm of birds is fleeing south. In the valley below, they can see hundreds of rabbits and deer running and stampeding through the wood, heading towards a cave system at the bottom of the valley.

'The birds are fleeing. The animals are hiding. They know something is afoot. We do not have much time. Come, Professor, let us consult the book of riddles,' Cassian sighs.

'Mais oui, I need a coffee,' the professor replies. Cassian whispers into the crow's ear, and it flies off again, on another mission.

They leave the balcony, and their footsteps echo as they go down a narrow, spiral, winding stone staircase. They brush past cobwebs and walk down a corridor while the professor wraps his cardigan around him to protect against the draft.

'Cassian, have you ever thought about central heating?' They walk past suits of armour, tapestries and old wooden boxes. Portraits of Romanian nobility adorn the cold stone walls, bearing a striking resemblance to Cassian. The professor studies the paintings, rubbing his beard, removing his glasses.

'Come along Professor, we haven't got time for da history lesson,' chides the count. He produces an old brass key from his pocket, and he opens a thick, solid oak door with strange inscriptions on it. The Professor looks at the ancient runes written in gold, on the upper part of the ancient door.

'They protect against unwelcome visitors, Professor,' says Cassian, reading his thoughts. The thick oak door creaks open, and Cassian looks around the room searching. Then he walks towards a huge wooden chest. He mutters some unrecognizable words, and the chest opens. He lifts out a huge book wrapped in leather. It has an ancient lock on it. He produces a golden key and opens the book.

Cassian blows away the dust. 'It's been a while since I looked at this ancient tome, professor, 200 years in fact. I got a bit bored trying to solve its riddles.'

'I have listened to you talking about it, but this is the first time I have actually seen it, Cassian.'

Professor Picard stands back in shock when he sees the tome being placed on a large wooden table. He touches the hard leather in reverence as he examines the ornate Greek letters embossed in gold on the cover. As he runs his fingers over it, he speaks to Cassian without looking up.

'It cannot be. Cassian, where did you get this?'

'I looked everywhere for it, including Alexandria.'

'You mean the ancient city of Alexandria?' the professor stands aghast and looks up from the book.

Chapter 23

SEARCH FOR THE BOOK OF BEROSSUS

'Yes, some 2000 years ago in fact. I had spent twenty years looking for this book before going to Alexandria. In Athens, I looked in all da temples. I travelled to Rome, I spent a year looking in all the libraries, temples and archives, but da authorities starting asking me questions, got suspicious. Then I heard it was in Alexandria, a centre of great learning and culture, in ancient Egypt.' He paused.

'But I got there too late.' He looks with earnest at his professor friend.

'There was a fire, when Julius Caesar attacked da city in 48 B.C. He was cornered by the harbour and lit a fire, it burned down da library. I thought all was lost. Then I heard another rumour, after a bit of persuading. I tracked down and questioned da librarians that had worked at the library.'

'You did more than question them, Cassian,' mutters Lucia in her East European accent.

'I discovered that many scrolls had been secreted away by da Romans to da Imperial library of Constantinople, the Eastern capital of the Roman Empire. They wanted their own great library. They wanted their second capital to be great. So the capital city of the

Byzantine Empire contained one of the last of the great libraries of da ancient world.' Cassian's eyes lit up.

'It was a magnificent place, columns stretched to the ceiling, great carved arches, murals and paintings on the walls and ceilings. Great rooms filled with scrolls, teeming with scholars, scurrying back and forth, studying ancient texts—you would have loved it, Professor!' The professor listens in awe as Cassian describes the great spectacle.

Professor Picard beams as he pictures the scene in his mind. 'Mais oui, mais oui, the book, the book, Berossus Book!' Professor Picard is beside himself with excitement. 'Berossus was a Greek Hellenistic-era Babylonian writer, a priest of Bel Marduk, a mystic, He was also an astronomer,' the professor enthuses. Cassian continues.

'Yes, da book, Berossus Book of Prophecy. I had discovered that an Arab scholar had bound the Berossus scrolls into leather covers, so this narrowed down my search from 100,000 scrolls to about ten leather-bound volumes. I stole into the main Imperial Library in da dead of night. The guards were sleeping, and I made myself invisible, so that I wasn't disturbed. It still took me an hour to find it, though.'

Professor Picard is in his element as his eyes water with emotion. He faces Cassian and Lucia.

'You know after the destruction of the Great Library of Alexandria, the Imperial library of Constantinople stood out as a beacon of ancient culture. It preserved the knowledge of the ancient Greeks and Romans for almost 1,000 years. The Emperor Constantius II established a Scriptorium so that the surviving works of Greek literature could be copied and so preserved. Incredibly, the library survived until 1453 when Constantinople was conquered by the Ottoman Empire, and everything was destroyed. A light went out in the world. Such a tragedy,' says the professor, shaking his head.

'It's in Greek, Professor. Ancient Greek. Now my ancient Greek is a bit rusty, so I will need your help,' says Cassian.

'Looks like Berossus wrote in the Koine Greek language—Hellenistic. The new testament was written in this language,' says the professor, running his fingers over the gold embossed letters on the front of the remarkably well-preserved tome, scratching his beard, his eyes full of wonder and excitement.

Βιβλίο της Προφητεία

"Professor, I'm looking for a passage about 'Flames of fire come down from the Sky… when the Gods come down from the Heavens.'"

Professor Picard puts on some white gloves and leafs through the book. His concentration does not waver as he totally immerses himself.

'Fascinating… such insight.'

He continues while Lucia brings him a cup of French roast. The professor does not look up as he sips his coffee.

'Thank you, my dear.' Lucia puts her hand on his shoulder.

'Found anything interesting, Uncle?'

'Oh here…here is the passage you're looking for, Cassian!'

'Flames of fire descend from the sky and blacken the earth, and it is burning and scorched. The gods come down from the heavens and create fear among the people. The nations are scattered, and confused, and they run beating their breasts. Their buildings are rent asunder as they wail and weep. The people flee from the demons in their chariots in the heavens above. They get on their knees and cry unto God.

But there is one who will come forth from the Isle of Albion, from Cymru, from the land of the mountains. A warrior with foresight and strength who will travel to the land of the eagles. And he will destroy the demons in their chariots.'

'That's it Cassian.'

'The land of Albion?'

'That's easy, it's the ancient name for Britain,' the professor says, scratching his beard.

'From the land of Cymru?'

'Wales.'

'Does this warrior have a name?' asks Lucia.

'It says here his name is Caius. He sounds superhuman 'No one man would be able to brave fire or water like him. He can run as fast as the wind and has the strength of ten men.'

'Sounds indestructible,' said Cassian.

'Caius can go nine days and nine nights without the need to breathe or to sleep, and can grow as tall as the tallest tree in the forest if he pleased. He radiates God-like heat from his hands. Furthermore, it is impossible to cure a wound from Caius's sword."

'He will travel to the Land of the Eagles.'

'Eagles…eagles…symbolism? Ah, the USA?' beams the professor.

'It is decided. We must move to da United States of America,' Cassian stands upright. 'We must meet with the leaders and find this warrior. We must seek him out.'

'He might even find us,' Lucia says, as she plays with her hair and imagines what this mighty warrior looks like.

They sit in silence at the ancient oak table in the cold, stone room adorned by hunting trophies and tapestries. On the table is a large map of the world. Professor Picard has another cup of coffee and Cassian helps himself too.

The professor smiles to himself—the humans would be amused to know that a vampire drinks coffee, but Cassian was full of eccentricities.

Cassian stands to speak.

'Our brethren are scattered all over da world. I have not spoken to many of them since the council meeting of the Vampiri in World War Two. It has been too long. It will be difficult. Old friendships will need to be renewed. There are old grudges and feuds among our clans, Professor. We must set aside our differences if we are to stand a chance against da oncoming threat.'

'Who are our main allies?' asks the professor.

'There is Lady Vesilia in England, Lord Aswerne in da Philippines certainly. Those are the ones we can count on— maybe Baron Titas in Germany, but he's a stubborn old fool. I need to hold a council meeting of da Vampiri—soon. Time is of the essence. He looks at Lucia.

'Lucia, make da arrangements. They are compelled to attend.' Cassian strokes his long chin. 'Professor, you need to come with us, to the United States of America, I need your help.'

'Mon ami, you know I found a tomb with a preserved alien in it, in Iraq, it's incredible. There are some cuneiform texts I need to translate and papers to write. I need to get back to the university to continue my research, but I will be in constant touch. Meantime I'm going to finish reading this ancient tome. I want to know more about this Caius. Lucia another coffee please, it will take all night.' Cassian puts his hand on his friend's shoulder, a look of concern on his face.

All of a sudden the professor looks up from the leather book, his face deadly serious. 'Cassian, keep this book safe, it might be useful to our enemies.' Cassian nods.

'I will keep it in my possession at all times,' a sense of urgency rising in his voice.

'We do not have much time, Professor, a storm is approaching fast. Da winds of fate are changing, my old friend, nothing will be the same anymore. Lucia, pack your bags, we leave in twenty-four hours.'

Then he puts his hand on the professor's shoulder. 'We may be too late already.'

Chapter 24

OF QUESTIONABLE CHARACTER

EAST END, LONDON

Peter had promised Vinnie he would meet him for a drink after his meeting with Sir Nigel, and he was wondering why he sounded so serious about it—unusual for happy-go-lucky Vinnie. As he walked through the city and down Whitechapel Road, Peter admired the contrast between the old and the new. Flash city skyscrapers and flash city traders in flash suits, drinking red bull and yelling into their mobiles. And old London—cobbled streets, ancient medieval pubs, a sanctuary of old history, wooden beams and cask conditioned ales—an oasis, away from the stresses of the world. As he looked around him, he realised that there was nowhere else in the world quite like London.

The old and the new.

The world was changing fast, but did he fit into this new world? How fast do you have to run to keep up? He thought about the visions he had: the Eternal Warrior, an ancient memory with a magical sword, the priest, and part of him was part of the new. How could he combine the two parts that pulled at him? He dismissed these thoughts as he approached his destination.

As he walked towards the Blind Beggar Pub he saw two huge, tough looking men outside, wearing Italian suits. People walking past avoided them, but they broke into a smile as Peter approached them. They both shook his hand and clapped him on the back.

'Vinnie and Reg are waiting for you.'

As he entered the pub, he could see Vinnie and his father Reg standing by the bar. Reg's normally hard-as-nails features cracked into a warm smile as he walked towards him.

'Peter, nice to see you again, anything you need, just let me know.' Reg turned his head towards the bar.

'Doris, two beers for Vinnie and Pete. We have some jellied eels left, they're lovely.'

With that, his face turned back to his normal granite features and the two mountainous men in suits joined him.

'I have a job for you two boys, someone's not toeing the line.'

Peter and Vinnie sat on two barstools by the bar sipping their pints of London Pride. Peter declined the offer of the jellied eels, they made his stomach turn; Vinnie took one and turned to face his oldest friend.

'I've travelled all around the world with this job but only in England can you get a decent pint of bitter,' Peter smiled.

'Heaven,' replied Vinnie as they looked at the dark golden liquid reflecting in the sunlight, almost in a trance. They enjoyed that moment of pure pleasure as they took the first few sips of real ale. A ripple of satisfaction showed on Peter's face as he looked at his old friend Vinnie.

'Spoken like a poet.'

'How did your chat with Sir Nigel go?' Vinnie narrowed his eyes, concerned.

'I have just been promoted to Captain.'

'Captain Morgan – well-done mate, do I have to call you sir? Maybe we should be drinking rum instead—Captain Morgan,' Vinnie joked. Vinnie walked around behind the bar, grabbed two glasses and poured them both a Captain Morgan. They raised their glasses then both downed in one.

Peter laughed and carried on. 'Ahoy shipmates, me hearties!' he added and they both laughed. Vinnie told a joke: 'Horse walks into a bar. Why the long face said the barman?' They both laughed, they had heard it before, but it was always funny. Then Peter became serious.

'Sir Nigel, he said he would give you a pat on the back.'

'Pat on the back? What the fuck does that mean?' asked Vinnie looking furious.

'Don't worry Vinnie. It's all sorted.' Vinnie frowned.

'I got a problem Pete, for some reason, 6 put a new handler in charge of me—you know, "shit face."' Vinnie looked unhappy and had that look about him that made ordinary mortals run for cover. Some called it the thousand-yard stare. Peter sipped his pint.

'Oh yes I met him Ratti. Very new. Doesn't know his arse from his elbow. I don't like him much either. He gave me a dressing down for not doing paperwork properly. Technically, I'm his superior, so I told him to fuck off. Later he found out who I really was, and avoided me like the plague.'

Vinnie moved even closer, as if he was plotting a war and wagged his finger.

"He said my father was 'of questionable character—moi?'"

Vinnie tried to look innocent and Peter smiled. Vinnie went on. 'Ratti says my methods are unorthodox. He stopped my bonus for Christ's sake.'

'Unorthodox? Stopped your bonus he really is a shit face!' exclaimed Peter.

Vinnie leaned in towards Peter and whispered. 'I saved your arse for Christ's sake. You know, the gig in Saudi.'

'Not for the first time mate,' Peter moved closer.

'It's a black op for Christ's sake, you have to think on your feet!'

Vinnie leaned even closer. He wagged his finger again and his eyes grew thinner, as his features changed. He looked fearsome. Peter recognized this as battle mode: Vinnie "The Terminator" mode.

'Oh yeah, Ratti, goes on about how he went to some posh English school, starts showing me these PowerPoint slides about how I'm going wrong. Says he's a CA.'

Vinnie paused for emphasis.

'What's a CA I said to him, cunt and arse?'

'No,' he said. 'I am a Chartered Accountant.'

'My uncle is a Chartered Accountant—good business brain. So he didn't offer you another job then, Vinnie?' Peter asked innocently trying not to laugh, imagining the scene.

'No, not after what I said to him after that.'

'What was that?' Peter was captivated and entertained.

'I told him to go fuck himself.'

'Oh Vinnie, you need to be more diplomatic mate.' Peter laughed, nearly falling off his stool and spilling his beer, as he looked at Vinnie's deadpan face.

'I told him to stick his PowerPoint slides where the sun don't shine.'

'Vinnie, you have to think about your career,' Peter was sympathetic; Vinnie was being true to character and he loved him for it.

'He tried to get me expelled from the Service.'

'I heard.'

'I don't know what to do Pete, I really don't.' Vinnie looked forlorn.

'Don't worry Vinnie, I put in a good word for you with Sir Nigel. He blocked it, your job is safe. I heard through the grapevine that it really pissed off Ratti, you will be happy to know.'

'Good thanks, Pete.'

'That's what mates are for.'

'What about my bonus, Pete?'

'I talked to Sir Nigel, and he's arranging it—tax-free of course. And he doesn't mind your father being a gangster. In fact, he quite likes it—he might use him.'

They hugged each other in a tight embrace. Then Peter looked Vinnie in the eyes.

'Vinnie, I know what you're thinking mate, don't do it, it's not worth it.'

'It's a matter of honour, Pete, he insulted me.'

'I know Vinnie, and I understand, I really do, we live by a code of honour, just don't do it.'

Vinnie seemed disappointed. They hugged each other again

'All right, I will give him a pass,' said Vinnie reluctantly.

'It had better be a good bonus, I promised Gill we would be putting a deposit on a house. After I get my bonus, I'm thinking of retiring from all this bullshit.'

'But Vinnie you're my wingman, I can't work without you mate! I told Sir Nigel that—it's both of us or nothing.' Vinnie hugged Peter then had a worried look in his eye.

'Rumour has they were going to transfer you to a test facility,' asked Vinnie.

'Who said that?' asked Peter.

'The boys at Hereford,' said Vinnie

Then Peter came clean. 'Someone from the CIA interviewed me. They wanted to find out how I can run so fast, be so strong like I was someone from a Marvel comic—the Hulk or something,' said Peter angrily, then added, 'I'm not going to be some test guinea pig, Vinnie, and be put on display. No fucking way.' Vinnie nodded. They hugged again before Peter walked out of the pub.

Peter stood outside the pub and looked around him. Then looked up as a huge flock of birds flew past, blocking out the sun. There was definitely a change in the air: *the winds of fate were moving.*

Chapter 25

Primordial Instinct

As Peter sat on the train on the way back to Wales, his mind wandered. 'Is it worth the stress? I should give up being a Secret Agent working for MI6 and become a farmer.'

The quiet life. Retire from all the bullshit—like Vinnie planned to do.

If it wasn't for Vinnie watching his back he would have given up years ago. It was like having insurance, having Vinnie around, despite his bulletproof reputation. His thoughts moved to Jennifer and his family. They would see him again, at last, it had been too long since he had been home, far too long. He missed the peace and quiet of his home in the enchanted wood. His little enclave of serenity and beauty, away from the mad world of guns, terrorists, and politicians. And politics. Here in this wooded valley, a spade was a spade, no grinning politicians to call it something else.

Home, the enchanted wood—there were all sorts of stories about that place, told to him by his grandmother and old Welsh farmers in the pub. He had never told anyone else about his experiences in the woods and desert with the priest, and the angel - not even Vinnie. As he walked up the garden path, there was no sign of anyone in.

He thought back to his waking dream.

Did he imagine it? As he looked out the kitchen window at the green countryside and the woods, he felt he was in a dream. Time seemed to stop, and all was quiet around him—the old black book with gold letters, the old, wise priest. The ancient warrior, a knight with a sword. He was holding a long silver sword that seemed to shine and illuminate everything.

A name repeated in his mind, Caius, Caius, he was standing on an island off the coast of Wales, looking out over a cliff, the breeze blowing his long hair as he looked out over the ocean. He heard a growling behind him. As he swung around, he saw a huge cat-like beast, a palug cat, ancient, wild and stalking him. Its evil eyes fixated on him as saliva drooled from its fangs. A deep growling came from deep within the beast; it was ready to pounce. Peter was cornered, nowhere to run; his heart pounded. He raised his sword, it was glowing blue with radiated light, and seemed to vibrate with power.

Then his wife was shaking him, 'Peter, what's the matter with you? What's the matter!' Peter came out of his trance, he was standing in his kitchen, and Jennifer was shaking him. 'I'm sorry, I was daydreaming.' He held her in his arms and didn't let go.

'It's good to be home. I'm not leaving again—not in a hurry.'

'Why don't you go upstairs and rest? You look exhausted,' she stroked his bald head.

As Peter lay on his bed, he saw a large black crow at the bedroom window, looking at him, its beady eyes looking into his soul. It tapped with its beak three times on the window. Then it was gone. He had a feeling in his gut that things were about to change, his life was about to change.

The world was about to change.

Gut instinct he called it.

It had saved him more than once, his sixth sense, survival instinct, an ancient sense of knowing. Humans had lost this primordial instinct, but Peter had it, in spades.

A warrior needs to be self-aware.

The atmosphere seemed different. People seemed different. The world was changing. Events were moving fast, his visions were more frequent now. Then he fell asleep. His children watched him, as Jennifer came into the room. Peter dreamed of ancient lands and ancient battles and a silver-blue sword. Then the landscape changed; he was standing on a hill overlooking a city, and above him was a huge, menacing black ship covering all in dark shadow.

And he was alone.

'Daddy's very tired, let him sleep. Help me cook him dinner.' As Jennifer stood in the kitchen something made her glance up. The sky was dark, but it wasn't storm clouds. She dropped her pan when she saw a huge swarm of screaming birds as they descended on the hidden valley, covering all the trees, screeching like the Hitchcock movie. It seemed all the birds in the world were seeking sanctuary in this hidden valley. Soon all the trees were covered in a thick layer of birds of all kinds and sizes, making a deafening noise. Jennifer hugged her frightened children as they watched the spectacle. Then she froze as a huge crow jumped onto her window ledge and stared at her with black knowing eyes.

Nature knows; nature was moving.

Chapter 26

VAMPIRE AND HUMAN SUMMIT

TOP SECRET US GOVERNMENT INSTALLATION
IN VIRGINIA – PRESENT DAY

Cassian and Lucia are flying over the Blue Ridge Mountains in Virginia. Their large leathery wings catch a mountain updraft as they soar through the air. Their red eyes glow in the dark as the full moon shows them the way. Their progress is swift but unseen, except for a group of outsized bats who follow them at a discreet distance. As the vast mass of bats passes the moon, the light is dimmed for a moment. Cassian gestures to Lucia that they descend, so they swoop down outside a military base near some pine trees and land in silence.

Their blood-red eyes slowly change to blue, and their wings shrink, as they transform back to their normal form. Cassian raises a hand to the bat escort, and they move off. They can see the perimeter fence two hundred yards away as they shroud themselves in hooded cloaks. Fifty yards in front of them, Rangers in black military fatigues raise their automatic rifles and shout a challenge.

Cassian looks at Lucia, their thoughts as one, for no soldier can withstand the will of a vampire, especially Cassian, the Prince of all Vampires. As Cassian and Lucia walk nonchalantly past the guards, Cassian waves his hand, and they stand transfixed, open-mouthed in silence. One soldier opens fire, the bullets hitting Cassian in the chest. Cassian stops as if annoyed by a mosquito bite, then swoops forward at lightning speed and throws the soldier a hundred yards into some trees.

Inside the Top-Secret US government installation, General Bill Scott walks with President Frank Wilson along a steel corridor. The general's short-cropped hair, ruddy face, and tall, straight frame sit perfectly in his immaculate four-star uniform. His disciplined tones echo down the hallway as he talks to his old friend, college professor and president, a dead ringer for Morgan Freeman.

'I don't know why you agreed to see these vampires, Frank - they are vermin. If the public ever found out, your ratings would plummet.'

'God has a plan for everything, Bill,' replies the President, taking off his glasses. His soft African-American features hide great wisdom, his short hair shows signs of grey, and his eyes show a hint of sadness, as if nursing a secret. General Scott thinks he sounds philosophical, not his usual self, not like him at all. He seems different, he appears to have lost some of his spark.

In a secure soundproof meeting room sits President Wilson, General Scott and vampire elders Cassian and Lucia.

'I have agreed to this meeting as an opportunity to explore common ground as a basis for more talks between humans and vampires. I am hoping this will be the first of many meetings,' says President Wilson, his hands open in friendship.

Cassian stands showing his thin, wiry and powerful frame. His long blond hair and sharp blue eyes radiate ancient wisdom and knowledge. He takes off his black cloak and reveals a black, medieval suit. Cassian speaks with a strong East European accent.

'Thank you, Mr. President of da United States. Very soon, we will hold a Council Meeting of our elders, our government if you like. I want to establish diplomatic relations with da United States of America. I wish to adopt a policy of cooperation with humans on a broad range of issues. I would have waited till after our council meeting to ratify, but events seem to be overtaking us.'

General Scott looks curiously at their vampire guests, turning his nose up at their presence.

'How can we be certain we can trust you, after the last incident in Texas?' asks General Scott. Cassian and Lucia exchange glances. Lucia stands, her beautiful black hair flows over her shoulders, contrasting with her sharp blue eyes and pale skin. She wears a tight-fitting black leather suit, her magnetism palpable.

'That was regrettable, and da punishment has been swift, I can assure you. We have an ancient law forbidding attacks on healthy humans. We will only feed on cattle or wild animals, besides we are now developing our own artificial blood banks, so we should be able to replenish ourselves without resorting to attacks on humans. It's early days with this project, but we're hopeful,' replies Lucia in her East European accent, looking at Cassian.

Cassian gazes levelly at the president and General.

'What do you mean—events seem to be overtaking us?' President Wilson's curiosity is piqued.

'Mr. President, if you will allow, there is another more pressing issue we need to discuss. We have become conscious of da threat of an old enemy. There are many orders of creation apart from humans and vampires, of which you may not be aware.'

Cassian casts his mind back thousands of years. He is inside a pyramid in the desert. He is leading a group of vampires against the aliens. The aliens wear battle dress and use hand lasers, and the stronger more agile vampires fight with swords and knives. Though better armed, the weaker aliens retreat to their spaceship and take off.

'Thousands of years ago there was a war between a race of aliens and vampires back in a land called Sumeria, which you now call Iraq.

These aliens are an ancient race, ten million years old. Their gene pool became depleted, so they came to Earth looking for new genetic material. First, they came in small numbers. They killed da men and kidnapped da women for their filthy genetic experiments.'

'What experiments?' asks the president.

'They set up laboratories where these women were held, strapped to tables. Yhey had long needles inserted into their head, arms, and stomach. Da aliens did not use anaesthetic.

'How do you know?' asks Scott.

'I was there, I witnessed it. I heard their screams of agony. I saw da look of terror in their eyes, their pleadings for mercy, but of course, they didn't get any.'

The president winces. General Scott's eyes roll.

'They took human samples of DNA, mixed it with alien DNA to try to create hybrid, half-human half-alien creatures. Their first attempts were like a freak horror show. I am a vampire, a demon, but even I was shocked at the grotesque creatures that emerged. They died, of course, da few that survived didn't live very long. They also performed experiments on muscle, bone and nerve regeneration of disabled aliens with transplantation of body parts from human to aliens. At first, I was ambivalent about humankind—they were just a food source to us, but when I saw da torture and mutilations my attitude changed. I began to feel sorry for them.'

'Sounds like the Nazi experiments during the Second World War,' the president shakes his head.

'Then they came in a larger ship and destroyed an entire village. I was there 6000 years ago. I witnessed it. You may think we vampires are da enemy of humans, yes in those days we fed on humans, mostly dead, as well as a few old or weak individuals, and not in great numbers. You must understand we admire humans for their spirit and courage. Anyway, they wiped out an entire village. You understand—we could not tolerate this, so there was a war.'

'Incredible, if it's true,' says the President.

'Mr. President, surely you cannot believe this nonsense,' says General Scott, smiling sarcastically.

'General Scott, we have evidence. An archaeologist found some artefacts from da ancient war recently. We keep an eye on these ancient sites. They are part of our history and heritage. He works at your University of da California, Professor Picard,' replied Cassian.

General Scott picks up the phone. 'This is Scott, get Professor Picard, University of California.'

'That was then—this is now, how does this affect us, here in the present?' asked the president exasperated.

Cassian looks at Lucia. He pauses, 'As I said, we have become aware of the threat of da old enemy. They are coming soon. In da next few days.'

'Mr. President,' says General Scott, scratching his head.

'What evidence do you have for an alien invasion?' asks the president, his eyebrows raised as he leans back in his plush leather chair.

'We have detected increased alien activity over the last year or so. Many of your human women have disappeared,' replies Cassian.

'Fifty thousand women in the US have disappeared over the last year.' The general looks at Cassian.

'Were they white, middle-class?' asks Cassian.

'Yes. How did you know? You think aliens are responsible?' asks the General.

Chapter 27

PHYSIC VAMPIRES

'Yes, we do. We are psychic,' says Cassian.

'We need hard facts,' says the president.

'We can see into other worlds you cannot see. We became psychic because we had to, to survive. The ability evolved naturally over time. For instance, did you know your ancestor, Neolithic man was telepathic? If danger was imminent, like a flood, for example, they had to communicate to survive—there were no telephones in those days. There was a symbiosis between man and nature, a direct connection—evolution did da rest. Humans have lost that ability, partly due to religious persecution and partly because they don't need it anymore,' explained a patient Cassian.

'Thank you for the information. We will investigate this professor's discoveries.' The President is uncomfortable now.

Cassian continues. 'That is not all. We have reason to believe there is a traitor amongst you. We are certain of it. He is high up in your military hierarchy.'

President Wilson and General Scott exchange glances, trying to hide surprise. 'Again, thank you for the information. I have another meeting now,' says the president, beginning to rise from his chair.

As Cassian is leaving the room, he turns to the President, looking sympathetic. 'You want proof that I am psychic President Wilson. You have a problem with your stomach, you need to see a doctor.'

The president stands aghast for a moment. How could Cassian know he needs to see a doctor unless he really is psychic?

President Wilson and General Scott stand outside the meeting room. 'I want this professor's discoveries investigated,' orders the president.

'Do you think what they are saying is true, Frank?' asks his friend, the General.

'There are more things in Heaven and Earth, Horatio, than are dreamt of in your philosophy,' replies the president.

'Beg your pardon, sir?' The General is confused. The President looks his friend in the eye.

'Bill, who would have thought a year ago we would be discussing an alien invasion with vampires? Real vampires, Bill, they told me something nobody else knows. There was something about what they said that rang true.'

The General shrugs his shoulders.

President Wilson holds his stomach as if in pain. 'Are you okay, Frank? You look pale.'

The President tries to sound confident, 'Yes I'm fine, just some indigestion.' Privately the President knows Cassian is right: he needs to see a doctor. If Cassian is right about that, *maybe he was right about other things.*

"Why would they come to us unless it was something that threatened both our races? Maybe we should trust Cassian and Lucia. There is an old saying 'The enemy of my enemy is my friend.' We need to trust our instincts on this, Bill." The President looks intense.

General Scott is thoughtful. 'If what they say is true—and I'm not saying it is—there is a clear and present danger to national security—global security for that matter.'

The President and the General stand silent for a moment, the President speaks first, 'They said these aliens would be coming in the next few days. I'm going to take a chance. Go to DEFCON 4. Give the order, just as a precaution.'

The General is shocked.

'But what do I tell the other joint chiefs?' as he opens his arms, exasperated.

'Tell them it's a training exercise,' answers the president.

'Yes sir, I hope your hunch is correct.'

CONSULTATION ROOM

President Wilson is in a private health clinic with a consultant. Secret Service agents wait outside the room, along with his wife Vanessa, the First Lady, in a smart suit, high heels and Jackie Kennedy-style brunette hair. Her pale white face looks scared and apprehensive as she paces up and down, biting her immaculate nails.

Inside the room, the consultant looks at him and tries to be reassuring, but his news is not good.

'We have done all the tests, and I have double-checked the results. Please sit down, Mr. President.'

'I will stand if you don't mind.' The President goes outside and speaks to his wife. 'Vanessa, come in please, I need you now.' Vanessa enters, and they sit down together looking at the consultant. She grips his hand so firmly he winces.

'I'm afraid I have some bad news, sir. The tests have come back, and you have early-stage stomach cancer.' Vanessa weeps, but the President sits stony-faced as the consultant continues.

The consultant puts on his most optimistic face as he addresses the leader of the free world. 'We have had very good success rates with these types of cancer. We have caught it early so there's every chance you can make a full recovery, if we start treatment, now.'

President Wilson puts his head in his hands, a sense of mortality and foreboding filling his body. He feels weak and helpless. He is the leader of the free world, but we are all at God's mercy. He feels fragile, but he needs to be strong. How can he tell his son he has cancer? Then he puts on his brave, resilient face and faces the consultant.

'You must keep this confidential.'

'Yes sir, of course,' said the consultant.

'When do we start treatment?'

'This afternoon Sir, there is no time to lose.'

Outside the doctor's office, President Wilson hugs Vanessa. 'We can beat this together, okay?' whispers Vanessa, the tears welling in her eyes. She smiles, trying to hide her feelings.

'If they start treatment now, there's a good chance,' says the president, trying to put a sugar coating on it. His young son, Michael, runs up to him and hugs him tight. The president looks down and puts his hand on his young son's head. 'Son, you need to be a brave boy. Daddy is sick. I have a problem with my tummy.' His son nods.

'I feel so bad. There's the charity event in New York, I should stay here with you,' says a tearful First Lady as she touches his chest.

'No, you go, Michael can keep me company.'

They kiss, but the president will ultimately regret his last words to her.

Chapter 28

INVASION

CANBERRA DEEP SPACE COMMUNICATION COMPLEX –PRESENT DAY

Two junior astronomers based in the communication complex are doing the night shift. Banks of computers and monitors line the walls. Nick, longhaired, scruffy, unshaven and hung over, nods off then sleepily gazes up at his screen.

'Huh?'

Nick grimaces at his coffee and then looks at his screen again. 'Chris, have a look at this. Is this shit coffee making me see things or can you see an object moving towards Earth?'

Chris, even more longhaired, and even scruffier, stares at his screen.

'You mean that object?

'Yes, I mean that fucking object—it's not an asteroid, it's too solid! Call the boss,' says Nick.

'You mean bell end?' asks Chris.

'Just call him,' orders Nick.

Chris is on the phone to his boss. 'Yes sir, we have a very large object moving towards Earth… about 100,000 kilometres distant and closing fast. Speed? Hold on a minute. 20,000 miles per hour. No, hold on. Sorry sir, it's changing, 19,000 miles per hour. Can't be right. How can it be slowing down?'

UNITED STATES SPACE COMMAND. PETERSON AIR FORCE BASE COLORADO

In Air Force Space Command (AFSPC) sits Chip, a young, muscular, crop-haired space radar operator. He is surrounded by other operators and banks of screens. In the front of the huge room is a screen twenty feet tall and fifty feet wide showing every single satellite and other space objects, and their position in Earth orbit, shown in real time.

Chip gets excited. 'Sir! I've picked something up on the space radar. It's coming in fast, sir.' His superior, General Grimbald, looks annoyed.

'Meteorite?'

'I don't think so, sir.'

'Why's that?' asks the General, showing his yellow teeth.

'Because it's slowing down, sir!' General Grimbald looks agitated.

'Must be a fault in the system,' he replies, his eyes darting this way and that.

Chip is frustrated. 'But sir!'

'Do a full system diagnostic. That's an order!' barks the general.

'But sir that will take three hours!' Chip is jumping with agitation.

'Do it! That's an order! The only reason you got this job, Lieutenant, is because that jumped-up asshole of an uncle of yours is in the White House.'

General Grimbald walks away. His greasy, black hair is in contrast to his pale, unhealthy-looking face. His dark, shifty eyes dart back and forth as if searching for something, he then checks his watch. Chip waits until the General leaves, then discreetly taps out a message on his mobile phone, then decides what he is going to do. Disobeying a direct order could mean a court-martial, but if the Earth was being invaded, he needed to do something.

He finishes the message to his uncle, General Scott, in the White House and decides to wait for an answer. Running a system diagnostic would consume a lot of computing resource. A bead of sweat drops from his forehead, as he looks at his colleagues, hoping he has made the right decision.

Chapter 29

PANIC IN THE OVAL OFFICE

WHITE HOUSE

General Bill Scott is walking down the corridor when he picks up a message from his nephew Chip. He raises his eyebrows as he walks into the Oval Office where his good friend President Frank Wilson is pouring coffee.

'Hello Bill, sugar?'

'No thanks, trying to cut down,' replies the General his thoughts occupied by Chip's message.

'Bill, sit down, please. There is something I need to tell you.' President Wilson pauses as he looks directly at Scott. The general hasn't seen that look in his eyes before, this is something new.

'I am only telling you this as you are a family friend, and we've known each other for many years, and I trust you. Now, apart from Vanessa and Michael, you will be the only person to know this. No doubt, the press will get hold of it sooner, or later. Anyway, I have been diagnosed with cancer—stomach cancer.' Bill Scott sits down in shock next to his old friend.

'Jesus Christ, Frank, I am so sorry. You should be resting and taking it easy.' The General, not one normally for showing emotion, put his hand on the president's shoulder. As the president looks out of the Oval Office window, he sees a huge crow looking at him, its black eyes piercing his soul. For a few seconds he is transfixed—then it waddles off, spreads its wings and flies away. The president looks at his friend.

'What is it, Frank?'

'Did you see that bird, Bill?'

'No.'

'Odd, I couldn't take my eyes off it.' The president shakes his head to regain his focus, but the image of the bird stays in his mind.

'It's in the early stages, so the prognosis is good. My doctor says I have an excellent chance of recovery.'

'That's good Frank, you have a chance,' says the General, cheered up by his friend's optimism, then he looks at his mobile again.

'You look preoccupied. What is it?' asks the President.

'Sorry Frank, it's just odd. I have a message from my nephew Chip down at Space Command. An object has been detected coming towards Earth.'

'Shouldn't we get notification direct from General Grimbald?' asked the President, surprised.

'Yes sir, that's why it's odd. It is just not standard procedure. I've asked Chip to schedule a conference call with Grimbald in ten minutes. Maybe it's just my nephew getting over excited—he is pretty new.'

'Do you trust him?' The President looks the General in the eye.

'Yes. Absolutely, 100%. He has made lieutenant already.' General Scott dials Chip on his mobile.

'Chip, don't run that diagnostic. Await further orders. That's a direct order.'

Scott is interrupted by the large red phone on the president's desk, blinking away. A direct line to all the world's leaders. Wilson and Scott look at each other as an aide rushes in excited.

'Sir, sir! It's the Chinese on the line!'

Wilson picks up the red phone.

'Premier Xin, what can I do for you?'

'President Wilson, we have picked up something on our long-range space radar, do you have any unofficial space missions that you have not told us about?' President Wilson hesitates.

'I can confirm we have no space missions, we, err… haven't had any official confirmation of any near-Earth object.'

'I find that difficult to believe, President Wilson, honestly.'

'Can I get back to you? We need to investigate this,' says a shaky president as he puts the phone down.

'Jesus Christ, Bill. The Chinese know before we do!' The President looks at General Scott.

'The Chinese have hacked into the Space Command network several times this year already.' The red phone blinks again.

'President Wilson.'

'President Wilson, this is President Yakimov, we are tracking an object approaching Earth orbit. Do you have any space missions you haven't told us about? Protocol dictates that you must tell us.'

'We are also tracking the object. We are awaiting further information, President Yakimov. Thank you for informing us. We will get back to you. Goodbye.'

President Wilson sits back in his chair, head in his hands. By now, the room is filled with most of the Defense Chiefs and military personnel. Wilson is angry as he looks at Scott, 'Get General Grimbald on the line NOW!' punching his desk in frustration.

The crowded oval office stands in silence. Scott gets on the line to his counterpart in Space Command.

'This is General Scott. Get me Grimbald now!'

Grimbald's assistant answers, 'He's not here, sir. We cannot find him.' General Scott is incredulous, as his face reddens.

Chapter 30

WHERE THE FUCK IS GRIMBALD?

'What do you mean you cannot find him? Where the fuck is he? This is an emergency!' shouted a red-faced Bill Scott.

'Sorry sir, Colonel Mack's not here either. Do you want to speak to Lieutenant Scott?'

'Yes, put him on the line!' he snapped.

'Sir,' said a nervous Chip.

'Where is Grimbald? Why didn't he notify us officially? We've had the Russians and Chinese giving us more information than our own guys, where the fuck is he?' The General's face is red and flushed.

'That's it, sir, we cannot find him anywhere, he didn't leave a message, it's like he has disappeared.' Scott pauses and takes in a deep breath trying to calm down. He looks at the window and sees the crow, its black eyes staring back at him. It gives him the creeps; a bead of sweat runs down his face.

'Right Chip, I'm putting you in temporary charge, I want a full status update. Now!'

'Yes, sir. The object is now 20,000 miles from Earth, and it's slowing down sir. It's slowing down. It's not a meteorite, sir.' General Scott is grim-faced. President Wilson pale. There is silence in the Oval Office as the senior military officers absorb the revelation.

'How big is the object, Chip? asked the general.
'Well, it appears very large, about one hundred miles across.'
'Jesus Christ.'
'Something else.'
'What else?'
'Sir, we're losing satellite communications! Only a few are working.'
'OK, thanks, Chip. I will call you in half an hour for an update.' General Scott turned to President Wilson.
'Where's Fraser?'
'The Secretary of Defense called in sick yesterday,' Wilson replied. The President and Joint Chiefs sat in conference. Wilson sat hunched on his desk, hands clasped, face white, and sweating as he spoke. An aide passed a handkerchief to the President's shaking hand.
'If this is what I think it is, we face a situation that makes the Cuban missile crisis look like a tea party.'
'The Defense Department, NASA and US Space Command have used global satellite tracking systems, telescopes, and radar to gather data on this space threat. Some satellites are still working. This object is one hundred miles wide and is not of Earth origin. It's slowing down. Is this what we have been afraid of sir, an alien invasion?' said a sombre Scott.
'This is what Cassian hinted at,' said a stony-faced Wilson.
'Who is Cassian?' asked one of the Joint Chiefs.
'He's the leader of the vampires,' replied the president.
'So they do exist!' said the Air Force General.
'Yes and so do aliens, probably.' Scott prompted him to be quiet so Wilson could continue.
'We don't know for sure, but there is no time to lose. Go to DEFCON 3. Notify NATO, we need to be on a war footing, just in case.'
President Wilson turned to his general.
'Set up a conference call with Yakoff and Xin. Also, British Prime Minister Johnson and French President Hollande. Let's try to establish contact. Notify the UN Office of Outer Space Affairs committee to draft a message, keep it simple. And someone get Fraser please, I don't care if he is sick!'

Chapter 31

Alien Contact

In Space Command, Chip punches up a program to transmit prime numbers. He presses a red button and numbers flash up on the screen; they are transmitted on all frequencies.

'I just hope they are friendly,' he mutters to himself, a knot of fear in his stomach. He looks around him, at his colleagues. Some are grim-faced, a few younger ones look like rabbits caught in a truck's headlights. His friend Leonard is dialling his girlfriend under his desk, trying not to be seen.

'Get out of New York now!' he whispers.

'But I have a hair appointment.'

'Forget your appointment. Get out of New York now. Aliens are coming!'

'Will they be friends with us? What shoes shall I wear?'

A military space shuttle flies out of the Earth's atmosphere into space. President Wilson and General Scott watch from the shuttle's onboard camera.

'What can you see, Commander?' asked Wilson.

'The object is approaching fast: 10,000, 3,000, 1,000 miles. It's slowing down—it's huge, sir!'

'Are you able to send a signal to it?' asks a white-faced Wilson.

'Trying on all frequencies. Sir my controls are frozen, I cannot steer the ship. I have lost control. I'm locked in some sort of tractor beam!' Wilson and Scott look at each other. The joint chiefs stand crowded around the screen.

'Sir, it's destroying all the satellites. The ship is opening—Fuck!'

Laser beams emit from the lower section of the massive spaceship. Satellites in the immediate vicinity are destroyed like a bat feeding on mosquitoes. The shuttle drifts helplessly towards an opening in the spaceship. The Space Shuttle disappears inside as the screen goes dark.

Back in the White House, an agitated Scott confronts President Wilson.

'Shall we launch a nuclear strike, sir?'

'We are not certain of their intentions yet, let's wait.'

'But they have destroyed a bunch of satellites!' the General exclaims.

The president looks pale and ashen.

'Shall I invoke the Sirius Protocol?' Scott looks Wilson in the eye.

'The Sirius Protocol? I didn't think that was real I thought it was just a ruse to get extra funding for the Defense Department.'

'Oh, it's real sir, a preparation for an alien invasion. After Roswell, we knew we had to prepare for this eventuality one day. With your permission, I am invoking it now sir. We have to move you to a safe location before it's too late.'

Wilson appears shaky and drawn.

'Do it. Fetch my son, he's in the East Wing. And my wife, she's at a charity event in New York. Do it now!'

As he looks out of the White House window, he realizes that the strange creature, Cassian, was right. The question is are they prepared?

The black monolithic spaceship stays in Earth orbit, unhindered. Eighty smaller, but still huge spacecraft, each one-mile wide, emerge from the mothership at precise intervals, each one as black and ugly as the mothership, making their way around the globe to all the main cities and population centres.

VIENNA

Jayesh Jindal, wearing a smart suit, pin backed hair and glasses, is sitting in her office in Vienna, her brain reeling. She is on her third cup of coffee, well beyond her normal limit of one a day. She is an Indian astrophysicist and works for the UN Office of Outer Space Affairs committee. The office is charged with making first contact with aliens, and Jayesh is its ambassador.

She wipes her brow with a tissue as she strides into the small control centre where her staff of five are in a frenzy of activity.

'Has the friendship message been translated?' Jayesh puts her hands on her hips.

'Yes ma'am. English to Spanish, Mandarin Chinese, Arabic and Hindi,' says a smart looking Chinese girl with glasses.

'Transmit now, Li.'

'Okay ma'am.'

'Where is your family?' asks Jayesh.

'Salzburg, ma'am.'

'I have a bad feeling about this. Leave now. It will be safer than Vienna. Same for the rest of you. I will pack up. Go!' she shouts. She watches as her staff grab their bags and rush out the door, then she walks to the window. Down below, crowds of people are running in the streets, in all directions, cops failing miserably to control the traffic, cars crashing, and shops being looted. 'This is how it starts', she thinks.

TRAFALGAR SQUARE, LONDON

Tourists standing underneath Nelson's column look up as a huge black ship darkens the sky above them, making a deep throbbing and grinding noise. People scream and start running as the object covers the sky, casting a shadow over Trafalgar Square. A man in an expensive blue pin-striped suit talks into his mobile checking his Bloomberg feed at the same time.

'It's getting dark, darling…people are running.' Then he looks up open-mouthed. 'Oh shit!' as he sees the black ship above him, making an unearthly grinding noise; windows shatter, Nelson's column wobbles.

As the sky darkens above him he calls his broker but no one is answering. 'Got to go short,' he mutters, 'Got to go short FTSE!'

Bloomberg man's mind races as he runs for the tube, intent on getting home to his wife and family in Berkshire. He pushes an old woman out of the way, and she falls, cursing him. A taxi swerves and crashes into a building. There is panic, shoving and shouting as everyone tries to get into the crowded tube entrance away from the menace in the sky.

Bloomberg man fights with the massive crowd outside Charring Cross tube. In the distance Nelson's column wobbles again, then it comes down with a crash – people scream as they run.

MANILA, PHILIPPINES

In Manila, it is a beautiful day, a cloudless blue sky - the sun is shining on the tourists and native Filipinos are strolling along Roxas Boulevard enjoying the day. A group of trendy Filipino teenagers are looking out over Manila Bay admiring the view. A boy tickles a girl, pretty with long black hair, she giggles. The rest of them dance and listen to music on their headphones as they look at the ships on the water and watch the sun come down for a beautiful Manila sunset. Then a teenage Filipino wearing a baseball cap stops dancing and looks in silence out over the bay, his body rigid.

Then he points out to the bay.

They talk excitedly as a dark spot gets larger and larger, 'What is that?' a girl asks the boy with the baseball cap. The boy stares, but does not answer. A small crowd gathers around them as the dark object gets closer, their laughter and joking now replaced with an air of disquiet, then trepidation, then abject fear, as the object grows larger, filling the horizon.

It is an enormous black ship, which darkens the sky above them. It moves over them, above Roxas Boulevard, casting them in shadow. The ground vibrates as it emits a deep throbbing and grinding noise, shattering the windows of the nearby hotels. People scream and start running as the object covers the sky; the hotel buildings shudder, and windows break as the ship takes up its position over central Manila, putting it into darkness.

There is panic as people run and scream, some going into churches, others going home to pray for deliverance. There is a huge traffic jam as people try to get out of Manila. The busy Manila traffic becomes deadlocked, and people abandon the cars and jeepneys – running in all directions - screaming.

Outside a church, an elderly nun gets on her knees on the pavement, rosary in hand, looking heavenwards towards the black monstrosity filling the sky, tears in her eyes.

'Diyos protektahan sa amin. God protect us!'

Chapter 32

Sirius Protocol

President Wilson, his young son and three rock-faced and black-suited secret service personnel are going down in a secure White House elevator, deep below the White House. Everyone looks tense. As the steel doors part, and they get out, they see a silver steel train with the American Flag and Seal of the President of the United States emblazoned on it. There are shouted orders and frantic activity as boxes and personnel are stowed onto the train, a stoney-faced Secret Service officer steps towards the President.

'This way sir.' Wilson and Scott are seated in the presidential car, along with boxes piled high with equipment. The President wipes his brow and gestures towards his staff, 'Leave us please,' as he leans forward to his friend General Scott, then faints as his head falls on the table. The knock to his head brings him around.

'Frank! Are you ok?' asks Scott.

President Wilson retrieves a pill from his jacket pocket, his hand shaking.

'Anything I can to do to help?' a concerned Scott helps the President get seated. The train moves away and accelerates to a tremendous speed as they are forced back into their seats. Wilson takes a drink of water and the colour returns to his face, but his voice is weak.

'Bill, protocol dictates that I should hand over to the Vice President if I'm incapacitated, but I don't trust him. He's a backstabber, unreliable, power gone to his head. Anyway, he is in London.'

'We managed to get him on an X-37D, but we've had no contact for 24 hours,' replies General Scott.

'The Secretary of Defense, Fraser? Nice guy, but I'm not sure he could cope—he's also missing. I need loyal and competent people by my side. But when the time comes I want you to take over,' he says, looking at his General. Wilson leans back and takes another one of his pills. Scott nodded.

'So Bill, what is this Sirius Protocol, and are we ready?'

'Well, sir.'

'You call me Frank in private from now on please - we've known each other long enough, and I don't know how long I've got.'

'Okay, Frank. The Sirius Project was first mooted in the 1950s after Roswell. It was classified Above Top Secret so not many people knew about it.'

'You mean you actually found a spacecraft—aliens?'

'An alien craft was found. It was damaged but we recovered it and we have been doing research at Area 51 ever since. The aliens were dead but we have kept them preserved for research. Then in the 1970s, there was a secret meeting of the five permanent members of the United Nations Security Council where it was agreed to set up and fund Project Sirius. Since then France, UK and China have pulled out, thinking it was a waste of money. Only Russia stuck with us. Surprised eh? Over the years we have built some ingenious weapons, some with technology we gained from the alien spacecraft. But to be honest we're not sure if it will work in practice, against the aliens I mean. Hold on…'

A panel and a blue phone flash. General Scott picks up.

'It's Chip again sir, multiple alien spacecraft have entered the Earth's atmosphere, satellites are down, most communications are down.' Wilson leaned forward towards Scott. 'How come space command can contact us?'

'Radio technology, the old-fashioned stuff seems to work best in these circumstances. Sir, can I launch the squadrons of F22s?'

'Do it,' ordered the President.

'What chance do they have?'

'We have equipped the F22s with the shielding technology we found on the Roswell ship. It's controlled from Sirius headquarters. That's where we're heading now,' Scott loosened his tie and took off his jacket.

The President's son, Michael, walks in with an aide.

'Dad, will the aliens be friends with us?'

'I don't think so, son.' Wilson stood up and addresses his son.

'You will need to be brave.' The president digs in his pocket and puts a Secret Service badge on Michael.

'You stick close to me, you're my new Secret Service agent. Here's your badge, son.'

They salute each other. General Scott smiles and salutes as well.

'Where's mummy?' asks Michael.

'She's in New York son. We're trying our best to find her and bring her home safe.' The President looks pale as he hugs his son.

The red phone flashes as an aide walks in.

'It's your UN Security Council conference call sir, not sure they're all there sir.'

President Wilson picks up the phone in eager anticipation of the events in other parts of the world.

'Prime Minister Johnson, hello Boris, how are you faring?'

The British Prime Minister sounds out of breath.

'Hello Frank, we've evacuated Downing Street and we're at a secure location - a Sirius base outside London. It's pretty chaotic, an alien spaceship has appeared over London, the population is terrified, scared the shit out of me, to be honest. We're engaging now with a squadron of Eurofighters, we're hoping this new Sirius technology you gave us will protect our planes. What's that? What's that noise? Christ! I've got to go!'

Wilson looks up at Scott, who shakes his head.

'Anyone else there?'

'Yakimov here!'

'Alexey! How are you faring?'

'Frank, not well. We have evacuated Moscow, alien craft are everywhere. Most of our Air Force is shot down. Were bunkered down in Siberia. We're hoping this Sirius technology will help us, our Sukhoi's have the new technology fitted, the shields, but it's not working against these alien bastards! I know we have had our differences in the past, but the world must unite now Frank, else we are doomed. To be honest …'

The line went dead. Wilson and Scott shake their heads in dismay.

'I need a stiff drink,' the president mutters, head in hands.

'Are you sure—in your condition?' as General Scott wanders over to a drinks cabinet.

'We need to find a solution to this alien threat, Bill.' Scott is silent as he pours them a glass of whisky from a decanter.

'Ice please,' says Wilson as his friend passes him a glass of single malt—Glenmorangie. They sat in silence, trying to comprehend the enormity of their responsibility to the American people, and to the world at large.

'You know Bill, when I was talking to Yakimov, I felt a sense of camaraderie, like I've never felt before. Like we're all in this together. Maybe this crisis is what the world needs to bring people together.'

'Assuming anyone survives of course,' replies General Scott, then adds, 'The enemy of mine enemy is my friend.'

'Yes Bill, I take your point, but it's more than that.'

President Wilson leans forward. 'I heard from Smith at the CIA of a British guy. Captain Morgan—an SAS soldier of superhuman ability, the strength of ten men. Runs as fast as a leopard, indestructible,' as he took a gulp of whiskey.

'They call him Bulletproof Pete,' smiled General Scott. 'We tried to recruit him before but failed. Smith put a request into the British Government to put him on an X-37D in return for Sirius technology. They agreed. The British stopped funding the Sirius project so they're short of kit.'

'We need answers Bill, and fast. I pray to God he's on his way.' The President looks earnest, like a father awaiting the safe delivery of a child.

'God speed Captain Morgan,' prays Frank Wilson as he finishes his whisky.

SECRET AIRFORCE BASE - NEVADA DESERT

An experimental, sleek-looking plane, black as the ace of spades, emerges from an underground hangar, X-37D emblazoned on the fuselage. It looks like a cross between a space shuttle and an SR71 Blackbird, brimming with stealth technology. It launches into the air and quickly accelerates to Mach 3. The skin of the plane shimmers and becomes semi-invisible. Destination: an air force base in the North of England.

Chapter 33

Sirius HQ

SIRIUS HQ COMMAND BUNKER - VIRGINIA

The train arrives at Sirius Headquarters built deep underneath the Blue Ridge Mountains. The presidential party steps out of the train into a cave-like structure, surrounded by bare rock. Their voices echo through the chamber as they enter a large, cold, steel lift. The lift hums as it moves at lightning speed through the rock. When the door opens, they face a large steel door built into the granite. It has a Sirius logo on the side, an S inside a three-dimensional triangle. It reminds President Wilson of NORAD, built deep inside a mountain. This was Sirius HQ, humanity's last stand against an alien invasion – 'it certainly has a feeling of permanence about it' thinks Wilson as the door slowly opens—the solid steel and titanium door is twelve feet thick. They are met with a blast of air.

'How far underground are we?' asks Wilson, his voice echoing in the chamber.

'About half a mile,' answers Scott.

They walk down a corridor, past more security and enter a large room full of computer screens. Air Force General Schmitt meets them. He is large, round-bellied and jovial by nature, but today he is grave and under pressure. Wilson shakes his firm hand.

Scott is shocked when he sees his colleague Schmitt. He only saw him last month at a Pentagon meeting, but he seemed to have aged ten years in the last month. His grizzled face looks shell-shocked as if he had gone ten rounds with Mike Tyson.

'So Mike, you're in charge of Sirius, what's the situation?' asks Scott.

Schmitt wipes the sweat from his brow with a handkerchief and points at the main screen where a camera mounted on an F22 shows the action. An alien ship is hovering several miles above New York. It's black ugly bulk is covering the city in shadow.

'The F22s have engaged 'Bogey 1'. So far the alien's shields are holding—we're having no effect.'

'What about our shields on the F22s?' Scott asks.

'That's the thing I don't understand, Bill—they're not working,' says Schmitt shaking his head. 'Our shielding is based on a fractal encryption code. We adapted the alien technology we got from the Roswell ship—the aliens shouldn't be able to crack it.' The President's interest piques.

'Who adapted the technology?' asks Wilson.

'It was Professor Picard.'

'Oh yes I remember now, the man's an absolute genius. Archaeologist as well. A polymath,' says an admiring Wilson.

'I have sent for him,' replies Scott.

'Are our F22s being shot down?' pressed Wilson.

Schmitt scratched his head, 'Yes sir, we have a screen here so we can see the F22s coming up on target.' On screen, hundreds of alien fighter craft emerge from the ship and the F22s are being shot down at will, the top gun F22 pilots are no match for the alien fighters' manoeuvrability and firepower.

Scott stands with his legs apart, his face slowly turning red.

'Only four other people apart from myself had access to those encrypted shielding codes, General Schmitt here, the President, Grimbald and Fraser,' a stony faced Scott stares at Schmitt, then he phones Chip at Space Command, and puts it on speaker phone.

'Chip, any sign of Grimbald?' shouts the general to his nephew.

'No sign of him. The whole of Space Command is searching for him, sir.'

'Where the fuck is Grimbald?' General Scott's face turns red.

President Wilson looks at the screen: 'At this attrition rate we will have no 22s left. Can we change the codes?'

'Yes sir, but as most of our comms are down, we cannot do it electronically. We will have to hardcode it manually. Shall I tell the squadron to abort?' says an exasperated Schmitt.

'Yes for Christ's sake, abort, abort!' replies President Wilson.

Chapter 34

A Rat in the Pack

General Scott sits in grim silence. Schmitt and President Wilson look at him. Scott closes his eyes and a bead of sweat drops from his forehead. The blood drains from his face as speaks. He goes white then goes from pink to red as his voice breaks.

'Frank, do you remember that meeting we had with Cassian? Maybe it's nothing…' Scott takes a pill from his pocket and drinks some water.

'They said there would be an alien invasion, and they were proved right,' Wilson is subdued. 'He was also spot on about me needing to see a doctor too.'

"Yes he was right, maybe these vampires aren't scum after all. But there was something else—something he hinted at, says the General. 'We have reason to believe there is a traitor amongst you.' Those were his words."

Wilson looks shell-shocked as he recalls the conversation and leans on a table for support. Schmitt looks as though he is going to throw up.

'My God, you think Grimbald is the traitor?' whispers Schmitt, recalling the Pentagon meeting between himself, Scott and Grimbald last month. 'Grimbald seemed pensive, evasive as if he was hiding something. Shifty.'

Scott stands up, his face turning a darker shade of red.

'I never did trust him back at the academy he was a Nazi sympathizer.'

'How the hell did he ever get to be a general if he was a closet Nazi?' asks Schmitt.

'I checked him out myself, he has kept himself spotless, his political and family connections helped him get to where he is today. They protected him.' replies Scott. 'Mike, do you remember that meeting we had with Grimbald last month. In the Pentagon?'

'Yes, he seemed shifty,' replied the Sirius Chief.

'Evasive,' whispers Scott, remembering,

'We will need to change all our nuclear launch codes—just in case,' Scott adds. President Wilson faces General Scott.

'Do it. What about Fraser? He's missing as well. He also had access to the nuclear codes, as well as the F22 codes.' The president looks ill. Schmitt is sweating with fear.

'But we don't actually know he is a traitor,' Schmitt says in a hoarse whisper.

'Who, Fraser or Grimbald? Do you want to take the chance?' Scott is incredulous. Wilson was frantic. 'Change all the codes! Change all the fucking codes!' The President steadies himself as he regains his composure.

'Now, what are our next steps, Gentlemen? Are you alright, Mike?' Wilson wipes his brow.

'Yes,' says Schmitt his voice now hoarse.

'I will handle the nuclear codes. Mike, you do the F22s. How many do we have left?' General Scott has regained control of himself but is still sweating.

'Around 200, they're flying back to base now. It will take thirty minutes to change the encryption codes. Then we can have them refuelled, rearmed and ready to attack again,' replies Schmitt as he wipes his face with a towel.'

'OK. Initiate the emergency broadcast system, we cannot rely on satellites for our communications anymore,' orders President Wilson.

'Schmitt smiles. 'Sir, we also have Morse code, the technology is too simple for the aliens to break.'

'Bill, any reply from the alien spaceships after our UN broadcast message?' asks Wilson.

'No, nothing sir.' Schmitt looked glum.

'Were you expecting an answer?' asks Scott, a hint of sarcasm in his voice. Schmitt ignores him as he looks at the main screen in front of them. It has gone blank and fuzzy.

'We have now lost nearly all satellite and electronic communications; switching to analogue.' General Schmitt presses a red button. A fuzzy black and white image appears on the screen showing the monstrous mothership in high Earth orbit. General Schmitt makes some adjustments, and the screen becomes coloured.

'I need to call my nephew Chip, see what's going on in Space Command,' says Scott, pouring himself a large cup of coffee.

'What about Grimbald's deputy, Colonel Mack?' asks the President.

'He's disappeared too,' answers Scott reaching in his pocket for his blood pressure pills. He swallows two, swigged down with his coffee, then sits down, wiping his brow.

Schmitt faces the president.

'Mr. President, in the Sirius project we predicted that we would lose all electronic and digital communications, even the internet. So we went back to basics. We have installed underground analogue lines to key installations and to our allies. London, Paris, Moscow and Beijing are now connected in the Sirius system.'

'Let's hope that gives us the edge,' says President Wilson as he pours himself and Schmitt some coffee.

Chapter 35

THE PRESIDENT'S SPEECH

President Wilson became solemn, 'I need to make a speech to the American people. Give them some glimmer of hope.'

'We will use the emergency broadcast system,' replied Scott. Generals Schmitt and Scott stood nearby. 'Bill, how do I look?' asked the President.

'You look like shit Frank.' Half an hour later Wilson nodded and smiled as he looked at the camera in front of him. His hand shook and he looked pale, then he began.

'People of America. The question about whether we are alone in this universe has now been answered. At 0100 today alien spaceships entered our atmosphere. I am not going to beat around the bush or try to paint a rosy picture. So far, they have destroyed many of our major cities, Washington is gone, Los Angeles is half destroyed. London and other cities around the world are being evacuated - I'm sure you get the picture. Our attempts to communicate with the aliens have failed so far. Their motives for attacking us are unclear. Our conventional forces are having no effect, so I have held these back. These forces are being utilized to assist people to evacuate to safer areas. We have been preparing for this contingency—an alien invasion—for fifty years; we developed new technologies to defend ourselves, but with limited success. Our best weapons are courage and patience. We will find their weakness and find a way to fight back. That is my promise. My advice to you is this: If you cannot leave your home and you have an underground basement, stay there for the time being. Alternatively, go to the subway stations, you will get food and water there. Stay off the streets, and keep calm. If you have any short-wave ham radios or walkie-talkies, use these and stay alert. Listen to radio messages. Now is the time for nations to unite. We must put aside our petty differences for the sake of the human race. Americans, Russians, Chinese, Arabs; east, west, Catholics, Hindus, Muslims, and Buddhists must unite to fight this alien threat. People of America, take courage, be resourceful, and pray to your God. In God we trust.'

'Good speech Frank,' said Scott patting him on the back.

'Someone get me a large cup of coffee.' The President sank back in a chair looking exhausted, the weight of responsibility heavy on his shoulders.

'It's always darkest just before dawn,' said Scott trying to cheer him up.

'Update, Bill?' The President sat down next to Scott. 'News just in. The Pentagon and the White House are gone. They have deployed an alien ship over New York, it's bigger than the rest, about three miles wide. But the city is intact—why? However, their main asset, their mothership, is in high Earth orbit.' General Scott rubbed his chin.

'Looks like they're making New York their main HQ. They must have a reason. Most of our other major cities are rubble,' pondered Wilson. Scott continued.

'I have ordered our troops to retreat while we organize ourselves. Los Angeles seems to be less well defended by the aliens than other western cities, maybe they are not expecting much resistance there. Chicago is lost, but we have a Sirius base there, so I'm planning to re-group for a new offensive, Washington is also completely destroyed. Our Mid-West has been left untouched by the aliens. Odd. They seem to be focused on our Eastern and Western seaboards. I haven't heard from our other major cities.'

'Bill, I think they have limited ships, and limited resources. That may be their weakness. What about our allies?' asked the President.

'News is patchy. London, and the eastern part of England is under alien occupation, but the western half is being fiercely contested, there is a full-scale battle going on in Birmingham. Moscow no news. Paris nothing.'

'I wish we could bottle some of that British fighting spirit,' the president drank his coffee and sighed.

'Frank, we've been promised some British SAS in exchange for some Sirius kit,' The general reminded the President, trying to cheer him up.

'Yes Bill, that is good news. I hope this Captain Morgan is as special as everyone says he is. Let us hope he can help us, be our silver bullet, God knows we need help.' The president sighed. 'It is times like this I wish we had Winston Churchill by our side. He was a great wartime leader. What was his famous saying? "Sometimes doing your best is not good enough. Sometimes you must do what is required."'

'Roosevelt was a great leader too. You are a great leader. Everyone respects your judgment,' said Scott.

'By the way, any word about our missing professor? I was hoping he would have some insights,' asked a hopeful President.

'I sent a Special Forces team to get Picard. I received a coded message saying they're holed up in the basement of his university.'

'My wife?' President Wilson looked worried.

'Sorry Frank. No word. We have two teams in New York looking for her, but movement is difficult.'

Wilson looked at a picture of the First Lady and his son Michael. 'Vanessa, come home safely my love.' But inside he felt guilty for letting her go to New York.

Chapter 36

VINNIE'S BUSINESS

EAST END LONDON PUB

Vinnie is wearing a leather jacket and jeans. He is persuading a frightened looking geezer to give him some money.

'Now we can do this the hard way or the easy way. Personally, I prefer the hard way cos I don't like you. You've got a boat race like a cow's arse.'

'Vinnie please, I promise I will pay, on my mother's life Vinnie, please!'

Vinnie head-butts the man who falls to the floor, holding his bleeding face. The pub telephone rings. The landlord calls Vinnie over.

'Vinnie, it's Gill for you. She can't get through on your mobile. Mine's not working either.'

Vinnie takes the phone.

'Speak up, it's a bad line. OK, sweetheart, I will pop to Tesco's later, promise. No, I won't forget.' Vinnie rings off, looking even more annoyed than usual. The frightened man cowers, and starts shaking. Vinnie picks him up from the floor and holds him by his lapels.

'Now then, Cow's Arse, give me the fucking money cos I don't want to keep my wife waiting, she has run out of washing powder. Do you know what they call me?'

'Er, I don't know. What do they call you?' Cow's Arse pleads with Vinnie.'

'They call me "The Terminator!"' Vinnie bangs the man's head against a wall, causing a framed photo to fall on the floor and smash.

'Now look what you made me do, that'll be extra,' he winked at the landlord and grinned. The sort of grin that would make most people run a mile.

'OK, OK, I'll give you the money!' The shaking man reaches for his wallet.

'Here's a monkey, the rest tomorrow.'

'That wasn't so difficult now, was it?' says Vinnie, tucking the money away. As he raises his finger, the man flinches.

'Tomorrow.'

But as Vinnie walks out the pub, everything is in shadow. People are running in all directions, in a state of panic. A man is running while looking up and knocks himself out on a lamp post. Vinnie looks up and his heart misses a beat as his mind tries to comprehend what he is seeing. A huge black object sits in the sky above. Huge, black and ugly. It emits a shrieking sound, then a deep throbbing noise every five seconds, as it turns slowly in the sky above. Nearby windows shatter and the ground vibrates as it groans and throbs again.

Vinnie tries ringing Pete on his mobile, but the network is dead. Then his bleeper goes—his SAS bleeper, carried wherever he goes, whenever there is an emergency, somewhere in the world that only the SAS can deal with.

As Vinnie looks up his brain tries to compute the object by reference to existing experiences, and fails miserably. Fear grips him as his bleeper sounds again. The SAS did not have a scenario for this, and he realises this will not be a normal mission.

Then his thoughts turn to Gill—where is she?

Chapter 37

Leaving Home

PETER'S HOUSE IN WALES

It is breakfast time in Peter's family home. He ducks his head under a low wooden beam in the kitchen and looks at his kids playing in the garden. The flowers are blooming and his vegetables are doing nicely. He sits down to read a letter from the Readers Digest, and dips toast soldiers into an egg. He sips his pint mug of tea trying to wake up, looks up and admires Jennifer as she stands in her skimpy nightie, her long brown hair flowing over her shoulders, looking like a Greek Goddess; elegant, beautiful and timeless.

The TV is on. Jennifer is admiring Peter's bald head, keen blue eyes and bullet-hard muscles through tight jeans and a T-shirt. Peter yawns as he admires Jennifer in her nightie, who is now looking out the kitchen window, the nightie riding up her legs, showing her knickers. His ancient warrior bloodlust starts to rise as he looks at her.

Peter's sharp blue eyes sparkle. 'My favourite colour is pink,' Peter's deep voice echoes around the kitchen as Jennifer pulls down her nightie, smiling, wagging her finger.

'Something's odd. All the birds have disappeared from the wood,' Jennifer becomes serious.

'That is a mystery. I have hardly slept the last couple of days—like I'm going on a mission or something.' He opens an envelope.

HERO—DOMINION FIRST BLOOD

'I keep getting these letters from Readers Digest telling me I'm going to win £100,000.'

'I don't know why you bother, you never win,' Jennifer complains and then crosses her arms. Peter looked at the unknown painting from Sir Nigel hanging on the kitchen wall. It's probably worth a fortune—a nest egg.

'How long are you going to be home this time? Me and the kids really miss you. I need you here.' Peter looks up at his wife, a guilty expression on his face. He knows he is in for a dressing down, much more frightening than a dressing down from an SAS Colonel, much worse. He pleads.

'I want to be here as well, but we've been very busy recently, especially in the Middle East.' Peter is trying to sound apologetic.

'You never talk to me about your work.' Jennifer knows very well that Peter cannot talk about his work, and she suspects he is working for MI6, but she asks the question anyway - *to make him feel uncomfortable.*

'Listen, you know I'm in the SAS, and quite often we work with MI6.'

'You work for MI6? That's dangerous,' Jennifer replied.

'So is the SAS. Jennifer, you know I cannot talk about my work. I would get into trouble if I did. You must not tell anyone else, okay? Listen, they have just given me six months paid leave, as a reward. Besides, they just promoted me to Captain. Pays a lot more too, we can get that kitchen you keep on about.'

Jennifer puts her arms around Peter and kisses him, her mood changes. Peter is always amazed at how quickly women's moods change, like the Welsh weather.

'Come here, you know that American accent turns me on.'

Peter grabs Jennifer's bottom and kissed her.

'Well Captain, It's your English accent that gets me hot and those hard muscles. Is that why they call you "Bulletproof" Pete?'

Jennifer rubs her hands over his sinewy muscles, then his crotch, then for some reason looks at the TV.

'Pete, something's going on, look.'

They both gaze at the TV. The reception is blurred and fuzzy.

167

"Reports are coming in from NASA and observatories around the world that objects are entering the atmosphere…"

There are blurred pictures of huge dark objects entering the atmosphere. Peter's bleeper goes off. Jennifer looks at him in a state of panic. He smiles that bullshit smile, as if everything is ok—but it isn't of course. Maybe that's why he hasn't been sleeping—his subconscious knows something is up. He dials a number on his landline, but reaches static. He tries the mobile, Vinnie answers, but its' a bad signal.

'Vinnie, do you know what's going on? The news!' he shouts.

'HQ said it's aliens. They're invading. There's a big fucking ship over London mate!' The line is breaking up.

'What aliens? What are you talking about? Speak up, it's a bad line.'

Then his SAS bleeper goes off again as he looks at a wild-eyed Jennifer. He has a sinking feeling in his stomach. On the TV he can see vague dark shapes suddenly become clearer. His heart skips a beat as he remembers his visions in Sir Nigel's office: dark, ominous, and alien. Déjà vu.

It's all becoming true.

'It's for real. We need to report to an RAF base up north in double quick time,' says a faint-sounding Vinnie. 'A helicopter will pick us up. It's…' Vinnie's voice is cracking up then the line goes dead. Peter and Jennifer look at each other.

'I have seen those shapes before Jenny in my dreams. I don't like it.' Peter pauses for a moment, looks at the TV, then Jennifer.

'I think the safest place is right here. Don't go wandering outside. Especially the kids. There's a stash of canned food, water and candles in the cupboard . You should be okay.'

Jennifer starts crying. Peter holds her in his arms and comforts her. Was this the last time he would hold her in his arms? He held her a little tighter, not wanting to let her go—to be with her forever, as tears well in his eyes.

'Everything's going to be all right. I will be home before you know it. It's probably just the Russians playing silly buggers,' trying to sound cheerful, but he knows his bullshit isn't fooling Jennifer.

Peter's two young children come running in from the garden, dirt on their hands and knees. They reach up to try to put their arms around his neck.

'Daddy, are you going away again?' says Sally, a sad look in her eyes. Peter feels heartbroken, again.

'Yes, but I will be back soon, I promise. Look after Mummy please,' as he hugs his young daughter, tears in his eyes. Peter looks at Robert, his young son, a sense of pride filling his chest.

And sadness.

'Robert, you're the man of the house now, so you have to look after Mummy and your sister. Okay?'

Robert looks at him with his blue eyes and says 'Yes, Dad.'

Peter puts his arms around them both. 'Now give me a big kiss, both of you.'

'Don't forget your little book.' Jennifer hands Peter his little book of poems.

'Thanks,' he kisses her. 'It will remind me of you. And keep me sane.'

Peter is in turmoil. He loves his family dearly. He has just got back from a mission, after a year away, and is leaving them again. It is the hardest thing he has ever had to do. Leaving them when they need him the most, at their most vulnerable. His instincts tell him to stay home, but Queen and country—duty comes first, doesn't it? Later, that decision to leave his family will tear him apart.

That look in Jennifer's eyes tell him everything he needs to know. Inside he is crying as he hears the sound of a helicopter approaching.

Chapter 38

This Cannot Be Happening

AIRFORCE BASE IN THE NORTH OF ENGLAND

A room full of SAS soldiers from 21 Regiment is being briefed. Peter and Vinnie, in military uniform, sit at the front. Straight-laced, white-haired SAS Colonel Bradley addresses the troops in his gravelly voice.

'Any question that we are alone in this universe has been answered. At 0600 UK time today alien spaceships entered our atmosphere. So far, they have manoeuvred their ships over major cities, including London and Birmingham and other major populations around the world. Our cities are being evacuated as I speak. Military law is now in force. The North of England is clear of alien activity but we may not have much time.'

Peter thinks he is dreaming—as if he was in a movie and he is an actor—but this was not a movie, this is real. He drinks his coffee, reassured by the presence of his brother in arms, and good friend, Vinnie. He hasn't slept well the last few days, and the coffee gives him the kick he needs.

'Is this really happening?' asked Vinnie.

'Yes Vinnie, this is real,' replied Peter.

'Their technology is far superior to ours, and aerial attacks by our fighters have proved futile, so we have called them off. NATO intelligence reports have indicated that we are looking at a complete destruction of our cities and military within a few days, if not less. Conventional weapons will probably be useless so we will be fighting a different type of war. More covert, more stealth. We will be fighting a guerrilla war, perfectly suited to our training, Gentlemen. We will join forces with the Americans and some of you will be flying to the US to be seconded onto Project Sirius.'

The Colonel glanced at Peter and Vinnie.

'I don't need to tell you that we face the biggest challenge this regiment ever faced in our history. I have had the honour of serving with many of you, so I know how good you are.'

'What's their objective, sir?' asks Peter.

'That's not entirely clear at the moment, Captain Morgan, but I expect we shall find out soon.' An aide whispers into the Colonel's ear, then his voice becomes more urgent.

'There are reports of an alien ship heading this way, so we need to move quickly. Best of British luck. Briefing over. Dismissed.' After the briefing, the colonel takes Peter aside.

'Peter, you are going to the US. The Americans—the CIA—specifically asked for you. Your reputation precedes you it seems, and I know you work with Corporal Carson, so he is going too. Des too. We've had the nod from Sir Nigel at 6, though he wasn't happy about it.'

'I should be fighting here sir, I'm British!' protests Peter. But the Colonel looks away, unable to look him in the eye.

Half an hour later, Peter and Vinnie in full SAS battle dress are in an aircraft hangar, with enough equipment and weapons to start a small war. They pack their weapons and equipment into their 40lb Bergens. Peter was offered an M16 rifle, but it runs off a gas system and jams or breaks every 30 seconds because of it. No, he has a Heckler and Koch G36, which is nearly as robust as an AK-47, and more powerful. It can fire straight out of mud or water, and it won't jam.

No dead man's click.

It is more accurate than the M16 and quite light; it can be field-stripped in under two minutes with no tools.

Just like Vinnie, dead reliable.

He looks at Vinnie who nods approval at his choice. They were to be issued some brand new Sirius PR7 rifles, but someone at the Ministry of Defence procurement had made a shocking cock-up, and some vital components were missing, so they were useless. They only have one working PR7, which Peter has managed to cobble together from other malfunctioning PR7s. Peter takes the PR7, one electro mag battery pack to power the rifle, and three PR7 magazines. The PR7 has a Sirius logo on the side—an S inside a three-dimensional triangle. He will take his G36 as well, as a backup.

Peter has heard all the stories, first hand, of non-functioning radios in Afghanistan, and useless jeeps, which was why the SAS don't use standard MOD equipment, but source their own. He remembers the bitter lesson in Yemen, when his radio didn't work because a Rupert, the traitor Ponsonby, didn't do his job properly.

Peter wonders if these weapons will actually be any good against aliens. Do aliens have force fields? Are they carbon-based life forms like us? Do they breathe oxygen? What are their weaknesses? Peter takes a swig from his water bottle, as he packs extra ammunition. Deep inside he knew this was coming, the foreboding the visions.

Now he must face it.

'Well, Bulletproof old mate, here we go again,' Vinnie sighs philosophically.

'Vinnie—aliens for Christ's sake. What do we know about aliens? It's an unknown, and I don't like it. We haven't trained for a war against ET.'

'We'll kick some alien arse,' says Vinnie. Peter smiles at Vinnie's eternal optimism.

'This will be a different kind of war, Vinnie, my old friend. A different kind of war.'

Peter and Vinnie look at each other, the smile of comradeship before they go into battle. They clasp hands.

'Strength and honour,' Peter recalls an ancient memory of battles in a hot and dusty landscape, spears and shields, running, cries of anguish, cries of conquest, clashes of shields, the smell of blood, then lying in the dust after the battle looking at a blue sky, the vultures circling above.

'Let's be quick about it Vinnie, an alien ship is on its way.'

They look out of the hangar door at the strange looking plane on the landing strip, black as the ace of spades.

'Would you Adam and Eve it. It looks like a Space Shuttle,' says Vinnie.

'A Space Shuttle and an SR71,' replies Peter. Vinnie looks worried.

'Hope we're not going into space. I'll get space sick.' Peter smiles at Vinnie, then adds:

'The Colonel says it's a new prototype—converted to carry troops—rumour has it that it contains alien technology, an X-37D. It's based on the X-37B. Flies bloody fast by all accounts.'

Vinnie raises his eyebrows and whistles.

'Tuck your shirt in, mate,' Peter slaps Vinnie on the back.

'As long as I don't get Tom and Dick, you know I don't like flying.'

They carry their gear from the hangar towards the X-37D troop carrier stealth aircraft, then stow it in the hold, get on board, and get seated. It is much more comfortable than a C130. Peter smiles at Vinnie.

'Don't be a pussy—it will be okay. Here, have a sick bag and stop moaning, you're always complaining,' nags Peter.

As they are sitting there, SAS Colonel Bradley climbs into the plane, out of breath. He finds Peter and Vinnie, who look up in surprise.

'Colonel?'

Chapter 39

BUCK HOUSE

'Slight change of plan Captain, you're going to Buckingham Palace to take the royals to a safe location. You will be leading the team. You will get more information on the way, good luck!—oh, and after that, you're going to the States.'

The top brass had made a difficult decision - Bradley had argued for Captain Morgan to remain in the UK fighting for the British, but in the end the US promise of X-37D stealth planes and Sirius technology in return for Peter had won the day. Peter was none the wiser—a pawn in a bigger chess game.

A few minutes later the X-37D was flying at supersonic speeds towards London. As Peter looked out the window he could see the wings and fuselage shimmer as the cloaking shield was switched on. His laptop bleeped, as he looked down and saw an encrypted message, which he deciphered. It was a briefing note of the location of the secret bunker they were being tasked to take the Royal Family to.

'We're going to Buckingham Palace Vinnie, so mind your P's and Q's and no swearing ok?'

'Buck House, The Queen,' sighed Vinnie.

'ETA to target twenty minutes,' the pilot spoke over the tannoy.

Peter recognised the pilot's voice and headed for the cockpit. He was greeted by a man with a bald head and sunglasses.

'Kojak—great to see you again!' smiled Peter.

'Likewise laddy. Good to see you're still in one piece.' Peter went back to his seat and looked at Vinnie, who was unusually quiet as they flew over London. They looked down, and saw the devastation below them, shaking their heads in disbelief.

'Thinking about Gill?'

Vinnie nodded.

'Reg will take good care of her…do not worry mate. Focus on the job.'

Peter looked around the X-37D for two other men to make up their four-man team. The rest would be deployed to guard the aircraft and ensure a corridor for the exfil. He nodded at Johnny Two-Times *(because he always said everything twice)*, a huge gorilla of a man, and Fag-Ash Phil, who smoked like a chimney, but was as fit as a fiddle. As they arrived at their destination, they could see two alien fighters hovering over the palace. The X-37D was invisible, but Kojak came over the tannoy, 'We're cloaked now, but I need to de-cloak to engage the two fighters. Hang tight.'

Vinnie and Peter watched as Kojak engaged two independent Sirius-modified Phalanx Gatling guns which whirred as servos kicked in to track the fighters. Kojak switched off their shielding, ready to fire.

The X-37D hovered as the Phalanx Gatling guns fired a wall of enriched uranium bullets at 250 rounds per second. The bullets bounced off the alien shields, in a blaze of sparks, but the fighters shuddered and vibrated at the bombardment. One fighter veered off, and the other lost control, as the fearsome onslaught continued, forcing the alien fighters to crash land in front of Buckingham Palace, in a blaze of sparks and fire.

The X-37D landed and they spilled out, ready to engage the enemy. Peter and Vinnie, were joined by Johnny and Phil. Three other men, led by Des, one of Peter's DS's spread out to guard the aircraft. Alien soldiers staggered out of the crashed craft, looking bewildered and dazed, they raised their laser weapons when they saw the SAS soldiers, who unleashed a firestorm of bullets and grenades. Vinnie fired with his Heckler and Koch G36, but the bullets bounced harmlessly off the aliens, their personal shielding holding. Then

Peter raised his PR7 rifle, and fired on automatic. The air moved around them at the sheer kinetic force of the rail gun technology as the depleted uranium bullets move at supersonic speed and hit the aliens, disintegrating their force fields, and exploding the aliens in a green haze of blood and body parts.

"This Sirius technology has fearsome firepower," Peter thought, as he and Vinnie sprinted forward and threw charges into each fighter. There was an explosion and acrid smoke streamed out.

'Come on, let's go, they will send backup soon. Let's retrieve our package and get the hell out of here!' shouted Peter, his deep voice commanding instant authority. Peter nodded at Des and the team guarding the aircraft. They knew the drill. The four-man SAS team find their way inside the palace entrance. 'Johnny and Phil, you stay here, cover our backs, until we get out,' ordered Peter. There seemed to be nobody about, as Peter and Vinnie made their way through ornate staterooms, huge with high ceilings, the throne room with its pink carpet and gold and pink tapestries and chandeliers. Vinnie's mouth opened as they made their way through the quiet blue drawing room with portraits of Kings and Queens, and Vinnie gasped at the beauty of the white drawing room.

'Wonder if Her Majesty would mind if me and Gill could come round for tea.' Peter shook his head, as they made their way down a long corridor, long and silent. It was deserted, as they made their way to the designated pick up point. Their footsteps echoed around the huge rooms as they make their way through, down an empty corridor, enamoured by the beauty of the place. Peter admired one of the enormous paintings on the wall, then moved on.

It was deathly quiet as Peter consulted his map. The Royal Party would be in the basement safe room. "Too quiet," Peter thought, as he looked around. The quiet before the storm. Peter's sixth sense kicked in as they walked down some steps and stopped as he came face to face with a group of aliens examining a large steel door. They studied one another as Peter's lightning sharp senses took in their appearance Tall, thin, pale green skin, looking patchy and flaky—a dermatologist's dream, large head, soulless black eyes and black uniforms. He took all this in a hundredth of a second. His training took over as a split second later he shot all the aliens, who didn't know what had hit them, their shielding failing under the fearsome firepower of Peter's PR7 on full automatic. Green blood and body parts smeared the steel door behind them.

'For Queen and Country,' said Peter.

'For 'er Majesty, God bless her,' replied Vinnie, as he removed the remains of the aliens from the door.

Peter knew who was on the other side of the door, they must have heard the commotion. He knocked three times on the thick steel door. A moment later, a telephone rang next to the door which he picked up.

'Hello, we've come to take you to a secure location.'

'What's your name?'

'Captain Morgan.'

'Password?'

'Balmoral.'

There was the sound of clinks and locks being unlocked, and creaking bars being lifted, and the large steel door opened to reveal some footmen and members of the royal family. Peter bowed his head as Queen Elizabeth came forward.

'Ah Captain Morgan, thank you for rescuing us, we are most grateful.'

She looked down in shock at the dead aliens for a moment but hid it very well.

'I see you had a spot of bother.'

'Yes, your majesty.' Prince Philip came forward.

'Good man good man, shall we make a move?'

Vinnie was dumbstruck as he took up the rear guard position. As they started to climb the stairs, Peter gave the Queen a helping hand until they reached the top. 'Thank you, Captain,' the Queen smiled.

Peter took point, Vinnie to the rear, as he whispered to the party, 'There may be more aliens about so keep quiet and stay between us, ok?' Peter stared at one of the footmen as he coughed.

The royal party nodded as they crept their way back through the palace. Peter stopped, held up his hand, and motioned for quiet. He thought he could hear talking. It was a low guttural language, an ancient form of Arabic he thought, he knew that language well, but the voices did not sound human. As they walked into the pink throne room, they could see two aliens in black uniforms sitting on the two pink thrones. They fired their laser pistols at the royal party, hitting one of the footmen. Peter retaliated on full automatic, shredding the two aliens and the throne behind them.

'Bloody cheek, sitting on the throne! Erm…sorry for swearing your Majesty,' Vinnie bowed.

'Apology not necessary,' said the Queen as she patted Peter and Vinnie on the back.

'Good man,' said Prince Philip. 'What's that rifle you're using Captain?'

'It's a PR7 kinetic technology rifle, sir. Our G36s are useless because the aliens have shields, but the PR7 can make mincemeat of them. As long as it's on automatic. Trouble is, we don't have enough. I've got the only working PR7 in the UK.'

The Prince's curiosity got the better of him, as he and Peter, walked over to the dead aliens.

Chapter 40

ALIEN AGENDA

Peter looked at the uniform - black jacket and trousers made of a strange material, light but very strong. It had a utility belt and a device which he thought must be the personal force field emitter. A holster for the laser pistol, which was on the floor. On its boot, it had a pouch for a knife.

He undid the uniform to get a closer look at them. The first thing that hit him was the smell. Like a cross between cat urine and bad body odour. Maybe sulphur; not pleasant. Then Peter noticed the large black oval eyes with a red hint.

Empty.

The open mouth showed razor sharp pointed teeth.

The skin colour was light green, the thin arms were wiry.

It wasn't the shock of seeing the skinny, unhealthy looking aliens with skin problems that would keep a skin specialist busy for a lifetime that shocked Peter so much, it was what they were wearing. The Prince examined the uniform, a look of horror on his face.

'I have seen these uniforms before—or something like them!' remembering his days spent in the Royal Navy during World War Two, and the time some Nazi SS Officer prisoners were brought on board his ship. They had been trying to escape the Allies driving north from Italy during the Italian Campaign. His heart skipped a beat as the memory flooded back. He remembered one SS Officer in particular: eyes as cold as ice, hiding the evidence of heinous crimes, defiant, duplicitous, his thin, pale face wearing a thin smile, as if he knew something others did not.

'There is something more to these creatures than meets the eye, Captain Morgan,' the shocked Prince exclaimed. 'What do these uniforms remind you of Captain?'

'If I didn't know better, your Royal Highness, I would say they look like a Nazi uniform—a modern version. The swastikas are a bit different, and the material, is strange and shiny, but unmistakable nevertheless,' replied Peter. The Prince was right, there was an agenda going on here, and he had to find out what it was, maybe he would find those answers when he flew to the states.

'We need to get out of here, quickly!' shouted Peter.

They made their way back through the Palace, and to their relief, met no more aliens. Peter received a message on his transceiver from Kojak.

'We need to leave now laddy!'

They made their way out of the Palace, Peter leading the way, Vinnie at the rear, taking tail-end charlie, and the footmen helping the elderly Royals as best they could.

As they took off in the X-37D and made their way out of London, the Queen looked out of the window and exclaimed her astonishment and shock at the destruction.

'Captain Morgan, we must stop these aliens, at all costs!'

Peter found himself on one knee kneeling before her, kissing her hand.

'Yes, your majesty, I promise.'

'There is something about you, Peter Morgan,' said the Queen softly.

Peter couldn't quite figure out why he made such a promise, but as he knelt before Her Majesty, he suddenly had visions of himself, in ancient times. Kay, Cai, a mighty warrior, strong as an ox, kneeling before a King, a great sword by his side, swearing an oath of allegiance, to fight for the King and save the land from a great danger.

As Peter looked up at Queen Elizabeth, he understood why the British people loved her and looked up to her. She was the glue that kept the United Kingdom together. She and her family were the over-soul of the nation. Imagine the UK without a Queen. It would lose its soul, its whole identity. Fuck the federalists, he loved his Queen, and he loved his country, and that was that.

Peter and Vinnie decided to get some shuteye until they arrived at their destination. Peter had learned early on to grab sleep any time he could, because you don't know when the opportunity will arise again.

He was dreaming of the Welsh hills, holding hands with Jennifer, smiling, laughing as they ran over the green grass and down into the wooded valley where they live.

The warm sun beamed down on them. The bluebells dazzled in the grass among pine and oak trees, but then a cloud appeared, looming, dark and ominous, its tendrils reaching for the ground. A whirlwind, black, and menacing, moved towards them. The wind hit them, the sky turned darker still, and they were running, running away from the tornado, rushing towards them, wind swirling around them - a knot of fear in his stomach.

Chapter 41

Queen's Speech

'Pete, Pete, wake up,' Vinnie shook him as the passengers, the Royal family, disembarked from the plane. Peter shook his head as he got up out of his seat, and went down the steps of the X-37D, onto green grass, and a blue sky, and a fresh breeze. He smelled the scent of a pine forest nearby.

A stupid dream, but it lingered in his memory. In the last year or so, he had gained the ability to remember his dreams. His psychic powers had increased so he could also, most of the time, tell what people were thinking. Certainly, he could tell if someone was telling the truth or not - *an internal bullshit detector.*

Nearby were some concrete steps, which went down into the hill. He followed the royal party down the steps until they all stood outside a sturdy-looking steel door. The door opened, and they walked down a corridor, with rooms on either side: sitting rooms, dining room, bathrooms—it was not Buckingham Palace, but it looked comfortable. Like a hobbit hole. The Queen and Prince Philip went into a cozy-looking room, a wood-panelled sitting room, with large chairs and some side cabinets, from which Prince Philip was pouring what looked like whiskey from a crystal decanter. He looked at Peter and nodded.

'Please join us Captain and your companion.'

'Please sit down,' said the Queen, 'You deserve a rest.'

Peter took a comfortable chair by a log fire. He felt the heat warming his bones, as Prince Philip handed him a glass of whiskey, which he sipped, and looked at his Queen. Vinnie stood awkwardly nearby, not sure whether to sit or stand.

'Sit down man,' Prince Philip looked at Vinnie and handed him a whiskey.

Peter bowed his head to the Queen, 'Your Majesty.' The Queen turned to look at the young, fit SAS captain, the one who had saved their lives, and brought them to safety, to their bunker.

'Sir Nigel told me about you, Captain. I remember now. Ah yes, at a garden party, yes that's right, they call you "Bulletproof Pete" don't they?'

Peter was a bit embarrassed, as the Queen smiled and Prince Philip gave out a guffaw of laughter.

'Yes, they do Ma'am.'

'We are deeply concerned about these alien invaders, and why they have come here, Captain.'

'And those uniforms, haven't seen the like of those since my days in the Royal Navy, during the Italian Campaign. It's like a bad bloody nightmare, Captain, it really is,' said Prince Philip, leaning towards Peter.

'We're flying out to the States directly, and I'm hoping to get some answers there, your Royal Highness. They have this Sirius program.'

'Captain, why aren't you fighting for England?' asked the Queen.

'It seems I'm just a pawn in a much bigger game, Maam.'

The Queen nodded and leaned towards Peter.

'Captain Morgan, if you meet with President Wilson, please give him this message. It is very important. Tell him to remember that it is in our darkest hour that we find the greatest courage. We British and Americans have always stood together, through thick and thin, through war and peace. We both uphold the same values of freedom and democracy, our abhorrence of tyranny and evil. We now stand on the brink of destruction. We must make a stand. We must find a solution. In the Second World War, Britain stood on the edge of destruction, London was in ruins, the German invasion force twenty miles away across the English Channel. Thus began the Battle of Britain, where a few Spitfire pilots stopped wave after wave of Luftwaffe through skill, grit, and determination. If we had not been resolute and wavered for just a moment, if we had not found that extra ounce of courage, we would have lost.'

The Queen paused, recalling her many conversations with Winston Churchill.

'In the words of Winston Churchill, "Sometimes our best is not good enough, sometimes we have to do what is required." '

The Queen, recounting a thousand years of history, looked at her husband, then at Peter.

'We are counting on you, Captain.'

Peter felt the heavy weight of responsibility fall on his shoulders.

'He is a wise man, he will understand the meaning,' the Queen added.

The Queen and Prince Philip nodded as the Queen looked directly at him. 'I will give the President your message, Ma'am.'

'Captain, in your time, working in the Special Air Service, and with the Secret Intelligence Service, have you seen anything like this?'

Peter was surprised that the Queen knew that he worked for MI6, but then again, Her Majesty was very well informed, about everything, it seems.

'Well Your Majesty, I have seen some things that are weird. Really weird. We were called out once, in the middle of the night to a site on Salisbury Plain. Air Traffic Control had reported some unusual activity, so we were sent to investigate and control the situation. We were told not to talk about it to anyone, not even other members of our unit, which was odd. Anyway, 8 Flight dropped us in the middle of this field, and there before our eyes is this glowing object. It was not standard military aircraft—not even the Russians have anything like this. It was saucer shaped and buried several feet into the ground as if it had crash-landed, but it didn't look damaged. There were glowing red, blue and green flashing lights. Brilliant. Dazzling. We had to shield our eyes. The metal it was made from wasn't steel, it was something else. I had a bad feeling about it, and stood back.'

'I was going to go inside Ma'am, I mean Your Majesty,' said a nervous Vinnie.

'Good job I stopped you, the radiation readings were off the scale,' said Peter to his friend.

'Then some MOD guys in white suits went in and pulled out some—what I can only describe as creatures, aliens, very tall, seven feet high, with long silvery bodies and large eyes. These were different aliens, not the ones we've just seen. They wore this kind of suit, a biological suit, that seemed part of their bodies. There were four of them, three dead, but one was still alive. He stood up and looked at me, just me, no one else, his big black eyes seem to speak to me. I had visions in my mind, of spaceships arriving and attacking us.' Peter got serious again, as he looked thoughtful.

'Then he told me very clearly, in my mind, that I was the one. One day the people of Earth would need me.' Peter looked at the Queen. 'I told no one except Vinnie.'

'He is your best friend?'

'Yes, Ma'am, we are inseparable, he is my right-hand man.'

The Queen turned to look at Vinnie and smiled. Vinnie was almost in tears as he smiled back at her, then bowed his head, in respect. He would have a lot of stories to tell Reg and Gill.

'Everyone needs their Batman,' chipped in Prince Philip.

They all sat in silence for a while, until the Queen stood up, smiled, and looked at Peter and Vinnie.

'When all this is over, please come to the palace for tea—both of you, bring your wives too, you will be most welcome.'

Vinnie beamed with pleasure as the Queen, and Prince Philip shook their hands, and the Prince gave Vinnie a wink.

As they walked back down the corridor, and up the steps, to the waiting X-37D, Vinnie kept saying, 'Tea with the Queen,' a look of great pride on his face. 'Just wait till I tell Gill and Reg.' Peter was happy for Vinnie, people from the East End of London always had a great affection for the Royal family, especially the Queen, and after meeting her Peter was most impressed, by her knowledge, perception, and charisma.

He felt blessed to have met her. They both smiled as they climbed back on the plane, Peter replayed the experience in his mind—a moment so rare, and forever savoured. He would have a lot of stories to tell Jennifer when he got home.

If he got home.

Chapter 42

It's a War, But With No Rules

They are back at the airbase, they refuel and pick up more supplies and ammunition before their flight to the States. Peter and his team are on the plane as it sits on the runway ready for takeoff. Then, out of the corner of his eye Peter can see what looks like a small aircraft, then he realizes it is not terrestrial. It's an alien craft, moving at tremendous speed and at impossible angles. It is heading for a civilian airport nearby. Vinnie joins Peter as they watch an Airbus A380 elegantly take off and start climbing skywards towards them, arching its back as it accelerates over a cluster of tall buildings—with the alien craft on an intercept path.

'Jesus that aircraft, those people,' whispers Pete as they lean nearer to the window. The Airbus A380 is hit by laser blasts from the alien fighter. It seems to stop in mid-air and move from forty-five to ninety degrees, flames erupting from the fuselage and two of its huge engines. Then it stalls, as its speed is too slow to gain height.

Time seems to stop as Peter's super-vision can see into one of the passenger windows—a young girl crying holding a teddy bear, then the huge aircraft plunges earthwards into a nearby road, jam-packed with cars. There is a tremendous crash; debris and flames erupt as a fireball and smoke fill the sky. Peter and Vinnie watch open-mouthed in horror through the smoke and flames in the distance, as a car comes hurtling through the air and smashes onto the tarmac nearby.

'Get moving Kojak!' screams Peter.

They suddenly lurch forward as the X-37D plane launches down the runway. Peter is pressed into his seat by the G-force as it glides into the blue sky, through the smoke, then quickly accelerates to Mach 3. 'Inertial dampers activated,' Kojak's voice announces over the tannoy.

Peter and Vinnie sit in silence trying to assimilate the horror they have just witnessed.

'They didn't stand a chance,' sighs Peter crossing himself.

'Those poor people,' says Vinnie, his normal cheerful disposition gone.

'It's a war, but with no rules, no hiding place. Total warfare.' Peter replies. He puts on his headphones and listens to Led Zeppelin: Dazed and Confused, his mind starts to drift as he listens to the lyrics. He is definitely dazed and confused, what the fuck is happening to the world?

'We have a bogey on our tail!' shouts Kojak over the tannoy. Peter can feel the plane accelerating through the blue sky. The speed is shown on a display as it increases to Mach ten: 7000 mph.

'At 7000mph, we can give those aliens a run for their money all right,' says Vinnie, some of his normal cheerfulness returning. 'What's inertial damping Pete?'

'Remember Star Trek? When they initiate warp drive, it stops the crew getting smashed into salsa.' Vinnie looks blank. 'If we didn't have inertial dampers all the veins in your eyes would burst from the acceleration Vinnie.'

Vinnie nodded, and Peter puts on his headphones again as he listens to Jimmy Page's genius guitar solo, trying to blot out what they have witnessed.

There is another audible warning: "Cloaking will be engaged in one minute, you may feel nauseous. End of message."

Vinnie goes white and reaches for the sick bag. Peter looks out of the window at the fuselage; the skin of the plane shimmers and becomes almost invisible. The plane quickly climbs above the clouds to 30,000 feet, then higher. Peter walks to the cockpit and chats to Kojak, the pilot.

'How high are we?' asks Peter, looking at the array of sophisticated instruments and dials in the cockpit. The co-pilot Jack nods at Peter.

'We're at 40,000 feet and climbing, laddy,' replies Kojak, sipping a black coffee.

'What type of plane is this, I have never seen anything like it,' asks Peter, his hands on the backs of the pilot's seats.

'It's an X-37D. It's based on the X-37B experimental space plane. It uses a mix of normal fuel mixed with hydrazine, that's rocket fuel, and ram air technology. The higher we are the more efficiently it works. We will climb to 60,000 feet—the edge of space—and then cruise at 20,000 mph until we get to our destination. In space, we can also use a new type of ion-engine called a Hall-effect thruster. This gives us higher thrust than traditional ion propulsion.'

'Thanks for the science lesson. Don't tell Vinnie were going into space,' says Peter, then adds 'What's ETA Sirius Base Mojave, Kojak?'

'About one hour, 6.00 a.m. local time. Get seated, we will be using ram thrusters shortly. And use a seatbelt, laddy, I don't want to be picking you off the ceiling!'

Peter looks out the window; he can see the dark of space and the stars above him and the quiet beauty of the Earth below. Peter closes his eyes and sleeps for a while. After waking, he strikes up a conversation with Vinnie who has just used a sick bag.

'Don't know how you passed selection,' Peter teases Vinnie.

'I'm the best shot in the regiment. Besides, who else is going to watch your back?' Vinnie retorted.

'How's your old man—still an East End Gangster?'

'I told you - he's a legitimate businessman.'

'Why did you quit the service, Vinnie, I had everything sorted with Sir Nigel?' asks Peter.

'After that trouble with Ratti I freelanced for a bit; 6 offered me a contract in Shanghai, but I didn't fancy it, prefer working for my old man. I always know where I stand that way,' replies Vinnie.

'I like your father, always tells you what he thinks. No double talk. He's very proud of you, he was over the moon when we both passed selection for the regiment. He doesn't want you to be a gangster, Vinnie.'

'You still working for 6?' asks Vinnie ignoring him.

'Yes, but Jennifer doesn't like it. Besides, MI6 and the gangsters—what's the difference? Different sides of the same coin. But I'm glad you're back.' Then Peter looks at Vinnie. 'This alien invasion means the old order will disappear, Vinnie. Nothing will be the same anymore.'

Vinnie nods but is pensive. 'I'm worried about Gill, I told my old man to collect her and go to the safe house; it's got a secure cellar. Not sure if the message got through; dog and bones are dead.'

'We can try and contact her later, these Sirius guys have great technology. Vinnie, I'm worried about Jennifer and the kids, they're at home in Brecon. I feel I should have stayed with them—they're my family for Christ's sake!'

Peter gets out his pocketbook of poetry. He found this little book of poems in the middle of the desert in Iraq: Keats, Byron, you name it. He has never been into poetry before finding the book, but now when he feels stressed out, it helps him relax. Peter reads a poem by Keats to himself: A Thing of Beauty.

> "A thing of beauty is a joy for ever:
> Its lovliness increases - it will never
> Pass into nothingness - but still will
> keep A bower quiet for us, and a sleep,
> Full of sweet dreams, and health, and quiet breathing."

He falls asleep again, still listening to a Jimmy Page guitar solo. He is dreaming. He is walking with Jennifer in the Brecon hills; they are childhood sweethearts. The sun is shining, the birds are singing, the flowers are blooming; he feels the warm sun on his face. They kiss for the first time; it tastes of bubblegum—they snigger. He looks at her sparkling brown eyes and long hair and loses all sense of time; then he chases her down a hill, and they fall over laughing in the lush green grass. 'I love you,' she smiles as she strokes his bald head and looks into his blue eyes. He looks into her eyes and thinks she looks like a Greek Goddess—perfect in every way.

He strokes her hair and kisses her on the lips, he can feel her heart pounding as he lies on top of her, 'Let's get married!' he says. She nods as tears fall from her eyes. Then he knows he will love her always. But in a strange way he feels that he has known her before, in a different life. It is a feeling, a knowing in the soul, that he has always known her; always loved her.

But in the distance, he can see a dark, forbidding shape looming in the sky, and it sends a shiver down his spine.

Chapter 43

Surprise Visitor

SIRIUS HEADQUARTERS VIRGINIA

There is a knock on the door. The president and General Scott look up as in walks Professor Picard, he has a few bruises and scratches but otherwise appears unscathed. He is in his early eighties, but fit-looking. He has a beard and glasses and wears a cardigan. He talks with a thick, French-cultured accent.

'Mon Dieu, what a difficult journey, do you have any coffee?'

President Wilson smiles in surprise.

'Professor, we were wondering what happened to you! I am very glad to see you. We were hoping you could shed some light on this alien invasion.'

Picard sits down, drinks some coffee and pulls a face.

'Sacre Bleu, if the aliens don't kill me, this coffee will!'

President Wilson gestures to an aide. 'Get some of that French Roast for the Professor, will you? We have a problem.'

'What is it?'

'The aliens have cracked the code on the F22s.'

'C'est impossible, I made those codes unbreakable. They were highly classified, only a few people knew about it!' the Professor threw his hands up into the air. He quickly drinks his coffee, then pours himself another cup.

'Those codes are très difficult to change, Mr. President, I will need to change the algorithm.' Wilson changed tack.

'So, professor was there really a war between aliens and vampires?'

'There was indeed a war—an ancient war, at the dawn of human history. There is evidence of this war from my excavations in Iraq, my research and from my conversations with Cassian...'

President Wilson is shocked.

'You know Cassian?'

'Oui, we go back a long way. It is a long story,' replied the Professor, looking distant.

General Scott looks irritated. 'Do we have time?'

President Wilson looks at his general and then at the Professor.

'Professor, please go on, take your time.' The Professor samples the French roast coffee, and smiles.

'Ahh - that's better. Do you have any croissants?'

General Scott seems annoyed again as President Wilson calls an aide. 'Get some croissants for the Professor. If you don't have any, bake some. You were saying, Professor...'

'Merci bien. It was back in 1938, I was a small boy then. We were living in Berlin. War was looming. My father had a jewellery business. It did well. The only problem was, we were Jews. Then the persecution started. The forced relocation. We were frightened. My mother pleaded with my father to leave Berlin before it was too late.' The professor pauses as he sips his coffee.

'Then the Night of Broken Glass. I remember heavy boots and shouting, so I clung to my mother. My father's shop was burnt to the ground. Then somehow, we escaped to France to a small village outside of Paris, where we had relatives. We took their French name, Picard, to disguise our heritage. We had false papers made, by the French Resistance. During the day, we slept in the attic. At night, I would read books by candlelight, anything I could lay my hands on really: chemistry, mathematics, physics, philosophy, history, anthropology.' The professor pours himself another cup of coffee and takes a bite from a croissant. He nods with approval.

'My uncle had a wonderful collection of books. Anyway, at night my parents worked for the French Resistance—they really hated the Germans and what they did to us. I remember one night they came back and my father had some strange people with him, who had helped them infiltrate a secret German base. But one night my parents didn't come back. My uncle sat me down and told me they had been captured by the Nazi SS. I was all alone and frightened…I was worried about my parents, but my auntie and uncle looked after me.'

The professor pauses, silent for a moment, recalling the bitter memory.

'My parents were due to be executed by the SS. I have never felt so alone in all my life. But at the last minute, they were rescued by one of these night creatures. I was overjoyed to see my parents again, and my father told me what happened.' Picard drinks some water.

"We were held in a cold stone cell; it was freezing. The water in the toilet froze. We huddled together for warmth. The only light was a small barred window. It was dawn, and a grim light shone through, a crow appeared at the window, looking at us. Then two soldiers came and dragged us out into the icy, cobbled stone courtyard, and tied us to two wooden posts. Opposite were six soldiers with rifles aimed at us, unsmiling, uncaring. A Gestapo captain appeared and shouted orders, smiling at us. We looked at each other and held hands. 'I love you, Heinrich,' Derica said. Time seemed to stop as we heard the firing squad cock their rifles. The crow appeared on top of my pole and cawed at me. Then faster than I can blink, Cassian and Lucia appeared out of the sky, and landed in the courtyard, red eyes blazing, black wings folding. Lucia picked us up then flew skywards. I looked down, and fast as lightning Cassian sliced off the head of the Gestapo captain with his sword, and then three of the firing squad's heads rolled onto the bloodstained cobbled courtyard. The rest fled. Then we fell unconscious, and the next thing I knew we were back home."

Picard continues. "I was so happy to see them again, I said, 'Let us go to the lake for a picnic.' On Sunday, we went to the lake. The sun shone, the birds sang, we were happy, so for one day a week we took the risk, it was our family day. I don't think I have ever been so happy.' The Professor smiles as he recalls the Sunday picnics by the lake. 'Ham, cheese, French bread, it was a feast.' Picard drinks more coffee then continues.

'But my parents wanted to rejoin the resistance; I pleaded with them not to go back, but it was no good. Soon after, they were captured again. I never saw them again. I convinced myself they were fighting for what they believed in. I stayed living with my auntie and uncle. Then one night, I couldn't sleep. This creature appeared at my window. He was kind. He told me stories about how brave my parents were, how hard they fought the Germans, and how much he liked them.' The Professor looks distant and melancholic. General Scott tries his best not to look bored, but Frank Wilson is fascinated.

'Go on, Professor.'

'He always came to see me at night time. He just appeared at the window. I was scared at first, but later he became my friend. He sort of adopted me. I stayed living with my auntie and uncle, but they were poor, so this strange man paid for my schooling. Later, when I was old enough, he told me he was a vampire. I wasn't shocked or surprised, I had sort of worked it out. He was like a father to me. After I had finished studying, I worked for him, as a historian, looking after and documenting the ancient vampire and alien sites in Iraq, and around the world.'

President Wilson leaned forward. 'This was Cassian?'

'Oui, it was my idea for him to meet with you, to broker a peace between vampires and humans.' The president reaches out to the Professor.

'Professor, we are alone in our fight against these damn alien invaders. Quite frankly, we face extinction as a race, we need a miracle.'

'Mr. President, Cassian likes you. You may not be as alone as you think. You may not know it but the vampires are very keen to help you; they themselves face extinction.' The president brightens a little.

'Perhaps these are the allies we seek,' the president smiles, looking hopeful.

'Cassian and the vampires—they are coming soon, very soon. Cassian—he is the most human vampire I have ever met,' the Professor finishes his croissant and smiles.

'Very approachable—for a vampire,' as he sips his coffee.

"There is another one who can help you, Mr. President. We are in possession of an ancient book of prophecy. It foretells this time 'Flames of fire come down from the Sky…when the Gods come down from the Heavens and create fear among the people.' That's the aliens. But it also talks of a warrior. 'But there is one who will come forth from the Isle of Albion, from Cymru, from the land of the mountains. A warrior with foresight and strength who will travel to the land of the eagles. And he will destroy the demons in their chariots. His name is Caius.' Cymru is Wales. Land of the Eagles—that is the United States. A warrior of extraordinary powers. Do you know of anyone like that?"

General Scott smiles. 'As a matter of fact, we do—a Captain Morgan. Smith from the CIA sent us his dossier. We specifically requested him from the British in return for some Sirius technology. An X-37D took off from England yesterday with the Captain on board.'

'I would like to meet this Captain Morgan,' says the president.

The professor beams. 'So would I, mon ami—formidable!' his eyes alight with curiosity and wonder.

Chapter 44

ALIEN HISTORY

In the desert in Nevada, a lonely, wooden ramshackle building stands, its red neon sign, "Juicy Lucy's", no longer flashing. A dustbowl rolled by as a jet-black alien ship landed quietly on the road outside. Two aliens in black uniforms walked confidently towards the building wearing a thin smile.

The tallest one remembered their glorious Emperor's speech just before they left home planet, Ergal Five, to conquer Earth. He was a full member of the Emperor's Narzuk Party, the equivalent of Hitler's Nazi Party, whom the Emperor greatly admired. As he was a member of the fanatical Narzuk Party, he was invited to the front of the throng crowd, facing their glorious Emperor, Herr Herg-Zuk.

All Narzuk party members wore a black uniform, with a Swastika symbol in a circle, on the sleeve, on the orders of their glorious Emperor. But his armband was red, being a member of—and Chief—of the Narzuk SS, specifically tasked for the harvesting and breeding campaign of humans with Sumeri. They received better rations and treatment than the ordinary Narzuk military, who had a white armband with a black swastika, not red like the SS. His name was Lord Grim-Uk, and he wore a thin smile as he popped a pill into his mouth. Red veins appeared in his eyes. Next to him stood his loyal brother and deputy, Himm-Uk.

As he was a member of the Narzuk party, he held Patrician status, one of the elite, which meant he was provided with a good home, in the Patrician neighbourhood, away from the stifling pollution, which plagued the planet.

He also held favoured status for any appointments to senior positions in the Sumeri Government. Good food was never in short supply, especially for the Narzuk SS, even though there was a food shortage, and he could get free holidays in Patrician holiday properties, in warmer climes to the south.

Life was good on Ergal Five if you were a Patrician, or a Narzuk.

The Narzuks were the minority elite who monopolized the military, and therefore, political power; fiercely loyal to the Emperor. Even ordinary Patricians, the businessman and politicians, did not get quite the same privileges as those who belonged to the Narzuk party, but nevertheless they enjoyed a very comfortable life. He also had access to the expensive *(and highly dangerous)* drugs and treatments necessary to produce children, which only the rich and powerful could obtain. But nowadays, very few Patricians had babies, even the rich ones.

However, the populace, the Plebeians, just withered and died. Some managed to get hold of illegal black market drugs and have children that way; sometimes the mother and child both died of the dangerous drugs, but people were desperate. The children that did survive were small and deformed, and did not live long. He knew the Sumeri race was withering and dying, and was increasingly populated by thousands of clones, slaves to the Patrician and Narzuk elite. The Sumeri DNA was dying, so clones were reproduced from good DNA, sometimes thousands of years old. Their race was ancient, ten million years old, and evolution had chosen their race for extinction. The clones were programmed from birth, in the learning chambers, to serve the Patrician elite, or become foot soldiers.

The clones were very pale green and had dark gray eyes, not black. It was unheard of for a clone to be disobedient, they were programmed that way, like machines, without emotion. But many were born with the personality traits of their DNA parent, some even had independent thought, but he enjoyed rounding these up for re-processing.

Behind the Narzuk SS, were the rank and file Narzuks, who did not look as healthy as their SS counterparts, and behind them were the Plebeians, who were the ordinary workers. They had homes near the smelly factories, but they had rights, and if they worked very hard, they could be appointed to serve the elite, and therefore be protected. The ranks of the Plebeians were thin, and they looked unhealthy, not having the wealth or connections to reproduce, or to regenerate their slowly decaying DNA.

Behind them were massed the lowest of the low, the clone soldiers and servants, greatly outnumbering their Narzuk and Patrician masters. The clones outnumbered their masters a thousand to one.

Patricians, including Narzuks, were not allowed to marry Plebeians, by law. The clone soldiers and slaves were not classed as citizens and lacked any legal rights whatsoever. There were two types of slave: There were clone slaves, the Grays, who were factory-built clones, and the Servi, who were prisoners of war, including women and children. The slaves were captured during Narzuk military campaigns on their near planetary neighbours, Ergal 6, and they were not Sumeri, but a different species. An inferior race. He regarded them as objects to be used and abused. Slaves were bought and sold freely, and regarded as the property of the owner.

Thus slavery was regarded as a circumstance of birth, misfortune, or war. Through hard work and service, a servi slave could become a Plebeian, with all the rights and privileges that came with it. The Grays, the clones, could never rise above their station and could never become a Plebeian, thus were classed as the lowest of the low. Being a clone was as an inescapably permanent condition, with no chance of progression.

All slaves who lacked skills or education worked in the fields or performed manual labour. Those servi who were disobedient or violent, would be sentenced to hard labour in the mines, where the conditions were not even fit for animals—in fact, the animals were treated better. If they were really unlucky, they were given a one-way ticket to the laboratories and torture chambers of Doctor Vlad-Uk, and were subjected to his horrific and diabolical experiments.

Nobody liked the doctor, but he was untouchable, being a member of the Narzuk party. Order was easily maintained on the planet by a visit from one of the Narzuks, and the threat of a Narzuk detention order in the doctor's laboratories was enough to bring even the most rebellious of detractors back into line.

Chapter 45

THE EMPEROR SPEAKS

Vlad-Uk was the mentor and master of Lord Grim-Uk, one of the few Sumeri to actually meet him. His laboratories were located deep in the depths of the cave and dungeon network below the Imperial Palace, and his activities were shrouded in mystery. Nobody knew much about him, except Lord Grim-Uk. Of course, everybody wondered at Vlad-Uk's unnaturally long life. If truth be known he had lived for centuries. Some Narzuks thought he had made a pact with a demon, and that was why he still lived. Lord Grim-Uk himself was over a hundred years old, only a few reached that age, the Emperor being one of them.

As Grim-Uk looked around him, he was shocked at the small number of Sumeri, both Patricians *(including Narzuks)* and Plebs that were left (there was double that number only ten years ago), and shocked at the growing number of clones needed to keep society and the military going. He looked forward again, as his Emperor was about to speak.

'Mighty people of Sumeri, I speak to you now as your Emperor and Leader, and I call on you to do your duty.'

A great roar came up from the crowd.

'We face a great crisis, as you all know our numbers have been diminishing slowly but surely, over the years. We are a dying race. All our women are barren. A small number of our men are still fertile, but that number is dwindling, at an exponential rate. Our scientists, those that are left, have done their best, but we still don't have a solution, we must preserve our race.'

The Emperor paused, as he sipped some water.

'We know of a planet, which we have visited many times over the centuries, where we can re-colonise, reproduce and make ourselves great again. That planet is called Earth. Our experiments on their human women have shown we can reproduce with a certain number of them if they have the right gene. But, we must preserve the purity of our race, to stop diseases and unclean habits. We will only choose pure-bred Earthling women, else our race will fail.'

The crowd became excited, and cheered as the Emperor raised his fist, The Narzuk cheering louder than the rest. Some of the Plebeians in the back row muttered and shouted comments at the Emperor. They were quickly picked out and carried off by loyal Plebeian guards, looking for promotion, or fanatically loyal Narzuk troops. They were never to be seen again.

'We will create a master race of half human, half Sumeri children, who will come after us. A purebred race, strong, clever who will continue our bloodline. We will be strong again. Our Empire will expand, our prosperity will grow, as we conquer new territories.'

The Narzuk elite raised their right arm, their hands in a fist, in a salute to the Emperor. The smartly dressed Patricians, the politicians and businessmen, clapped and smiled.

'Herr Herg-Zuk! Herr Herg-Zuk!'

Behind them the Plebeians half-heartedly raised their arms, murmuring, glancing nervously at the Narzuk guards lined up on either side, waiting to pick out any detractors.

Chapter 46

ATLANTIC STORM

ATLANTIC OCEAN

Peter and Vinnie were in the X-37D flying across the Atlantic, but they were losing height rapidly. Vinnie reached for the sick bag as they hit severe turbulence. Peter could not sleep, he had too much on his mind, as he looked out at the grey skies and white-topped waves below him. Kojak's voice came over the tannoy, 'Captain Morgan report to the cockpit.' Peter knew instinctively by the tone, it was not going to be good news, as he ducked his head into the small cockpit. He had heard that tone before, in Yemen.

'Pete, we have a fuel leak, we're losing height rapidly, must have been that firefight over Buck House,' the stress lines showed on Kojak's face. 'How much fuel left?' asked Peter tentatively.

'About enough to fly five hundred miles laddy.'

'We're in the middle of the fucking Atlantic, Kojak, what are our options?' asked Peter controlling the fear in his stomach. *Even Bulletproof Pete couldn't swim the Atlantic.*

'We could fly south to Terceira in the Azores, but that's 600 miles due south – we could glide the last hundred. But it's possible there's alien activity there, it's a military base after all. Alternatively, we could try for an aircraft carrier that I'm picking up, 450 miles due west. But...'

'But what?'

'There's a low-pressure area, fifty miles west between us and the carrier.'

'How bad?'

'It's a bad one. The radar indicates a conjunction of two low-pressure systems. Means we have to fly right through it, not around it. Not enough fuel laddy.'

'Go for the carrier. At least we'll be heading in the right direction,' replied Peter.

'Seatbelts on!' shouted Kojak over the tannoy.

The X-37D slowed to Mach one to conserve fuel, but Peter's eagle eyes could already see the waves getting bigger; the troughs getting deeper.

'Vinnie, get your seatbelt on mate, were in for a rough ride.'

Vinnie was quiet as the turbulence started.

Then as they hit the storm, a category four hurricane, they suddenly dropped a hundred feet as they hit a downdraft. Rain splattered the window, and visibility was zero.

'Can't we fly around it?' asked a white-faced Vinnie.

'Not enough fuel—just hang tight,' Peter tried to sound reassuring, but the solid frame of the X-37D was taking a battering. Then the plane lifted fifty feet, then dropped like a brick again. Des, one of the SAS team shouted, 'Pete we need to get out of this storm!'

Peter staggered to the cockpit.

'Can we fly above the storm?' asked Peter grabbing Kojak's chair to steady himself. The visibility from the cockpit was near zero, just driving rain.

'To do that we will use more fuel!' replied Kojak.

They were both silent for a moment, weighing up the risks.

'We could fly to 60,000 feet, that's the safest we can fly without pressure suits, we will run out of fuel, then glide the last few hundred miles. We would be well above the storm,' suggested Kojak in his most reasonable Scottish accent.

'Ok Kojak, let's do that—good call.'

Peter felt they had made the right decision and was glad that Kojak was flying the X-37D—one of the best, which explained why he was flying a Sirius project plane. It climbed quickly and the turbulence gradually lessened as they climbed above the storm.

As they got to 60,000 feet Peter could make out the storm centre below, the huge swirling mass of the hurricane with an eye in the middle. He could feel the plane gradually level out and then slowly descend. He felt calm as he watched the sunshine through the clouds and could see the curvature of the earth below – as he looked up, he could see the dark sky of space above him. Below he could see the Atlantic Ocean and the eastern seaboard of the United States.

The aircraft was silent now as it glided down through the clouds on the edge of the storm front. The plane was buffeted as they descended through the clouds until they could see the whites of the sea below. Peter's eagle eyes could pick out a ship in the distance. As they got closer, he could make out it was an aircraft carrier. Not just any carrier, a Nimitz class US aircraft carrier, its huge bulk slicing through 50-foot waves.

Kojak spoke over the tannoy: 'Brace for landing.' He wiped the sweat from his brow as he looked at the fuel gauge.

Empty. They were flying on vapour.

'USS Ronald Reagan, this is Sirius flight zero zero alpha. We have no fuel, were coming in for a crash landing. Repeat we have no fuel!'

'Roger that zero zero alpha, stay on your approach. We have been tracking you.'

He was 500 feet above the carrier about a mile away. He lined up as best he could, the hurricane had spent most of its force but the winds were still strong. The plane veered to the left, Kojak struggled with the controls and wiped his brow again. He could see the landing lights, but the carrier was moving up and down in the waves. If he didn't time it right they would crash into the carrier and be killed. The wind stopped, the aircraft carrier came up on a huge wave; he was now level. The X-37D landed just as the carrier lurched again, and came to a sudden halt as giant rubber bands laid across the deck stopped the aircraft.

They staggered out of the plane thankful for their lives. Peter crossed himself and said a silent prayer of thanks—his prayer to the entity he met in the desert had worked. Kojak came down the steps, 'Great flying,' said Peter shaking his hand.

'We need to get going again soon laddy, there's a lot of alien activity.' Kojak rushed off to talk to the deck crew about getting the X-37D patched up and refuelled. Peter and Vinnie stood on the deck of the huge aircraft carrier, glad to walk on something solid, even if it was a ship. 'I will make a brew, don't trust these yanks to make a cuppa,' shouted Vinnie above the noise of the wind as he scurried off.

Later, he joined Peter on the deck, handing him his steaming mug of Yorkshire Tea. As Peter sipped his brew the wind died down a bit and the waves became calmer; they were over the worst of the storm. He stood on the huge carrier deck and started to relax a bit as he watched the sun come out from behind the clouds, feeling the warmth on his face. He tasted the salty sea air and breathed in deep. He took another sip from his mug, Vinnie's tea always tasted great and he loved him for it.

But then, his Caius instincts kicked in.

Danger was approaching—fast. Loud klaxons sounded on the deck.

Chapter 47

INCOMING

'Incoming – Incoming Action Stations!' came warnings over the speakers.

Deckhands rushed here and there—a single F22 slowly descended on a lift. Peter and his team rushed to get below. But then Peter stopped in his tracks. Their craft must be protected at all costs.

The mission.

'Get below!' shouted Vinnie.

'Get below decks!' warnings sounded, but Peter retrieved his PR7 and loaded a magazine and grenades, then stood on deck next to the X-37D and gazed out into the distance, over the choppy foam-topped ocean, seeking his enemy.

Then he saw them.

Action stations sounded as three alien fighters sped over the ocean towards the carrier. As the alien craft approach the carrier, skimming the now calm sea in a V shape—*low-level attack formation*—two onboard Sirius-modified Phalanx Gatling guns were prepared for the incoming fighters, their radar tracking the fast-approaching alien crafts. The captain on the bridge looked out, adjusting his binoculars. These new Gatling guns had never seen action, and that worried him.

The Gatling's whirred, as the servos kicked in at lightning speed, acquiring their targets, firing specially modified enriched uranium bullets in a wall of lead at 250 rounds per second. One alien fighter veered off, the other fired, causing severe damage to the carrier's hull. The whole ship shuddered at the impact as flames erupted from the impact zone. Sirens wailed as fire crews ran about deck attending the fire. Another fighter was heading straight towards Peter and the X-37D. The Gatling's fired a wall of uranium bullets, but the fighter continued on its path, charging its weapons, glowing orange.

Peter loaded a grenade into his PR7 launcher: aimed and fired. Two in quick succession. The fighter was hit just two hundred yards from the ship; it veered off and span out of control as it crashed in a blaze of sparks and orange fire onto the carrier deck, setting it ablaze. Fire crews rushed to put out the fearsome blaze.

But the danger is not over.

One fighter is still heading towards the ship, its weapons glowing orange. Deck hands look in fear as it approaches. Peter is out of grenades.

Options. Think man!

Then he remembered the desert. The Holy Desert, and the Archangel Michael, and the Ancient Sword of Power. Then an ancient memory – an instinct overtook him.

Peter's mind entered an altered state - he knew instinctively how to do this, for he was Caius, the Eternal Warrior, come to defeat the alien menace, for that was his purpose, his mission, in this incarnation.

He cleared his mind, earthing and balancing himself before he spoke the invocation.

His mind wandered, contacting the dimension beyond time. Time itself seemed to stop, the deckhands and approaching craft, frozen in the moment, he had a vision of a sword, a large silver sword, with a golden pommel and jewels, amethysts, embedded into the pommel.

'Caliburnus!'
'Caliburnus!'
'Caliburnus!'

Three times he said the words, as he closed his eyes, his mind focusing on the sword, and when he opened them, he was holding it in his hand. It felt heavy, powerful, and it vibrated with enormous power, as it gave off a blue light - all around him was a blue light. It was one of the seven holy swords of Prince Michael, Lord of Angels. For indeed it was an object of immeasurable power, which could only be wielded by one such as Caius.

"The sword will give you power, strength, and the will to succeed and conquer your enemies," he remembered Prince Michael's words.

As Peter admired the blade, it vibrated in his hand, the power running through his body – he felt invigorated. And yet he was not alone, for there was another entity, standing beside him, a figure in robes, blue and purple robes, he had a smile so beautiful, and he radiated such raw power, such infinite love, that Peter knelt before him, in silence. He now had a sense of the power and majesty of God.

As the being laid his hands upon Peter's head, he felt a rush of power to his body, he now felt at peace with the world, as the energy surged through him. Michaels' eyes flashed a fierce blue, and then he witnessed an emotion - infinite power, limitless and unstoppable, and when he looked up again, the entity was gone. He now stood, his eyes shining blue and as he raised his sword the atmosphere changed. Dark clouds gathered as the sword shone like the sun and lightning sprang from it - thunder rolled in the distance as the deck crew stood back frightened. Lightning sprang from the sword, with a light that blinded the eyes and struck the oncoming craft, it caught fire and veered toward the carrier then at the last minute plunged into the sea. Peter looked at his sword – then it was gone.

Sailors looked warily at Peter, not quite believing what they saw. Then they slowly approached the smoking craft on the deck, carefully examined the wreckage and pulled out an injured alien, holding their noses, and looking at the strange creature, its pale green flaking skin, and large black eyes, half open—an alien on the border of life and death.

'Gee these aliens stink, don't they use deodorant?' said one sailor. Peter walked up to the smouldering fighter and looked inside. He could see strange writing on the controls, reminding Peter of ancient Arabic, and examined the metal structure of the craft, which was unlike anything else he had ever seen. He found what looked like a communication device and examined the markings. One soldier touched the alien metal with his bare hands, then took it away as a rash appeared on his fingers, then his hand. A medic rushed to his aid, scolding him.

'You were explicitly told not to touch anything without protective gear!'

Vinnie rushed up to Peter. 'You're a fucking nutcase!'

'No Vinnie, I am Caius,' replied the warrior as he put the alien device inside his backpack. Then he took Vinnie by the shoulders and looked him in the eye.

'Caius is my secret name, of which only you and I will speak.'

Chapter 48

NEW YORK

Peter and his team piled back into the X-37D and then it took off streaking into the grey-blue sky, quickly accelerating to Mach 4 as Kojak spoke over the tannoy. 'We've got new orders from Sirius HQ. We've been ordered to New York to observe and report. An alien ship is there, but the city is intact. Do not engage the enemy—observe and report. We land in thirty minutes. Message Over.' Peter looked at his encrypted radio. Orders were confirmed.

Peter nudged Vinnie awake as Kojak shouted from the cockpit, 'I canna concentrate with his snoring!'

He looked out the window at the New York skyline as the shimmering X-37D made its way to a landing spot near Brooklyn Bridge, across the Hudson River. It hovered, then landed. Above the X-37D the monstrous black mothership slowly turned making grinding noises, and dropping bits of debris on the city below. Peter and his team got out and they looked up, mouth's open, as a huge section fell into the river, making a huge splash in the river, and creating a wash, which came up to their feet.

As they stood shell-shocked on the grass by the river bank, Peter looked at his watch. It was 2 pm local time, but the alien ship blocked out the sun like a solar eclipse, covering the area in semi-darkness.

Peter gathered his four-man team for a briefing. Johnny Two-Times, Fag-Ash Phil and Vinnie. He handed round cigarettes and took one himself, Fag-Ash lit it for him. He looked up at the ship, then at his men. Vinnie burped loudly as Peter started talking.

'We've been diverted here to get intel, to observe and report. Do not engage the enemy. Repeat, do not engage the enemy. Des and his team will stay here to protect the ship. Any questions?'

'I need a brew,' said Vinnie. 'Later, Vinnie, later,' chided Peter. 'We will wear all-black gear, I'm hoping the enemy won't spot us.'

Peter took point as they walked off, Fag-Ash taking tail-end Charlie as they strode along the river bank towards Brooklyn Bridge. 'Strange the buildings are intact,' observed Peter as he looked at the New York skyline. Why?'

'It is strange Pete,' replied Vinnie, taking a swig of water as they walk in the semi-darkness.

'Bradley said their ships are one mile wide. This one looks bigger—more like three miles wide.'

'It's definitely bigger than the one over London,' added Vinnie.

'Maybe this will be their HQ,' observed Peter.

They walked in the shadows as they left the river and started to cross the Brooklyn Bridge into New York City. There was no alien activity on the bridge as they crossed, looking this way and that, trying to stay hidden. As they crossed the bridge they could see people milling about, looking confused, trying to escape, and in the distance they could see alien patrols and fighter craft.

They crept silently into the city, the alien ship hovering several miles over the Empire State Building. It was so huge that the whole of New York City was in its shadow, its massive black shape like something out of a horror movie, invoking a darkness of spirit among the people.

Day became dusk. The atmosphere of fear among the people was palpable, Peter's sensitive hearing could hear the screams of people in the distance.

Anguished screams, blood-chilling.

Peter and his team hid out in a shop below the Empire State Building. From their hideout they peered out of the window and observed the chaos: crowds of people wandering, running, and the alien foot patrols, killing or kidnapping them.

There were fewer people left on the streets now as they stared up open-mouthed, fear etched on their faces. Every five seconds the monstrous black ship emitted a deep, grinding, throbbing hum which made the ground shake, windows shatter, and roads crack. Every time the spaceship hummed and vibrated, small bits fell off it.

'Why are people just standing there?' asked Vinnie.

'Rabbits staring at the headlights,' replied Peter.

People were running in all directions trying to escape, screaming as they were hit by falling debris from miles above. Suddenly a twelve-foot piece hurtled down and crushed two cars, smashing a hole in the road. Water burst from a main, and a gas pipe hissed invisible gas. A small crowd looked up in fear, as the circling mothership made an ear-blistering grinding noise like someone scraping their nails across a blackboard. People ran in panic as they saw a much larger piece of the ship come hurtling down towards Earth.

A young girl stood transfixed looking heavenward as the black section of the ship became larger in the sky. Her mother grabbed her and ran for her life as the ship section crashed into the top of the Chrysler building, destroying the top twenty floors. Glass, dust, and steel were everywhere. Crowds ran in panic as debris and huge clouds of dust fell from the building, like a replay of 9/11—but of course, this was worse.

Much, much worse.

Peter watched as state troopers launched missiles which exploded harmlessly off the massive alien spaceship's shields. The wreckage of F22's were strewn on the streets. Alien fighter craft now dominated the sky, whizzing around the ship, like bees around a nest—a huge nest.

People were now fleeing the city in panic, in any way they could—bicycle, motorbike, car or lorry. A toddler being carried by her mother dropped her teddy bear. Shops were looted for supplies. A man tried dialling 911 on his mobile, then made a run for cover into a coffee shop. Breathless, he ran in; a group of New Yorkers were cowering in a corner. '911?'

'Are you joking, even the police and soldiers are running away!' says a large African-American woman in a smart business suit.

'Grow up boy! Find your family—find a safe place to hide!'

Peter and his team moved out of the shop into the dusty darkness, the haze penetrated by searchlights from the alien patrol craft, looking for humans. They made their way to Central Park as they watched larger alien fighter craft land there. The fighter craft design was less monstrous than the ship above, but still looked sinister, and the darkest black you could think of in your worst nightmare, looking as though it was designed to scare the inhabitants of invaded planets.

The soldiers hid in the undergrowth as they watched alien troops, pale green, patched-up skin, large black eyes and thin, wiry bodies, wearing black Narzuk uniforms, with swastika-style armbands, start spilling out of the craft. Peter had a sinking feeling as he gestured—waving his arms—for the people to leave, but curiosity seemed to get the better of them. Some people are just stupid; he had risked exposing himself; he had learnt a lesson that day.

Some of the elderly in the crowd, stood open-mouthed recognising the uniforms, sending shockwaves through those old enough to remember. Some people just stood mesmerised by the spectacle, too frightened to move. Out of the ships walked growling, muscular, alien dogs, with yellow eyes, and spines on their backs, eyeing the escaping humans, saliva dripping from their large fangs.

Terrified women were running. But it was too late as they were being kidnapped by Narzuks, and any men who got in their way were shot. A long line of women—filthy, with torn clothing—were being scanned and taken aboard the larger fighter craft and shuttled to the behemoth of a ship above them.

All about was panic and terror.

'We must do something!' shouted Vinnie.

Chapter 49

Nazi Speech

'Observe and report - those were our orders!' replied Peter. Vinnie wondered if Peter had lost his bottle. A group of Special Forces Rangers crept along, behind some bushes near to them, waiting for an opportunity to strike at the parked alien craft. A patrolling fighter spotted them and a few laser blasts later, they were burnt husks, smoke rising from what was left of their bodies.

'Sit tight,' whispered Peter. Vinnie nodded.

'Hold on, something is happening,' added Peter.

A terrified crowd was being herded into a group. A high-ranking alien in black, surrounded by alien soldiers and robots stood on a platform, addressing the crowd. Peter noticed he has a red armband with a strange black swastika symbol. He had red streaks running through his eyes like he was on something. The alien used a headphone translator as he spoke.

'Orgvod…People of New York, your attention, please. I am Lord Grim-Uk of the Imperial Sumeri army. Please salute your new leader.' A human man in a black uniform stood on the platform. His lank, unkempt, black hair was in contrast to his pale, unhealthy face. His shifty coal-coloured eyes looked at the crowd.

Peter nudged Vinnie, 'I'm sure I have seen that guy before – he's in the US military. I'm sure of it!'

'People of New York, do not be afraid. This is a period of change—great change.' The crowd fell silent. A large crow settled on the platform a few feet from the general and stared at him. Then it turned around and stared directly at Peter hiding in the bushes, its black eyes penetrating. Peter saw the crow but was not afraid, it was as if the bird was communicating with him. An image came into his mind of a tall blond being dressed in black clothing and piercing blue eyes, powerful and malevolent.

There were other forces at work here. The man spoke.

'We are entering a new system. Our new national breeding program will abolish the liberalistic concept of the individual and the Marxist concept of humanity and will substitute, therefore, the folk community, rooted in the soil and bound together by the bond of its common blood.'

'What the fuck is he talking about?' said an African-American man in the crowd.

'Of all the tasks which we have to face, the noblest and most sacred for mankind is that each racial species must preserve the purity of the blood which God has given it. The purest of you will be preserved for our new race. Others will be transported for resettlement.'

The African-American man in the crowd shouted,

'Are you a racist Nazi?' Others booed at the general. The crowd were shouting and waving their fists. An elderly Jewish man with glasses, supported by a walking stick, was crying as he pointed a bony finger at the speaker, old memories resurfacing like a nightmare, 'Are you Hitler?' he cried. 'Are you a fucking Nazi?'

The aliens started splitting up the crowd, African-American, Jews and disabled to one side, white people to another. Women of breeding age were herded into another area, and scanned by machines which looked like airport scanners. Any who protested were executed where they stood.

On the outskirts of New York, larger craft were lowering huge, black sections of wall, 200 feet high and 30 feet thick. The alien engineers were constructing a huge wall around New York. Thousands of people were at the base of the barrier screaming and looking up in desperation, their shouts of terror could be heard for miles. They gazed up at the wall, all hope evaporating from their faces.

A group of men see a gap in the wall and hide behind building rubble, as they edged closer. They waited until the alien patrol moved away before making a dash onto open ground, and through the gap in the wall. Just as they crossed the gap, their hearts pounding with adrenaline, alien robots detected them and fired, blowing them ten feet into the air, their limbs scattering everywhere.

Four soldiers fired in vain at a robot towering three meters tall, bullets bouncing in all directions. If it were possible, the robot looked annoyed, as if a mosquito were biting it. It hovered towards them and armed its laser cannons, which sparked violently, glowing orange, ready to fire. The soldiers fled in panic, eyes wide in terror, but were blown away by a fiery laser blast. One of the soldiers, agony etched on his bloody face, dragged his pain-filled body behind some rubble, his legs in fleshy tatters, the bone protruding, and blood soaking into his trousers. Alien dogs ran after and caught escaping men and women. They savaged the men, biting their necks, leaving the women to be captured by the black-uniformed Narzuks, where they were lined up in a queue and put through a scanner. The dogs finished their prey, eating the men alive.

Their screams could be heard for miles.

On the alien mothership, high above in Earth orbit, naked and drugged women were being passed along a conveyor belt, being scanned for defects and diseases, their blank eyes showing no emotion. A white woman with red hair was scanned showing a lump on her breast; a red-light and flashed, there was a beep, and a chute opened up underneath the conveyor belt. She disappeared down the chute never to be seen again.

Peter's radio beeped twice. It was a message from Des. Peter whispered to Vinnie. 'We have to get out, they're building a wall around New York!'

They slowly edged their way out of Central Park, back the way they came, knowing at any moment it could 'go noisy' and they would have to fight their way out. Peter's sensitive hearing could hear men's screams; a vision came into his mind of men being eaten alive by dogs. Strange dogs. As they reached the outskirts of New York they could hear the shouts and screams of thousands of people — anguished people. They turned a corner—then they saw it. A wall.

A huge black wall, hundreds of feet high.

Impregnable.

Their hearts sank.

'How the fuck do we get out Pete?' asked Vinnie. Peter's mind raced, searching for a solution. Their X-37D was on the other side of the river, and this wall blocked their exit over the Brooklyn Bridge.

'Let's get closer,' ordered Peter.

They crept around piles of debris and abandoned cars until they were only a hundred feet from the bottom of the wall. They hid behind a huge pile of concrete from a collapsed building. Through gaps in the concrete, they could see white alien robots patrolling the perimeter near the wall. Crowds stood around looking forlorn and panicked, looking for a way to escape.

But of course, there was none.

Then Peter remembered the bird—the crow, the image of the blue-eyed being with fangs. The image talked to him: "Noble warrior, do not give up hope, help is on its way."

Vinnie, Johnny Two-Times, and Fag-Ash Phil all looked at Peter for salvation. Their situation seemed hopeless. 'How are we going to get out?' asked Johnny. 'How are we going to get out?'

'I have the feeling we're going to be ok,' said Peter.

'How?—We're surrounded!' exclaimed Fag-Ash.

'Look to the skies,' replied Peter.

'Do as he says,' adds Vinnie, trusting Peter's instincts, but then, there was a huge explosion as their concrete hiding place was blown apart by a robot laser blast.

They had been spotted.

Peter looked around him, his head splitting, dust in his eyes, Fag-Ash and Two-Times lay injured, crushed under the rubble, moaning in agony. Vinnie was unconscious. His head was spinning as he pulled his friend out of their hiding place, right out into the open. Then he pulled huge lumps of concrete off Fag-Ash's and Two-Times's legs, ignoring the aliens hemming them in.

They were surrounded by white alien robots, and a few black Narzuk troops closed in, leading fifty grey uniformed troops behind them. But above them, Peter spotted something. Two black winged beings descended out of the darkness, red-eyed and white-fanged. Then he was hit by a laser blast from a Narzuk sharp-shooter and fell to the ground. He watched through glazed pain-filled eyes as one of the red-eyed winged creatures picked him up and shot up into the sky.

'Nightcrawler!' shouts one of the alien soldiers.

The next thing Peter knew he was aboard the X-37D, and they were flying away at maximum speed. Des was shaking him, 'Pete, Pete you ok?'

'Yes, what happened? One minute we were surrounded then we were here.'

'You're not going to believe this, but two strange creatures came out of the sky carrying you. They were not human. If I didn't know better I would say…*they were vampires!*' exclaimed Des.

'What did they look like, was one a tall blond creature?' asked Peter.

'Yes, the other was a woman, black hair, red lips, a real knockout.' Then Peter became solemn. 'Phil and Johnny?' Des nodded, 'Badly injured, but I think they will make it.'

Who were the creatures? And the woman – he had seen her before, deep in his subconscious an ancient memory stirred. He had a vision of an ancient city and a herb garden, the smell of rosemary, and the soft touch of two women as he lay between them on a white cotton bed, and he knew them both. Rays of a warm sun shone into the room from a garden as he looked at them. One an elegant Greek Goddess, with long brown hair, the other a dark fiery beauty – a touch of Spanish gypsy about her, as they kissed him on his body, then his lips, their naked breasts touching his body. Pictures flashed through his mind as the centuries passed - then he drifted back to sleep. There were other forces at work here. Good and evil.

Chapter 50

DOMINATION

CENTRAL LONDON

An alien ship hovers over London, emitting a deep, grinding, humming sound. The Houses of Parliament are in ruins, city skyscrapers are burning. People are fleeing the city any way they can. Rampaging mobs are looting, shops are being ransacked, Alien fighter craft have complete control of the skies and are destroying buildings at will. The wreckage of Eurofighter jets is strewn over the capital.

There is no electricity, no water. There is panic in the eyes of a young father carrying his toddler daughter as he barges past two men into a wrecked and dimly lit supermarket. He puts water and tinned food into his rucksack. 'Where's mummy?' asks his frightened daughter. The father kisses her, makes his way out of the back exit of the supermarket and heads down into a dark, eerie tube station. He lifts her over the ticket barrier and climbs over.

The man and his daughter make their way down the stairs of the escalators, navigating via emergency lighting. The vast London underground network has become a home for thousands of people. People find a home wherever they can, wrapped in blankets. The man carries his daughter down to the lowest level, by the platform. The emergency lighting is dim but he can see people lining the platform, sitting on deckchairs or sleeping bags.

An elderly couple in deckchairs listen to Vera Lynn's We'll Meet Again on a CD player. The man sits down next to them and gives his daughter some water. The elderly man gives a blanket to his wife and wraps a blanket around himself, then he smiles at the young girl and gives her a sweet. She looks up at them returning the smile, hoping she will see her mummy again soon as her father hugs her close.

'I remember the Luftwaffe bombing London, I remember those days, you never forget. Sirens wailing, people shouting in fear, the whistles of the bombs as they get closer and closer, wishing it wasn't us,' says the old man looking at the younger man.

There is a long trail of weary, filthy, hungry and dejected, troops and refugees, evacuating London. Some find shelter in house basements, others make for woods and forests, anywhere they can find concealment from the alien menace. Cars and troop transports head for the Welsh mountains and other isolated spots where the invaders cannot find them.

HONG KONG

On a hillside overlooking Hong Kong, a Humvee with a broadcast satellite dish targets an enormous alien craft hovering over the centre of the city. It has a Sirius logo on the side, an S inside a three-dimensional triangle. Inside the Humvee, a technician adjusts his targeting computer and wipes his brow in the humid atmosphere.

'Initiating microwave cyber-attack. Let's hope this jams their signals.' The technician presses a red button, and there is a loud, vibrant hum from the roof of the Humvee as the microwave dish blasts powerful waves of microwaves at the alien ship, hoping to disrupt their electronics and communications. The heat and humidity inside the Humvee increase, as the dish gives off heat, the technician gulping down water and pouring it over his face. The Humvee continues to blast the spaceship with microwaves but to no effect. After a short while, a small alien fighter emerges from the main ship, accelerates towards the Humvee, its weapons locked, and blasts the Humvee to pieces. The technician didn't know what hit him, as the alien fighter circles and headed back to the ship.

LOS ANGELES

In the dry hills overlooking Los Angeles, hidden amongst a cluster of trees, a large laser emerges, protruding from out of a protective steel cannon, it has a Sirius logo on the shiny metal as it fires a four-inch beam of green light—a laser—at the huge, ugly, alien spaceship dominating the skyline. The powerful laser is deflected by the spacecraft shields in a blaze of light. Two alien fighters approach and blast the hillside destroying the laser cannon.

MANILA

An alien ship, black and menacing, one-mile wide, hovers over the massive conurbation of cities known as Manila. Alien fighter craft patrol the blue skies unchallenged. The city is burning. A firestorm has started which is raging through the cities of Manila, helped by a heat wave and strong winds.

A Filipino man carries his baby daughter in his arms as his young, eager eight-year-old son runs alongside him. They run along Roxas Boulevard by the sea wall facing Manila Bay, avoiding the dead bodies, and rubbish strewn along the street. Their clothes are rags and their faces dirty. The baby is crying for milk as the father turns to his son.

'We will make for the US Embassy, we will be safe there.'

'Where's mummy?' The boy asks. The father does not answer as they run past the hotels on the boulevard, most damaged, collapsed or burning. They get to the embassy and walk over the broken remnants of the walls into the grounds. Parked on the lawn is an alien ship, the bodies of US soldiers strewn all about. An alien guard, on patrol, his personal shield glimmering, looks at them menacingly; they freeze as they stare at the alien.

'We must get out of the city!' cries the father to his son. He looks around and sees an abandoned tricycle, it looks intact. Does it have petrol? They run to the tricycle, and the boy gets in holding the baby, while the father starts it up.

The alien guard walks slowly towards them, laser pistol raised. The tricycle doesn't start. In a panic he tries again and it fires up, he guns the tricycle and they shoot off weaving in and out of abandoned cars. As soon as he feels safe, the father turns round to his son, 'Son, I'm heading for Uncle Bill's house in Quezon City, we will be safe there.' He heads down R-7 avoiding burning buildings, taking detours to avoid the fires and any alien foot patrols.

The sun sets over Manila Bay, alien ships doing their evening patrols, then darting back to dock with the huge black ship dominating the city; a cloud of fear and oppression hangs over the city.

People flee to the sea and to the mountains, to get away from the fire and escape the invaders. Filipino soldiers, marines and communist rebels lead refugees into the hills outside Manila. There is a resolute look in their eyes as they live to fight another day.

Planning their revenge.

Chapter 51

FIGHTING A LOSING BATTLE

SIRIUS HQ COMMAND BUNKER - VIRGINIA

General Schmitt was pacing up and down, wiping his brow.
'Has the X-37D left the British airbase yet?' The general asked the communications operator.

'Yes, sir. Eighteen hours ago.'

'Has it had its shield encryption codes changed so the aliens cannot breach its shields?'

The operator hesitated. 'I don't know sir. I am attempting to contact the pilot now. They call him Kojak.'

'Yes. I understand Captain Morgan is on board?'

'Yes sir, they refuelled on the Ronald Reagan destined for New York. No contact since sir.'

General Schmitt's face goes red as he sucks on a cigar.

'Goddamn it! There are troops onboard. Battle-hardened British SAS troops come to join our boys here in the fight, including a certain Captain Morgan. They're worth their weight in gold. Keep trying!' General Scott walked into the control room looking disconsolate.

'I don't know how much longer we can hang on. I think we're fighting a losing battle here Mike. Anyway, give me an update,' asked a grim-faced General Scott.

'We're waiting for Captain Morgan's Intel report on New York. Nothing so far. No news on the SAS team. Frankly, I'm a bit worried. The alien bastards are building a wall around New York. It's a fortress—maybe they can't get out.'

'Keep trying,' replied Scott. Schmitt continued.

'With our Sirius technology we've had some successes, but many failures—but we're keeping them busy, while we regroup our forces. The PR7s are working well, we just don't have enough of them. Goddamn budget cuts. The Gatling gun on the X-37Ds and carriers seems to work well also. It doesn't breach their shields, but it has such kinetic energy, it forces their fighters off course, sometimes crashing them. But again, we don't have enough of them.'

'Maybe we can modify them for our F22 fighters,' said General Scott.

'I will see what I can do,' said General Schmitt as he picked up the phone. 'Colonel, how many Sirius Gatling units do you have in stock—can you modify them for our F22s?'

Chapter 52

New Horizons

GRAND CANYON

Peter and Vinnie managed to catch one hour's sleep on the plane, and just as important, get some food down their necks from the galley. Peter was wondering about the strange creatures who rescued them from certain death, in New York. Vampires—two of them—a pale man and a black haired beauty, that much he remembered. They would meet again, of that he was certain. Events now seemed to be taking on a momentum of their own, all sorts of forces were at work here. Good and evil.

They were now watching the view from the window in the X-37D as it flew down the Grand Canyon at near supersonic speed.

'Wow what a view, first time I've seen the Grand Canyon. Kojak's a great pilot,' said Vinnie like a schoolboy on his first field trip. 'They've got lamb curry Jalfrezi!' as he brought Peter his food.

Peter was pre-occupied with his thoughts: How is Jennifer? How are the children? Are they staying indoors as he told them before he left? He looked at the wing of the X-37D. It was almost translucent, shimmering as the shield generators cloaked the surface of the plane. Peter was shaken out of his thoughts as Kojak's voice came over the tannoy.

'Alien activity over Las Vegas. We're taking the round-about route to Mojave. Diverting North to Death Valley. Fasten seatbelts, we'll be flying low and fast. The aliens are monitoring our comms, so I'm running silent from now on.'

The X-37D shot out of the Grand Canyon and increased speed. Soon it was flying fifty feet above Death Valley. The dust billowed behind the plane as it hugged the desert floor. Peter wondered at the huge white salt flats and dry lake beds as he put on his sunglasses to shield his eyes. He could see the shimmering heat haze from the hottest, and lowest, place on earth. Then he spotted sand dunes, he had a memory flashback of Yemen; next he saw a lush green oasis, then got a view of the surrounding mountains. At any other time, this would be an exhilarating adventure. Peter jumped as he saw an alien fighter hovering near the plane. It seemed to fly level then it veered off. Kojak gunned the X-37D to full speed as it flew at low level between the mountains in Death Valle. The landscape became a blur, and there was no sign of the fighter.

They were flying through the green valleys of the Sequoia National Park, its majestic redwood trees reaching up towards the plane. It looked beautiful in the sunshine, 'I must take Jennifer and the kids here,' he thought. The X-37D hugged the valleys as it wove in and out, to avoid detection. As it came out of the forest, gaining height, it gunned forward to full speed again.

Soon, they were in the desert again: the Mojave Desert. As the shimmering X-37D made a landing approach, Peter could make out cacti, and strange trees, which he had seen before in one of his geography books, but couldn't quite remember what they were.

The plane slowed, and where there had been bone dry desert and dustbowl, there was now a runway.

The plane landed smoothly, but Peter thought they were going to crash into a rock face, then an opening appeared, and the plane disappeared into the rock; the runway had gone back to the desert. Peter smiled, 'Looks like the take-off runway for Thunderbird 2!' Vinnie grinned, they were so much alike, boys at heart.

Inside the plane, Peter breathed a sigh of relief, and then turned to Vinnie, who looked heavenward and gave a sign of thanks at their safe arrival at last. 'I'm worried about Jennifer, she has a habit of acting on impulse.'

But Peter had a sinking feeling in his stomach, and that wasn't good.

Their SAS training had prepared them for all types of situations, but nothing could prepare them for what was coming; their lives would never be the same again.

Chapter 53

KIDNAP

BRECON BEACONS

Jennifer was pacing back and forth in their family hideaway in the Brecon Beacons. The house was concealed in a wooded valley and could not be seen from the air. There was no electricity, but there was a wood-burning stove, which heated the house and cooked food. Jennifer's children, Sally and Robert were playing with a puzzle in front of the burner as Jennifer talked to Peter's sister, Ruth.

'I'm fed up with staying indoors all the time!' Jennifer moved her arms around in frustration, a fire burning in her eyes.

'Peter did the right thing to tell you to stay here, you'll be safe, but don't wander outside. There have been reports of alien patrols,' said Ruth, trying to calm Peter's emotional wife.

'How could he just leave us here? He always leaves us, he's never at home when we need him!' Jennifer shook her fist at no-one in particular, her long brown hair flowing over her shoulders.

'When's daddy coming?' asked Sally.

'Soon,' lied Jennifer. 'I'm going to get some fresh air!' Jennifer grabbed her coat and walked out the door.

'Come back!' cried Ruth as she ran after her. 'Jennifer come back!' she screamed. Peter had warned her about Jennifer's impulsiveness. Ruth tried to stop her, but then Sally shouted to her, and she ran back to the children, shaking her head. 'Stupid woman!' sobbed Ruth.

Jennifer walked through the woods and onto the hills at the top of the valley. It was a bright, sunny autumn day, the air was fresh, and she took in long lungfuls of it. She felt alive and happy as she remembered the times she spent walking with Peter in the hills; good times. She closed her eyes as her imagination ran riot: Peter hugging her and kissing her in the long green grass, the birds singing, She felt a gentle breeze and the warm sun on her face.

Then the birds stopped singing.

There was an eerie silence. All she could hear was the soft breeze. Her heart pounded as she opened her eyes. Her blood froze, and she couldn't speak. In front of her were two Narzuks in black uniforms. As they grabbed her, she screamed in fear, sobbing, begging for mercy, Peter's words ringing in her head, "Don't leave the house." She yearned to be back in the safety of her home, with her children.

But it was too late.

Now her children were without a mother and a father.

As the alien grabbed her with its thin, wiry arms she looked at its large black soulless eyes, which had red veins running through them. It had light green flaking skin. Its long sharp teeth chattered in excitement as it got closer to her, drooling saliva.

She gasped as another alien put a device into her neck and she became unconscious. They dragged her into a ship and placed her in an incubation capsule, along with a hundred others in the hold of the ship. The ship took off and accelerated at an astonishing speed. It sped over the green hills and mountains of the Welsh countryside, heading for Birmingham.

Hovering over the now-devastated city was a black alien ship over a mile wide, dominating the city, putting much of it in the shade. It emitted grinding and screeching noises, as if it had a cog loose, as much smaller craft of all shapes and sizes navigated back and forth around the ship, like bees around a nest.

Jennifer woke up and was shunted from the small alien ship. Her eyes were open, and she could hear herself screaming, but nobody took any notice. Her arms were strapped down so she could not move. She saw an alien commander in a black uniform, with greenish skin and big black eyes, looking at her perfect skin and well-bred features, like a scientist examining an animal in a laboratory.

She noticed a red armband on the sleeve, then her heart skipped a beat as she recognized the symbol. A swastika?

He ran a DNA scanner over her which beeped and flashed green; he nodded, smiling, his sharp teeth chattering. He pressed a button on the incubation pod and she fell asleep again, sedated. The craft landed, and the alien commander pointed to a larger transport ship.

'Mothership,' and pointed upwards. They looked up to see the mothership in high Earth orbit, like a small moon passing through the sky. The incubator pod moved through the air, controlled by another alien soldier in a grey uniform, who looked different from the others, subservient to the black-uniformed Narzuks. Jennifer's incubator was stowed on the transport ship along with a thousand others from all over the UK. They all had perfect features like Jennifer, perfect skin hair, teeth, nails, and body: perfect DNA.

But the drugged women's faces were expressionless and empty.

High above the United States Eastern seaboard, in Earth orbit, the massive black mothership, one hundred miles wide, hummed and ground away. Transport ships from all over the world docked to the ship and offloaded their precious human cargo. Thousands of women were being taken inside the black monolith spaceship above them, taken from every continent, all with perfect skin and facial features.

Untarnished.

Jennifer, half-conscious, was aware of being transported down a long corridor, before falling unconscious again. When she woke, her heart pounded as she tried to move, but she was strapped down, covered by two wide straps, covering her now naked body. It was humid, hot, and she was lying flat inside a clear incubation pod, she could just move her head sideways, and she could see another pod, with another woman, next to her. She tried to speak, but no one could hear her. She looked into the eyes of the woman next to her—a look of terror, helplessness, and a mouthed "Help me!" A shiver went down her spine, and she took a sharp intake of breath, as an alien, green-skinned, with a white medical type uniform looked at her. She looked into the black eyes, and she thought she could detect a smile as the alien pressed a button, and a metal tube slid into her arm.

She screamed in pain, as it extracted DNA samples. The being collected the tube, smiled again and walked to the next pod. When she moved her head to the left side, she could see two tubes, one coloured blue, with a water symbol next to it. She sucked it and cool water trickled down her throat. Next to it was another wider tube, which she sucked and a porridge-like substance came out. 'I will survive,' she whispered in the hot sticky atmosphere.

As she looked up she could see she was inside a huge cathedral, cave-like structure, with a high roof. Lights flickered, and there were multiple floors on either side going up to the roof, like some huge, grotesque Italian Opera House, but on a vast scale. An eerie light shone about the cavern, the incubation pods muffling the screams of a million women. If only she had listened to Pete, her hero, strong blue-eyed, rugged and handsome. He had something of the red-blooded warrior about him. And the name he kept whispering in his sleep. Caius, Who is Caius?

Chapter 54

Roman Mistress

He has an aura about him, charismatic, sexually magnetic, and she remembers their lovemaking. Hot and passionate, she thought she would faint with the intensity of it. 'Rescue me Pete, rescue me.' Then she falls unconscious and starts dreaming, she is going back in time, to a former life.

She is a teenage girl and she is in a wooden cage with many other slaves—women, men, and children taken from her village in Gaul—taken by the Roman soldiers. She looks around terrified, searching for her mother, but she is not amongst the dirty, exhausted people crammed into the cage. The smell is awful. She is hungry and she starts to cry, the tears rolling down her dirty cheeks. She brushes her long brown hair and looks around her. She clings onto the cage as she looks out, there are large stone buildings all around, and there is a crowd of well-dressed Romans looking at the slaves in the cages, asking questions of the slave trader from Gaul, who has a whip in his hand. He is looking forward to making a lot of coin this day.

Only a week ago she was taken from her village by Roman soldiers in Gaul and sold to the slave trader, who now smiles at his potential customers. She can see a woman, looking at her with long black hair and piercing blue eyes, she is beautiful, she has something of the wild beauty of the desert travellers. The lady is wearing a purple silk dress; her hair is made up, and she wears a gold necklace. Jennifer brushes her long brown hair and smiles at the lady. Then their eyes meet and she smiles back. 'I want that one with the brown hair,' the black haired lady beckons to the slave trader.

'She is free from disease?' she asks. The trader nods eagerly as he unlocks the cage and brings her out. The lady looks at her, runs her hands through her hair, over her body, stares at her, smiles, then puts some coins in the greedy trader's hand. 'What is your name girl?'

'Juliana.'

'I am now your domina—your mistress. I own you. Follow me.' They walk from the centre of Rome, past the forum, and through the streets, filled with people in a hurry. She is bombarded with scents, smells, sights and sounds she has never known before. She looks at her mistress, and she returns a smile. They walk through a market then up a hill; she can see a villa there and a guard stands outside. She enters the villa and is taken by another slave to a bath pool. She washes away the filth and grime from her long journey, enjoying the new experience, then she gets out and is given a robe and a brush as she brushes her long brown hair. She never expected such good treatment as a slave—for that was what she was. The other slave points to the garden, she walks past flowers and herbs to a seating area, under the sunshine. Her mistress is sitting there, drinking wine, and eating grapes. She looks so beautiful under the sunshine.

'You must be hungry,' her mistress smiles at her. 'Come sit with me,' she says patting the seat beside her. Juliana sits down and helps herself to roast lamb, grapes and other fruits, and smiles at her new mistress, her cheeks turning red, as her mistress gets closer to her, and touches her long brown hair, running her fingers through it.

'Thank you domina,' she can feel her heart beating faster.

'You are very pretty, like a Greek goddess. You are from Gaul?' Juliana nods. 'It must have been a difficult journey.'

'Yes mistress,' the tears flow down her cheeks, as her mistress places her head onto her breasts, comforting her, brushing her long brown hair and kissing her head. Juliana can feel her heartbeat as her head rests on her soft warm breasts, she can smell her perfume, as her mistress pulls her closer, and kisses her head again.

'Come rest,' says her mistress. They walk together through the garden to a bedroom. There are white sheets and drapes; she lies on a soft bed, next to her mistress. She is nervous; she looks at her mistress, her long black luscious hair, and soft blue eyes, lying next to her. Her perfume is evocative. Juliana is excited, and her heart pounds as they both undress, and they smile at each other as their red lips meet and they kiss passionately. Juliana can feel her mistress's tongue in her mouth, and her strong hands on her bottom.

'My name is Lucia,' she whispers, then kisses her on the lips. Juliana feels the heat on her back from the warm sun outside, and the pleasant smell of herbs and flowers, as she lies on top of the woman, moving her hips. They join hips, and moan with pleasure, as they writhe and kiss, their tongues locked together.

Then she hears a man come into the room, behind her. It is the husband of her mistress. 'Husband, join us,' smiles Lucia. He takes off his toga and her heart skips a beat as she feels his manhood on her round bottom, his hard muscles gripping her and his soft kisses on her back. She moans as he kisses her neck, feeling his manhood grow harder. Then she gasps with shock, then pleasure, as he enters her. After all, it is her first time.

Chapter 55

TERROR IN THE FOREST

CALIFORNIAN REDWOOD FOREST

A boy and girl in their early twenties were hiking with backpacks through the Californian Redwood Forest. They walked up a path between two huge redwoods. The sun was shining, and they were laughing and joking as they came to the top of a ridge and admired the view. Nearby, a sparkling stream trickled its way down into the valley.

'We'll camp here,' said Gregg.

After setting up the camp, Gregg fiddled with a fire stick, tinder and twigs trying to get a fire going.

'Why don't you use matches?' said Anne teasing him.

'Because this is how hunters and survivors do it,' grunted Gregg as he watched the sun go down.

They ate their meal of beef stew by the crackling campfire, warming their hands, and smiled at one another as the air grew cooler in the dark night. Gregg handed Anne a Budweiser, and they looked up and gazed in wonder, as the stars came out, a brilliant tapestry of light.

Dazzling and magical.

But Gregg noticed something odd as he looked up and pointed at a section of the sky.

'What's that?'

A large object moved across the North Star.

'Where?' replied Anne.

'Just below the North Star, it's moving for Christ's sake. Is it a meteor?'

'Oh yes, I see it. I wonder what it is?' said a curious Anne.

'I wonder how big it is?' Gregg stared with his mouth open.

Anne yawned, 'anyway, I'm going to bed.'

'Be right there. Meteor? No, too slow, too regular, too large,' Gregg muttered.

'Hurry up Gregg, it's getting cold, and I have a job for you.'

As Gregg went into the tent, smaller objects left the main one and headed towards Earth, like stars shining in the night sky.

Gregg and Anne woke up, wriggled out of their tent, and looked up at the sky. Gregg rubbed the sleep from his eyes and looked at Anne, recalling the object he had seen the previous night.

'Good morning, Beautiful.'

'What's that up there?'

'Where?' asked Gregg.

'There, look you idiot!' said a frightened Anne. Gregg shielded his eyes from the sun.

'It's heading this way. Can't be a helicopter, it's too fast. What is it?' As the object became closer the realization slowly dawned on him.

It was not terrestrial.

'Christ, it looks like a UFO, run for it!' shouted Gregg.

The object moved towards them at lightning speed and landed one hundred yards away. Tall, gangly beings in Narzuk uniforms walked awkwardly out of the craft, their features disfigured by mutations and sores. One of them pointed at Anne and two alien dogs leaped after her. They were on her in thirty seconds and had her pinned to the ground. Gregg hovered near the dogs, which bared their teeth at him, growling, but did not attack as he waited for an opportunity to rescue her, his gold crucifix necklace glistening in the sun.

'Leave her alone you alien bastards!'

He watched helpless as they dragged his love, Anne, screaming onto the ship, her eyes wide in shock, mouthing something to Gregg, the tears streaming down her face. Her arms reached out to Gregg, begging him to do something. Another Narzuk stepped towards Gregg. He looked at the alien, then at Anne, uncertain.

As the alien stepped forward, it hesitated when it saw his crucifix, a look of fear in its eyes. Gregg ran towards Anne, but it was too late, as thirty seconds later, they were gone.

Gregg screamed at the fast disappearing spaceship, 'Anne!'

Chapter 56

TERROR IN THE WHOREHOUSE

NEVADA WHOREHOUSE

The two Sumeri Narzuk officers, wearing smart black uniforms, medals gleaming in the sunlight, walk into the run-down building. They look more healthy, more lean and muscular than the average Narzuk, for they are Narzuk SS, the Emperor's own fanatical elite.

'Bael has smiled upon us, we shall have some fun today brother,' says Lord Grim-Uk, smiling to his brother Himm-Uk, as he toys with a black figurine around his neck. Their Sumeri women may be barren, but there is nothing wrong with his libido.

'It has been a long journey, let us taste these human women,' replies Himm-Uk clapping his brother on the back.

They look patiently at an elderly lady standing behind a wonky wooden desk. She is wearing bad makeup and cheap clothes and has uncombed hair. As she looks up, her brain tries to make sense of what she is seeing, then she screams in horror. The Narzuks ignore her, and take red-coloured pills. Their black eyes turn reddish as the veins stand out, like their swastika armbands. They smile with pleasure as the old lady shakes with terror.

'My god, don't hurt me, please!'

She hides behind the desk, then peeps over as they adjust their translation devices.

'Most of our girls have run off, but there's Jane available.'

The maid points in the direction of Jane's room upstairs then hides behind the desk again. The tall Narzuk, Grim-Uk, leads the way up the creaky wooden stairs, and they search the rooms for females. Grim-Uk looks in one room and sees an African-American woman, lying on her bed, in a black nightie, red curtains on the window. He turns up his nose, then without a second thought, shoots her, the blast making a clear hole through her chest. Some blood lands on his face, but he doesn't wipe it off. He looks at her cold lifeless eyes then walks out.

Purebred. The human females must be purebred, said the Emperor, shouting hysterically, pointing at his copy of Mein Kampf. 'No African-Americans, no Jews, no disabled, no DNA flaws for our new master race. White women only; kill the rest.'

He is simply following orders after all. It is for the greater good, his emperor has told him.

If he had a soul he would have a conscience, but of course, he doesn't have a soul, and his mind is clear. He has turned his back on God, for he worships another entity, more diabolical and evil than Hitler ever was.

The bloody alien walks along the creaky wooden landing. There is a room with a sign, 'Jane' on the door.

A skinny, unshaven man, with unkempt hair, smelling of body odour, walks out of Jane's room, the door half open. His trousers are undone and he is wearing a dirty singlet. He runs down the stairs as he sees the alien, a look of disbelief in his eyes.

'Bye, Handsome, come again,' Jane calls after the man.

Grim-Uk walks into Jane's room to see a beautiful brunette with a Rubenesque figure; the Narzuk grins.

'Ohhh Gud tuk.'

Jane is terrified, as the alien walks towards her. 'Ahhhh! What are you going to do with me?' Grim-UK starts to remove his black uniform. He is disobeying orders of course, he is supposed to capture and transport selected females for further testing, and if they pass, they are to be inseminated surgically. But hell, who would know? And he was the chief, after all. Perks of the job, and he wants his fun.

And he wants it now, as he climbs onto the bed, his sharp teeth chattering excitedly.

Jane screams. 'Don't hurt me, please!'

Jane hides under the blankets. 'What are you? Are you human or some kind of alien? Please don't hurt me!'

After a few moments, Jane pokes her head out.

'Are you an alien by any chance? I saw it on the TV.' Then Jane's mood softens. Compared to the last client, this alien wasn't too bad looking. 'You're quite handsome for an alien I suppose. A bit smelly, though, aren't you going to take a shower?' she asks, holding her nose.

Grim-Uk takes off his undergarment and grins again.

'No money no honey. I don't care if you are an alien. We have rules.'

Grim-Uk ignores her, grins wider, grunts and drops his undergarment to the floor. He swallows another pill, which takes immediate effect, and Jane puts her hand over her mouth as she looks at his member.

Grim-Uk's eyes glow red with lust.

'Oooh, you've got a big one! What are you going to do with that?'

The Narzuk climbs on top of her, studying her anatomy.

'Oh, not that one silly, this one here.'

Himm-Uk walks into a door marked 'Bathroom.' In the bathroom, a woman is having a shower, singing to herself. The door opens and shuts, but the woman does not notice as she soaps her body, singing a Dolly Parton song. "Stand by your man..." she covers her mouth as a horrible stench hits her. She retches.

'Oh, what's that stink?'

She sees a dark shadow outside her shower curtain. She freezes as she looks at the shadow; it doesn't seem human, and the naked woman is terrified.

'Who is that?'

She starts shivering, as the shadow grows larger and darker against the curtain. She hears a grunting noise and heavy breathing.

'This is not funny!'

The curtain opens, and she sees a tall, ugly, evil-smelling green-fleshed alien, its large eyes glowing black in its angular head, red veins standing out, its long incisor teeth chattering in excitement as it gets closer, drooling saliva.

She cannot move, her eyes are wide with terror, and she shivers uncontrollably and then screams as Himm-Uk goes to grab her, but there is no-one to rescue her.

Chapter 57

Terror in Virginia

VIRGINIA

In an isolated pine cottage in the woods of Virginia, a man in his mid-fifties is reading last week's newspaper. His young, attractive wife, Susan, is nagging him about doing some DIY.

'I wonder why there's no power. I can't watch TV,' Fred complains.

'Get off your lazy ass and do some painting!' Susan replies.

'I'm retired now, that's why I am sat on my ass!'

'Get up and do something!'

'Oh get ye to a nunnery woman! Get ye to a nunnery, and leave me in peace!'

A Narzuk SS Stormtrooper walks silent and unseen past the kitchen window as Susan is doing the dishes, still talking to Fred, from the kitchen.

'Honestly, this kitchen is such a mess. If I didn't do the dishes, who would?' she nags. Fred has his head buried in his newspaper ignoring her. The alien walks into the kitchen, and Susan looks up from her dishes, but too late, as the alien puts a small device to her head, to silence her.

She opens her mouth, but no words come out, as she falls to the floor, half-asleep. The Narzuk struggles carrying her out the door, where a robot carries her off through the woods. She falls asleep as she is kidnapped. Fred is oblivious as he reads the Sports column.

'Ah, peace and quiet at last,' as Fred sighs, looks up, then resumes reading his paper.

Chapter 58

TRAITOR UNCOVERED

SIRIUS HQ COMMAND BUNKER - VIRGINIA

President Wilson was pacing up and down.
'Have the nuclear launch codes been changed?' General Scott wipes his brow. Professor Picard winced as he drank a coffee and nibbled at a croissant.

'Yes I did it myself at this end, but I am hoping the verification process still works for our subs. I'm not sure the National Military Command Centre still exists. We cannot do it electronically, we will have to use the old telex system. General Schmitt, do we have a telex machine here?'

'Yes.' General Scott picked up a call from Chip at US Space Command.

'Sir! I have found a device in Grimbald's office, it looks alien, sir, some sort of transmitter. It has a list of messages, some in English and some look alien, sir.'

The professor looked up. 'Take a picture of the messages!'

General Scott's eyes grew wider as he looked at President Wilson; he spoke in hushed tones to his nephew.

'Chip, try and retrieve the English messages if you can.'

'There's one here, sir, it's just a series of numbers and letters, four sets of four characters. Shall I read them out?' President Wilson and General Scott gathered around the phone, a look of anxiety etched on their faces.

'Yes, please do,' spoke his general, trying to maintain his composure.

'9A3E 2F7Z 1Y4D 301A,' spoke Chip to silence at the other end, The general scribbling down the codes.

As Chip was reading the message from the alien device, it started smoking, then went up in flames, as Chip dropped the blackened remains to the floor.

'Jesus Christ! They sound like…' General Scott, shaken steadied himself on a table.

'Oh my god, they're the gold codes!' President Wilson's eyes water and his hands start to shake. Then he composed himself and got out the card that was kept on a chain around his neck. The President broke the plastic biscuit covering the card and read the codes, gesturing General Scott to do the same.

'The code is third from the top, Bill.'

General Scott nodded and read the codes on his biscuit, checking them against the codes on the piece of paper. He went white and had to sit down. A bead of sweat ran down his forehead, his voice a hoarse whisper.

'I think I'm going to be sick.'

'When were the codes sent?' asked President Wilson, pale and ashen, now sitting down, sweating, breathing in gulps as his heart pounded.

'Chip, did you hear that?' asked General Scott.

'Eight hours ago, sir, just before General Grimbald went missing. The alien device has self-destruct. But I took a picture as the Frenchman suggested. Will send now.'

The president raised his hands: 'they could use our own weapons against us!'

A technician ran into the room, in a state of excitement. 'Sir,' he tried to regain his breath. 'What is it, son?' asked the President.

'Sir, we have had a confirmed launch of an ICBM. It's heading towards Colorado Sir!' General Scott fixed his eyes on the technician.

'What is its trajectory?'

They all walked to the technician's terminal; they can see the flight path of the ICBM.

'On its current heading, NORAD sir!' the technician replied. The president is apoplectic with rage.

'How the hell were safety protocols overridden? The NMCC. The two-man rule. Myself and the Secretary of Defense…The Secretary of Defense!' The president paused trying to digest what he just said.

'… must jointly issue the order to the Chairman of the Joint Chiefs of Staff, that's you, Bill!'

'Not Fraser. Grimbald had the codes,' an angry looking General Scott banged the table.

The president regained his composure and looked at General Scott.

'The aliens have somehow over-ridden the safety protocols. Can the launch be terminated?'

'No sir, I'm sorry, I didn't manage to change the codes in time. In any case, I can't use the coded destruct signal as it needs to bounce off a satellite, and they've been destroyed,' the General was apologetic, head down.

Schmitt turned to Scott. 'The aliens have the nuclear launch codes!'

'Mike, they shouldn't be able to launch anymore, hopefully,' Scott replied.

The technician looked at his superiors, a look of disbelief in his eyes.

'Sir - NORAD's been taken out – it's gone!'

They stood there in silence, trying to absorb the information.

President Wilson looked at Scott.

Scott took the president by his arm in a vice-like grip.

'The game has changed, we need to retaliate, sir. A full nuclear response. We cannot use the ICBM's, they have been compromised, use the subs instead.'

'Okay, but we need to respond quickly,' the president said with more confidence.

'Are we going to target the New York asset?' asked General Scott.

'No there are millions of people still trapped there. The aliens knew we wouldn't target our own people, they have been cleverer than we thought.' The president was deep in thought looking at the floor.

Generals Schmitt and Scott waited for their president to respond.

'Has Chicago been evacuated?' asked the President quietly.

'Yes, sir!' Scott replied. Professor Picard shook his head looking sad.

The decision weighs heavily on the President and Commander in Chief; the room is silent as everyone looks at him. He looks at the Professor then looks up.

'Initiate Trident launch at their Chicago asset—full nuclear response.'

'Yes, sir!' Scott brightened.

The launch missile case was placed on a desk. A technician plugged a telex machine into the launch briefcase with a digital/analogue adaptor. The president and General Scott retrieved keys from around their necks and inserted them into the launch panel. They entered separate codes. The president's finger hovered over a red commit button.

'How can the missiles fly without satellites?' asked the President.

'They are self-guided, they don't need satellites. The launch codes will be sent to the sub by the telex system. It is analogue so should work and not be detected by the aliens.'

'Mr. President,' Scott urged.

The President then pressed the button as Professor Picard made the sign of the cross, looking heavenward.

Chapter 59

LAUNCH DEPTH

TRIDENT SUBMARINE - NORTH ATLANTIC

The submarine is running at launch depth, below the ocean surface. On the bridge, the executive officer watches as a telex machine prints out some codes. The grim-faced captain, in his cabin, opens a safe and retrieves a red book, then hurries to the bridge. The young executive officer tears off the telex print and approaches the captain, as he enters the bridge. The captain compares the codes in the red book to the printout. The executive officer does the same.

'Codes are verified. Do you concur, Executive Officer?' spoke the Captain.

'I concur.'

'Launch codes confirmed. Enter target coordinates and initiate launch procedure. Maintain silent running,' orders the Captain.

The Trident submarine releases a Trident II ballistic nuclear missile. It is ejected from the tube by an explosive charge. The energy from the blast is directed to a water tank, which is flash-vaporized to steam. The pressure spike is strong enough to eject the missile out of the tube and clear the surface of the water.

The missile breaks the ocean and launches into the air in a burst of spray. Its engines then ignite, and it streaks heavenwards at supersonic speed. The Trident II ballistic nuclear missile carries nearly 3.5 megatons of destructive power. The weapon breaks apart into multiple independently targetable self-guided warheads and attains a low altitude orbit just a few minutes after launch.

The missiles re-enter the atmosphere over Chicago. All eight warheads converge on the alien ship, closer and closer to their target, alien fighters attempt to intercept the missiles, but they are too fast as they impact the alien craft in a blinding, blaze of light.

Within a millionth of a second, the splitting of uranium in the nuclear warheads leads to the temperature inside each warhead similar to those in the centre of the sun, roughly 15,000,000 Celsius.

A millionth of a second after the detonation of the missiles, a fireball erupts. A man in Tinley Park, Illinois, twenty-five miles away from the epicentre, shields his eyes from the new sun in the sky. Those people and aliens, looking directly at the blast, are blinded, as their retinas are burned. A group of refugees on the outskirts of Chicago, looking up at the ship, shield their eyes as the blast wave spreads out from the epicentre. Skyscrapers disintegrate like matchsticks from the blast shock wave, which spreads out from the epicentre.

The fireball begins to grow, engulfing the surrounding air, rising, like a hot-air balloon. Within seven-tenths of a millisecond from the detonation, the fireball is 500 feet across, within ten seconds the fireball increases to a radius of 6000 feet.

All buildings, humans, and aliens, within the radius, are vaporized, reduced to dust. The nuclear cloud rises miles above Chicago, five miles from the point of burst, forming a doughnut shape, the colour of the radioactive cloud slowly changes from red to white as the fireball cools and condensation occurs.

The blast completely flattens Chicago for a radius of ten miles, but the alien ship, high above Chicago, emerges intact after the explosion. After a few minutes, fighters emerge from the black groaning, spaceship, and buzz around like angry wasps which have been disturbed, looking for revenge.

Chapter 60

NAZI BLOOD

In a private room, at the end of a long day, a tired President Wilson and General Scott were sitting with open-necked shirts drinking single malt whiskey.

'Frank you shouldn't be drinking—not in your condition.'

'There are many health benefits to whiskey you know.' They both smiled and clinked glasses, then turned their attention to a computer screen.

Scott pointed at the screen.

'Have a look at this photo of Grimbald. From the side, and this one of Hitler.' President Wilson looked at the picture of Grimbald, his lank, unkempt, black hair, dark as coal eyes and pale, unhealthy face. He looked confused, then his eyes and mouth open wide.

'My God, if I didn't know better...' The president took a large gulp of whiskey, feeling the warmth going down his throat. 'I wish I had a daughter, so I could forbid her to marry him.'

Scott grinned then became serious.

'I've had my suspicions about Grimbald for a while now, I just didn't have the proof. I've had a team working on him for six months. We checked his birth records. Julian Alan Grimbald's father, was Wilhelm Grimbald. Born 1940, he travelled to the US from Germany after the war, and worked as an insurance salesman in Chicago. It all checks out. Wilhelm's father, Martin Grimbald was a German banker from Berlin—that's what it said on his German birth certificate. But we couldn't trace him.' Scott took another gulp, getting into his stride.

'We tracked his records back to Germany but drew a blank. There was no Martin Grimbald in Berlin. No Martin Grimbald worked at any Berlin bank. Then by chance we came across some declassified Nazi papers saying that Martin Bormann had a secret son but had changed the name of the father on the birth certificate to Martin Grimbald to hide the fact he was the father. Why? Martin Bormann was Hitler's private secretary. Hitler was fond of Martin Bormann and was a trusted member of Hitler's inner circle, but he was very protective of his sister.'

'Go on,' urged Wilson.

'It was rumoured that Martin Bormann had an affair with Paula Hitler, but it was all hushed up, as Bormann knew Hitler would be furious and send him to the Russian front. Wilhelm Grimbald was the illegitimate son of Paula Hitler and Martin Bormann. Paula Hitler is the full blood sister of Adolf Hitler. Julian Grimbald's grandmother is Paula Hitler, sister to Adolf Hitler. That's the connection.'

President Wilson's mind tried to work out the implications of this shocking revelation. The invasion, the Nazi link… he gasped.

'Good grief, he wants to start a new Third Reich and the aliens are going along with it. Same ideology. Jesus, they must be desperate. Cassian was right, there are parallels here.'

'How did he get away with it, for so long?' asked General Scott, shaking his head.

'I found out too late Frank, I'm sorry.'

'He's protected. He has a lot of political friends and connections. That means we don't know who else is in on this,' replied the President.

'His deputy vanished, Mack. So has Fraser,' added Scott. 'It's a conspiracy. We cannot trust anyone now.' General Scott shook his head.

'It all makes sense now,' said the president. 'I had a shortlist of two for the Chief of the Defense Staff: you and Grimbald. You both had excellent experience and, on paper, you were both outstanding. His political connections tried to sway me—he has friends in the Senate and several prominent business figures as supporters. But I have a long memory. Remember military school, Bill? He was a Nazi then, and not the only one, I suspect. I could never appoint a Nazi to a senior position.' The president refilled his glass, adding ice.

'Jesus, Bill. I reckon there are prominent Nazis lurking in the Senate—when things get back to normal we need to have a clear out.'

'Not just the Senate, Frank,' Scott gulped his whiskey.

Scott leaned towards his friend. 'I never told you this before: My grandfathers' Jewish. I am half-Jewish on my father's side.' The President nodded.

'During the Second World War he spent time in a Polish concentration camp, Auschwitz, he was lucky to get out alive. It was a miracle he survived! My grandfather was so traumatised that he only started to talk about his experience ten years ago. Do you know what they did to him?' Tears were in General Scott's eyes as he recalled the discussion with his grandfather.

'They, they experimented on him. There was this Nazi doctor, Josef Mengele, they nicknamed him the Angel of Death. He pulled out his fingernails, one by one. He said the pain was unbearable.' the tears welled up in his eyes as he gulped down some whiskey. 'No anaesthetic, Frank. Then they injected chemicals into his eyes, to see if they would change colour. He hinted that they performed terrible experiments on twin children, but he refused to elaborate. That bastard Grimbald—I will shoot him myself, with pleasure.'

'You have my permission, Bill, he is a traitor to this great nation.'

They both downed a full glass of whiskey and lay back in their chairs. Scott closed his eyes and thought back to his college days—and Grimbald.

RICHARD MANN

WEST POINT MILITARY ACADEMY - 1980

A young Julian Grimbald is in his study at West Point military academy. An athletic Bill Scott walks in and sees him reading Mein Kampf, which he tries to hide under his bed.

'Grimbald, why are you reading that book, are you a Nazi?' asks a red-faced Bill Scott.

'Bill, welcome. Have a whiskey.' Julian pours Bill a drink, his black eyes smiling.

'You know the Nazis were misunderstood. In their time they were the most advanced nation on Earth.'

Bill is incredulous, 'Really? Advanced? You should be ashamed of yourself. They were murderers, Julian! My grandfather is Jewish! During the Second World War, he spent time in Auschwitz for Christ's sake—it was a miracle he survived!'

'Listen, why don't you come to a meeting? I'm sure we can convince you,' Grimbald says as he wiped his greasy black hair.

Before Julian can react, Bill Scott punches Julian in the face, blood pouring from his nose.

'You'll regret that Bill, believe me you'll regret it. I have connections, powerful connections!' Grimbald uses a handkerchief to stop the bleeding.

'I'm going to report you, Julian—unbelievable,' Bill slams the door as he heads to the commander's office.

Julian smiles, the commander is a regular participant at his secret Nazi meetings. The commander will deal with Bill Scott.

Bill knocks on the wooden door of the study of the Professor of Military History - Frank Wilson. Bill waits patiently as he looks at the brass nameplate. If there is one person he can trust, it is the Professor. An expert in military strategy and consulted by the Pentagon on military matters, he also had a way with people—everyone says Frank has a great future.

Frank opens the door and smiles when he sees the ruddy-faced Bill. Frank listens as the likable student, only ten years younger, recounts his confrontation with Julian Grimbald.

'*He has something of the night about him but he has a lot of friends in high places. Be careful Bill, and take care of that temper of yours.*' His soft African-American features smile.

'Thanks Professor Wilson you're a wise man. I can learn a lot from you.'

Chapter 61

SHAPESHIFTER

A Filipino man walks along a mountain path, overlooking the smoking ruins of Manila. It is a hot and humid evening, but the mosquitoes do not bother this particular man. He is taller than most Filipinos with the muscles and build of a grizzly bear. He transforms himself from a human to a vampire were-dog and makes a 'tik-tik' sound. His name is Aswerne and is one of Count Cassian's closest allies. He is a half-vampire, half were-dog shape shifter, and huge in stature—over seven feet tall. Sinewy, sabre-toothed and terrible.

A few hundred yards away is a group of soldiers around a campfire cooking roast lechon—roasted pig, a Filipino favourite. A soldier pricks up his ears listening to a sound. He motions to his comrades to be silent, then listens again. He jumps up, looking around, eyes wide—the other soldiers look around in the darkness.

'Tik-tak! Alert Aswang!' says the frightened soldier. The terrified soldiers look around; into the clearing strides a huge fearsome half-vampire half-dog creature.

'Do not be afraid. My name is Aswerne. I will not harm you. I am here as your brother to fight the alien invaders. More of us are helping our human comrades in the fight. Come, let us go down to the city, take back what is ours—as proud Filipinos!'

The terrified soldiers follow the creature down the mountain track towards the city. As the shape-shifter walks down the track, the noisy night air of the jungle becomes silent. A group of shrieking bats hovers overhead, forming a macabre escort.

Once they reach the outskirts of Manila, the soldiers spot some black-uniformed Narzuks with aggressive looking, yellow-eyed growling dogs, saliva dripping from their fangs. The aliens are threatening a group of young women in short skirts, who are stood outside a run-down bar. The women scream in terror as the aliens advance.

Lord Aswerne launches into the air, his black leathery wings stretch wide as he swoops down the mountain, gathering speed. In silence, Aswerne appears out of the night sky and attacks the aliens, his talons ripping them apart, tearing their uniforms, their flesh, and their shield emitters to shreds, leaving them exposed.

The following Filipino soldiers run behind him and shoot the alien dogs, and there is a firefight between the Narzuks and the soldiers, who have a better vantage point at the edge of the jungle—they win the day. The screaming women run for safety towards the jungle, and follow the men, back up the mountainside to safety, before the alien invaders can call for reinforcements.

As the soldiers walk back up the mountain path, some other militias walk past them through the jungle, while four aswang vampires fly above them.

'Good hunting, brother,' says the soldier to the NPA militia.

As Aswerne regroups with the Philippine soldiers in their hideaway base on the mountainside, he sits down with them while they share their Lechon pig with the women from the bar. 'Even the National People's Army are joining us, it is a good sign,' one of the soldiers comments.

Aswerne nods. This invasion by the alien filth has brought people together—a good sign. Maybe there is hope for the humans after all. Maybe they will set aside their petty conflicts and unite in a common cause.

Chapter 62

VAMPIRE LAIR

COUNCIL MEETING OF THE VAMPIRE ELDERS

Deep in a cave in the catacombs of the Blue Ridge Mountains of Virginia is a secret vampire base. A complex of rooms is carved out from the rock. There are rooms for weapons, bedrooms *(vampires do sleep)*, storage rooms, a generator room and the council meeting room. In this room, around a long old oak table, vampire elders and nobility from around the world are assembled. There is Baron Titas, short and stocky, from Germany, Lord Aswerne from the Philippines, a tall and powerful shape shifter, and the elegant Lady Vesilia from England, who exudes charm and good manners.

There are many others from around the world. Some of them are chatting, while others cast suspicious stares at their assembled colleagues, memories of old rivalries, and vendettas, still fresh in their memory. Count Cassian rises to speak.

'This council meeting is in order. This is da 101st session of da Vampiri. Thank you for coming at such short notice. We have a quorum of twelve, so our decisions here today are legal and binding. On our agenda is the proposal to help da humans in their conflict with da aliens. Lucia, your report please.' Lucia rises. Cassian is glad he made Lucia his second in command, her strong personality and strength are a great asset to him, and above all, she is loyal, not like some of the two-faced vampires assembled before him.

'I managed to capture a Narzuk commander on one of their raids last year. I persuaded him to talk, and before he died, he told me they were a dying race, and needed new humans for their program. Da Sumeri, da old enemy, have invaded Earth, this time in force, to restart their destructive biological experiments. Their gene pool has become depleted, so they have come to Earth for new genetic material, to restart their failed breeding program.'

Lucia and Cassian look around the table, trying to gauge their commitment.

'As well as destroying the political and military infrastructure they have killed many humans. We cannot allow this to continue. We cannot protect all humanity. We are symbiotic to da humans, we cannot survive without them, our artificial blood bank project is a failure, we have no other food source. We cannot survive alone. Da humans will not survive this invasion.'

'Thank you, Lucia. Why are they attacking in such large numbers this time? Six thousand years ago it was a raid here and there, snatch a few women, kill da men, then they were gone,' asks Cassian, although he has a good idea of the answer he wants the assembled vampires to hear.

'I think last time their needs were limited, to supplement their poor DNA. Now they are desperate, they are a dying race. They live on a dying planet. They want to take over da Earth, take our resources, our food, our mineral wealth, our water, but primarily to capture human women for their hybrid breeding program, to genetically re-build their race, at da expense of the humans. From what I can make out their women are all barren, they have all but lost the ability to reproduce. With each successive generation, fewer and fewer children are born,' replies Lucia. 'The prisoner confirmed as much before he died.' Cassian smiles.

'I was almost going to say they are an ungodly race but that would be rich coming from us.'

'Maybe God has turned his back on them, like us…' Cassian ponders.

'We should not feel sorry for da Sumeri filth,' Lucia adds.

'Maybe we can redeem ourselves with God, maybe Professor Picard is right. I think we should help da humans. I do not fancy sharing Earth with da Sumeri filth,' Cassian adds.

Lucia agrees, 'Neither do I. I like da humans, they have great spirit.'

Baron Titas, an old, wizened vampire elder raises his hand. His leather jacket creaks as he puts his elbows on the oak table. 'Count Cassian, old friend, we have survived these crises before, and we can survive them again. You cannot trust the humans, they don't care about us.'

'Baron Titas, da alien filth's intention is to become the dominant species on Earth.' Cassian, in a rare show of emotion, bangs his fist on the table, looking at each of them in turn, his eyes now a frightening shade of red.

'They want *dominion over Earth.* They won't stop this time, and remember, they drew first blood so feel no mercy for them, they will hunt you down. Don't think you can hide in some dark cave. None of us can!'

Cassian calms down and becomes more conciliatory. 'I have detected a change in da humans, they are more open to talks now. They are more willing to trust us.'

Lucia nodded in agreement.

Lady Vesilia chooses her moment to speak. She stands up, showing her long pleated black hair and elegant, Victorian style dress. She licks her lips and smiles at Cassian. There is a sparkle in her eye of old memories as she looks at him.

'Count Cassian, you have always been a reliable ally and a good friend - more than a friend.' Baron Titas smiles.

'England is no longer our home. It is red with the blood of murdered humans, it has been defiled by this alien vermin! This time, the Sumeri will stop at nothing. We have no choice but to help the humans, you can count on our support.'

Lord Aswerne now stands. He is a half-vampire, half were-dog shape shifter and huge in stature – over seven feet tall, and built like a werewolf. The other vampires eye him warily as he is a close ally of Count Cassian. Those of them who oppose Cassian, and are even considering deposing him, now have second thoughts. Lord Aswerne looks around the table in silence before speaking, gauging their motives. He will speak to Cassian in private later. He now speaks with a deep guttural Filipino accent.

'Cassian, my old friend,' looking around the table again for emphasis.

'We have not spoken for over twenty years, but you have always been a trusted friend and brother to me. I will never forget how you helped us in our war with the Spanish invaders, some three hundred years ago. And then helping us to fight the Japanese in World War Two, the secret war. But that was then, and this is now. It was difficult to get here from the Philippines, the alien ships are everywhere. Our country is now overrun with the alien plague, we have the advantage of the jungle, so we have been fighting a guerrilla war, hiding out in the mountains, and valleys, biding our time, then attacking, here and there a war of attrition. But I think we are wearing them down Cassian. We are using the same tactics as we did against the Japanese.' The assembled vampires nodded, regarding Aswerne with respect. 'The humans are so innocent, they cannot survive on their own. Cassian, know you can count on us.'

'Thank you Aswerne.' Cassian stands up and looks at all the vampires in the eye before speaking.

'All is not lost – there is one who can help us. An ancient human warrior foretold in the Book of Prophecy. Caius.'

'Pah old wives tales,' grunted Baron Titas. Lucia grimaced and showed her fangs. Cassian continued. 'We will meet him soon. I'm sure I can convince him to join with us. The sword he carries belongs to Prince Michael himself.'

If it were possible the assembled vampires all grew paler at the mention of that name. 'The one who banished the fallen angels from heaven. The fallen are our comrades. Can we trust this Caius?' asked Vesilia.

'He is our only hope,' said Lucia. She felt a tear run down her eye as she thought about him. She had seen him in New York, she remembered him from somewhere, and he touched her soul, an ancient happy memory perhaps. A stone city, a grassy hill, the smell of lavender, a warm evening. She had lived for thousands of years and she knew she had she had met him before. But this ancient warrior had reincarnated now in their time of need. She knew she needed him. They all needed him. Humans and vampires alike. She broke out of her trance as Cassian spoke.

'I think we should vote. All in favor of the motion to help da humans raise their right hand.'

Six of the elders raise their hands.

'Now against.'

Six of the elders raise their hands. Cassian is furious.

'This is outrageous!'

The elders are arguing among themselves as Cassian shouts above the throng.

'I have da casting vote. The motion is carried! Let it thus be recorded. Lords and Ladies, please leave the room. We will meet again in four hours. Lucia, you stay, we have some planning to do.'

Cassian sits down, hands on his forehead, worry lines on his face.

'Lucia, my divinations tell me US President Wilson and his staff are nearby in their base in da Virginia Mountains. We must visit them tomorrow, if we are not to be too late. Time is of the essence. I should rest now, but there's too much to do. I have another meeting, and work to do tonight!'

Lucia touches her master's arm. He is like a father to her, and she loves him like one. As she puts her arm around him Cassian almost smiles.

'Cassian, go rest, I will finish tactical planning before da next meeting. Go.'

As Cassian enters his private quarters in one of the caves he climbs into his four-poster bed and covers his head. The centuries weigh heavily on him, as he places his hands over his chest, closes his eyes and ponders the day's events. He now knows who his friends are, and who are his enemies amongst the vampiric clans, but he won the vote and his rivals have now reluctantly agreed to fight the alien filth: *all ancient vendettas are on hold.* The Vampiri are committed to helping the humans, there is no going back now. They must throw in their lot with them and fight the alien filth together, or both their races will die.

Former enemies, both human and vampire, must become friends. That's the rub of it. But can humankind learn to set aside their petty conflicts and unite in a common cause? Issues of race, religion, class and skin colour are now irrelevant in a fight against a common and vicious enemy.

And one human holds the key: Caius.

Chapter 63

Vampire Moon

It is night-time. The moon is full. Cassian is standing tall on top of a mountain near their base, the sky is clear and the stars shine above him in the velvet night. Magical. His mind reaches out to vampire elders scattered around the globe who could not make it to the meeting: Baron Alexander in Russia, Raja Vamdevi in India, Sir Elijah in Australia and Viscount Vinicius in Brazil. Images flash through Cassian's mind as he makes contact. Pictures of old friends and allies, old rivals, old grievances, *old vendettas*.

'Brothers and sisters. A moment of crisis faces us, the old enemy returns, da alien filth. We must unite and put aside our differences and oppose this threat otherwise we, and da humans, face extinction.'

Baron Alexander replies, 'Cassian, old friend, we are fighting a vicious guerrilla war here in Russia in the major cities, Moscow, Leningrad. That's where the vermin are centred. In the countryside, there are very few of them, but then Mother Russia is very large. We will help the humans as we fought the Nazis in the siege of Leningrad. You can count on me.'

As he stands there and looks at the Moon he is joined by Lady Vesilia, in an elegant scarlet Victorian-looking dress which touches the floor, her hair flowing over her shoulders, she smiles at Cassian and holds his hand. Cassian returns the smile, 'Sweet Vesilia,' he whispers. As he holds her hand, Cassian remembers the time they spent together in Victorian England, near Old Baker Street, walking in the cobbled streets of Old London in his elegant clothes, top hat and tails, and cane. She was wearing the same scarlet dress. She looked so beautiful, so elegant, she is wearing the same musk perfume, it fills his nostrils as he smiles; the memories come flooding back, strong emotions burnt indelibly into his mind.

They had many happy years together.

Could a vampire feel love?

His eyes water as he looks at her. The night at the opera in the Royal Opera House, it was Puccini's Madame Butterfly, he looked into Vesilia's eyes as the opera came to its climax, the violins playing, then he kissed her red lips. He held her hand tight, promising never to let her go. Then she smiled as she read his mind.

'Puccini,' she whispers as she kisses him.

But that was then, and this is now.

'I have contacted the rest of da Vampiri nobility. They will fight da filth on their own turf. We will fight night-time when our powers are strongest.' He touches her hand, then kisses it.

'I am leaving soon, sweet Vesilia, but I have a task for you, a great responsibility. When I am gone you must look after this stronghold; also I have another task. In da strong room is the Book of Borossus.'

Vesilia gasped, 'I thought that was a fairytale - you mean you actually have it? Why didn't you tell me?'

'Some things are best-kept secret, my love. I want you to study it—find out if there is any other information we can use in our coming battles. Be warned, though, it is something of a Pandora's box, it has a life of its own. Tell no one else, for they may attempt to use it for their own ends. I have put a charm on it to stop thieves, and this is da key.'

'I will need to brush up on my Greek,' Vesilia replies.

Cassian's eyes shine blue as he speaks. 'Keep it secret. All our fates are intertwined with that book!'

Vesilia's eyes became watery. 'Why are you leaving me?'

'I seek the one called Caius – before it is too late!'

The story is continued in
VENDETTA

DOMINION
First Blood Series Book Two

OUT NOW

(Buy it quick else Vinnie the Terminator will pay you a visit – I'm joking)

Sign up on my website for new book releases, free books, stories behind the books, competitions, news and gossip, sample chapters www.richardgmann.com

Give feedback on the book email: richardgmann@yahoo.co.uk

Follow me and Like my Facebook Page:
facebook.com/richardgmann.author
Join my Richard Mann Author Sci-Fi Group on Facebook
Sign up for news and book releases at www.richardmannblog.com
Follow me on Twitter: @richardgmann

Search Dominion First Blood on Google and Youtube

Amazon Review

If you like my book, I would be eternally grateful if you could give a ☺ review on Amazon. To submit a review is quick and easy:

1. Go to the product detail page for the item on Amazon.co.uk (*search Amazon for Dominion First Blood*)
2. Scroll down to the customer reviews section
3. Click Write a customer review
4. Rate the item ☺ and then write your review.
5. Click Submit.

(**Note:** You need to have an Amazon.co.uk account that has bought something to post a review). After submitting your review sign up on my website for my newsletter and priority early bird previews and free ebooks. If you are using a kindle then I suggest you post the review from the main amazon website.

Acknowledgements

My thanks go to Dennis Turla and Jose Pepitojr for their help with the book cover. To my patient wife Brenda as I spend endless hours in front of the computer on my book as she gently asks, when will it be finished? To my son, David for his suggestions on various things. For Celine Byford, Chris Robbins and Kevin Berney for their eagle eyes. To Allison Wright my editor, you are always right. And thanks to Led Zeppelin for keeping me sane during the long hours at my keyboard.

Appendices

Cockney Slang	Rhymes with	Meaning
Cream Crackered	Knackered	Very tired
Pen and ink	Stink	Stinks
Tom and Dick	Sick	Sick
Bees Knees	Business	Effective
Adam and Eve it	Believe it	Would you believe it?
Boat race	Face	Face
Tom Tit	Shit	Going for a shit
Alan Whickers	Knickers	Women's Knickers

VAMPIRI COMMAND STRUCTURE

COUNT CASSIAN OF ROMANIA *1

LUCIA

VISCOUNT VINICIUS OF BRAZIL *2

LORD ASWERNE OF THE PHILIPPINES *2

BARON TITAS OF GERMANY *1

LADY VESILIA OF ENGLAND *1

RAJA VAMDEVI OF INDIA *3

SIR ELIJAH OF AUSTRALIA *1

BARON ALEXANDER OF RUSSIA *2

*Notes number of legions commanded

Sumeri Alien Command Structure

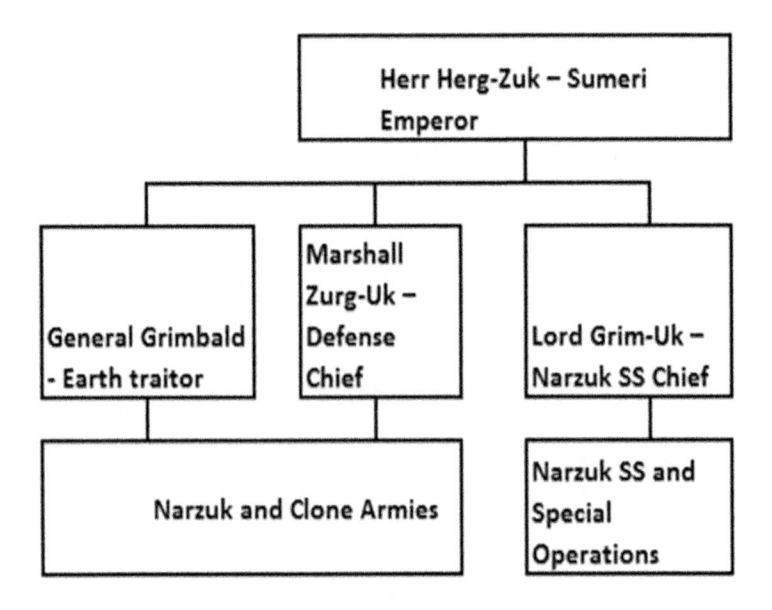

- **Herr Herg-Zuk – Sumeri Emperor**
  - **General Grimbald - Earth traitor**
  - **Marshall Zurg-Uk – Defense Chief**
    - Narzuk and Clone Armies
  - **Lord Grim-Uk – Narzuk SS Chief**
    - Narzuk SS and Special Operations

About the Author

Richard Mann grew up in being an avid reader of books, even from an early age he loved the literary giants JRR Tolkien, Michael Moorcock, Frank Herbert and Douglas Adams. *(If you like this kind of books you will love Richards books)*. He started writing at 16 and started a book called tales from Mellyms Tarc, with a character called Gluloidic. The dream of becoming a writer faded until a few years ago when he started writing again. During his twenties, he studied business studies and accountancy. During this time, he also studied Shaolin and Wing Chun Kung Fu and even started a school with a friend. He has worked as an accountant, Software developer in the City of London for banks and insurance companies, and is now an author.

His mercurial work is action packed, fast-paced, and guaranteed to keep the reader turning pages to the end. This wholly original book falls within the Sci-Fi Post-Apocalyptic, Superhero genre with elements of thriller and horror. It combines incredible action, hair-raising scares, and big laughs. It will shock the reader into thinking about his own place in the world. Warning: This book may keep the reader up all night!

Richard is a Fellow Member of the Association of Accounting Technicians, Member of the Institute of Analysts and Programmers and a Member of the British Computer Society. He is in his late fifties, married, has two sons and lives in Berkshire.

The best way to keep up with his latest news is to sign up for his newsletter.

www.RichardGMann.com
www.RichardMannBlog.com
www.DominionFirstBlood.com

Feedback to the Author

If there is anything you would like to see in my books, please send me an email.

Give feedback on the book email: richardgmann@yahoo.co.uk

Follow me and Like my Facebook Page:
facebook.com/richardgmann.author
Join my Richard Mann Author Sci-Fi Group on Facebook
Sign up for news and book releases at www.richardmannblog.com
Follow me on Twitter: @richardgmann

Sign up on my website for my newsletter for book updates, new book releases, stories behind the books, competitions, news, and gossip. You can easily signup by entering your name and email.

Book Movie Trailer

See the Movie Trailer for this book
Please share – Your friends will love it!
https://tinyurl.com/y8nksqmw
(or search google for Dominion First Blood).